TED TAYLER

QUICK TO ANGER

VINCI

BOOKS

By Ted Tayler

The Freeman Files

Red Herring Season
Gathering Clouds
Still Standing

Vinci Books

vinci-books.com

Published by Vinci Books Ltd in 2025

1

A CIP catalogue record for this book is available from the British Library.
Paperback ISBN: 9781036705077

Chapter One

"DO YOU HAVE ANY REGRETS?" asked Suzie.

"That's a tough question, darling," Gus said. "I've hardly had time to wake up. Do you mean about asking if you'd like to have lunch with me one Sunday afternoon in April?"

"That wasn't what I meant, and you know it," she replied as she poured his first cup of coffee. "Well, do you?"

"Not for a minute," said Gus.

"I was thinking of something more recent," said Suzie.

"The trip to Burnham-on-Sea?" asked Gus.

"It probably caused more problems than it solved," said Suzie.

"You can't win them all," said Gus. "A bit like the case we've just tackled."

"But you found the killer of those two young girls in a matter of days," said Suzie. "Surely that's a win? Or it should be when it gets to court."

1

"Nobody wins in a case like that," said Gus. "Why wasn't Sam Bean diagnosed earlier? Were Rob and Laura Bean aware of their son's trauma and ignored it? Could Rosemary Oram have done more once Sam bared his soul before leaving school? How is she feeling now?"

"I'd forgotten Immie Henderson was her goddaughter," said Suzie. "Rosemary had known Immie's mother, Elaine, since childhood. But nevertheless, that conversation between Rosemary and Sam was confidential. If Rosemary had breathed a word, it would have had ramifications in every school in the land."

"Yet, if Julie Kemp had learned there was an ex-student with gender issues, mightn't it have led her and Alan Quinn to alter their approach?" asked Gus. "A few hours checking Sam Bean's whereabouts to confirm an alibi rather than ploughing on with the tried and trusted methods."

"It's what we do, Gus," said Suzie. "We play the percentages."

"There were too many instances where police and public weren't working together as a cohesive unit," said Gus. "Nobody came forward with information despite extensive media coverage of both murders. Those message boards beside the roads didn't produce a single positive response. What does that tell you? Kemp and Quinn ignored the murder site itself in both Tammie Kenyon and Immie Henderson's murders. It proved to be key, as I suspected."

"Why, though?" asked Suzie. "What made you so certain that was where you would find the answer?"

"Because nothing else they had gone through with a fine-toothed comb had turned up a possible suspect. There-fore, the killer had to have a connection to somewhere they didn't place under the microscope."

"What do you have planned for the weekend?" asked Suzie.

"I'm free this morning for whatever you're building up to ask. I need to visit the allotment this afternoon, and then tonight, I think a trip to the Lamb is in order. Tomorrow will be a day of rest, as it should be. I've done enough running around this week."

"Mum wants a hand moving a few bits and pieces from my brother's bedroom, ready for Grace's arrival next weekend. Then, if we leave in half an hour to do the weekly shopping, we can drop by the farm on our way home. I don't think it will take that long, but Dad muttered something about fence repairs last night. So Mum reckoned that means she won't see him before sunset."

"No problem," said Gus. "I'll be showered and dressed in fifteen minutes. Then, if you get your skates on, we'll be in Worton before eleven."

Monday, 29 October 2018

"RISE AND SHINE, GUS," said Suzie.

Gus opened one eye and tried to focus on the clock on the bedside table.

"How can it be seven-thirty already?" he groaned.

"Your turn to get breakfast," said Suzie. "I'm off for a shower."

Gus eased himself out of bed gently. When Jackie Ferris said a few bits and pieces needed moving, she hadn't explained how heavy they were. No wonder John made himself scarce. After an hour of struggling with heavy furniture items, two hours on the allotment hadn't done Gus's back any favours. He was feeling all of his sixty-two years on Saturday evening.

Sunday was every bit the quiet day he and Suzie had planned. Gus pottered around the bungalow, trying to keep moving. They dined at home and spent the evening listening to Greg Allman and Carlos Santana. After a few glasses of Malbec, Gus was mellow and relaxed when he went to bed.

Suzie emerged from the bathroom to find a bowl of fruit and fibre ready and waiting.

"That looks good," she said. "What did you have?"

"One slice of toast with honey," said Gus. "My new regime, starting today."

He finished his cup of coffee and headed to the shower.

Thirty minutes later, he and Suzie stood outside the bungalow.

"Usual time tonight?" asked Suzie.

"I sincerely hope so," said Gus.

Suzie edged through the gateway into the lane, followed by Gus in the Focus. A leisurely drive through the lanes followed until they reached the main road into Devizes. Suzie turned off for London Road while Gus carried on towards Caen Hill.

As he parked behind the Old Police Station building, he wondered what lay in store in the days ahead. Despite leaving Urchfont at twenty-past eight, he was still last to arrive. The others were upstairs, awaiting his arrival. Gus gave a deep sigh and called the lift.

"Morning, guv," said Neil.

Lydia, Alex, and Blessing all looked up from their computer screens.

"Grace is fetching coffees for everyone, guv," said Neil. "We knew you wouldn't be long."

"I'll give her a hand," said Gus. "I hate to interrupt people when they're working."

"We're putting the finishing touches to the Burnham reports, guv," said Lydia. "You'll have everything you need for your meeting with the Chief Constable before your coffee gets cold."

If I get the call, thought Gus. I'm not sure if he's still speaking to me.

"Very considerate, Lydia," he said. "I hope you did as I suggested?"

"Yes, guv," said Alex. "We took every opportunity to remind him that you pointed out that all roads led to Burnham-on-Sea in the original reports on the Fennell and Roker case."

"Right. That might tame the storm," said Gus. "What about last week's enterprise?"

Grace was already on her way back from the restroom.

"Morning, Gus," she said. "I'm handling those reports. I'll pass you the files in an hour, and you can check I haven't missed anything. If the boss doesn't want you at London Road until lunchtime, you should be able to take two sets of completed reports with you."

"Amazing, Grace," said Gus.

She gave him an old-fashioned look as she handed him his cup of black coffee.

"The pause was for a comma," he said.

"I'll believe you. Thousands wouldn't."

Gus finally found time to reach his desk. No sooner had he sat down when his phone rang.

"Saved by the bell, guv," said Alex with a grin.

"Freeman speaking," said Gus.

"Morning, Gus. Kenneth is expecting you at a quarter to twelve."

"That's very precise, Vera," said Gus. "Tell him I accept the challenge."

"You know what he's like, Gus," said Vera. "He has meetings scheduled throughout the day. But, somehow, he always manages to find time for you and Geoff Mercer."

"It keeps him grounded," said Gus. "We provide a generous dose of common sense to counter the rubbish he has to endure from his peers and superiors."

"I hope this phone isn't tapped," said Vera. "That's dangerous talk these days."

"They can cancel who they like," said Gus. "Just as long as Geoff and I can get our bacon baps and chicken wraps."

"See you later, Gus," chuckled Vera. "Don't worry, your lunch has been ordered, and Kassie spent yesterday baking."

"Don't tell me Number Eight has been given the elbow," said Gus.

"Not by Kassie," said Vera. "Noah caught a stray elbow in the face not long before the end of Saturday's match. He was having his nose straightened in Swindon yesterday."

"Ouch," said Gus. "It puts my bad back into perspective."

"Old age creeping on," said Vera. "You need to slow down."

"That's quite enough from you, Ms Butler," said Gus. "Blame Jackie Ferris for not persuading her two strapping sons to take their bedroom furniture with them when they flew the nest."

"I heard Amazing Grace was moving to Worton Farm," said Vera.

"You don't need to wonder what lay behind the switch. Monty is still in Grace's good books," said Gus. "He wasn't charging her over the odds or looking for sexual favours.

Instead, Grace simply felt isolated on the edge of Salisbury Plain with no friends nearby."

"Grace won't have any shortage of conversation with Jackie and Blessing under the same roof," said Vera.

"I fully expect John Ferris to find urgent tasks as far from the farmhouse as possible," said Gus.

"He'll never change," said Vera. "Anyway, I must get on. Bye for now."

Gus sat drinking his coffee. There was nothing to do but wait for the promised reports.

"I've finished, guv," said Neil. "Shall I start the big clear-up?"

"We didn't have the street maps and murder scene photos on the walls for long, did we, Neil?" said Gus. He glanced at Neil's folder and finished his drink.

"Come on. We may as well do it ourselves while the others are playing catch-up."

The residue from the Kenyon and Henderson files didn't take long to remove. When Gus returned to his desk, Neil pulled up a chair. He had news.

"I escaped for an hour on Saturday night, guv," he said quietly, "and went into town for a drink. I was in the Cavalier on Eastleigh Road."

"I remember it well, Neil," said Gus. "Although, I haven't been back since we were there with your Dad."

"I avoided it for months," said Neil. "But several of my mates still use the place, so recently, I started meeting them there for a pint before we walked into the town centre."

"Is this another Amelia Cranston story?" asked Gus.

"Heavens, no, guv," said Neil. "I haven't seen her for ages. Thank goodness. Rick Chalmers was slumped in a corner. I reckon he'd been drinking since lunchtime. Rick wasn't making much sense but wasn't a happy bunny."

"I'm still waiting to hear where they're sending him next," said Gus. "DS Mercer thought the south coast operations were too expensive concerning the number of people they intercepted. So I don't think Rick will return to the Jurassic Coast anytime soon."

"Avon & Somerset won't be keen on taking one of ours on an undercover gig again," said Neil. "Not after what happened with Luke."

"Water under the bridge, Neil," said Gus. "So, what could Rick tell you?"

"He's off to Gablecross, guv. Jake Latimer got his promotion through. I rang and confirmed it with Jake yesterday. He's moving to Winchester to join Anna Cromwell's team."

"You need to get a move on, Neil," said Gus. "Jake's a good detective, but you're every bit as capable. Don't fall into the same rut as your Dad and get left behind."

"Got it, guv," said Neil.

"Why would Rick be unhappy with a move to Swindon?" asked Gus.

"I think he was hoping to join the Crime Review Team, guv," said Neil.

"I suggested that to DS Mercer, but he reminded me the Chief Constable wanted Amazing Grace to stay with us until the end of the year. I can understand the thinking. Kenneth Truelove will retire sometime next year, and if the CRT were to carry on, it would be more palatable for the powers that be if there's a DI in situ ready to assume command when they award me the DCM."

"Don't Come Monday, guv," said Neil. "Yes, I remember."

"That's why you need to look after Number One, Neil.

If they pull the plug, I want you to be on the next rung of the ladder or ready to take the leap."

"Forewarned and all that," said Neil. "We don't want to see you go, guv. Why would they dismantle a winning team? It's not as if we have many of those; wherever you look across the country."

"It's all politics, Neil," said Gus. "I steer clear of it as much as possible."

Grace and Blessing were collecting empties on their way to the restroom. As she passed Gus's desk, she picked up his cup and nodded to his monitor.

"You'll find everything you need in your inbox, Gus," she said.

"Thanks, Grace," said Gus. "I'll read, mark, and inwardly digest before leaving for London Road."

Neil returned to his desk and started reading Grace's report. Things were on the up; she hadn't taken credit for the positives from Wednesday's trip to Bradford-on-Avon. According to Grace, old-fashioned, solid teamwork had brought results.

Neil was interested in the interview sessions Gus and Grace held at the custody suite on Thursday and Friday with the killer of the two teenage girls. He didn't profess to understand Samantha Norton's condition and wouldn't want to be on the jury when the case reached the Crown Court in Swindon. Still, Grace had provided a suggested checklist for colleagues to consider when facing similar problems. Say what you like about her; Grace was a sensitive soul at times, no matter how hard she tried to hide it.

Gus couldn't find fault with Grace's report either. Armed with a hard copy of the relevant files, he was soon ready to leave the office. Only a slow-moving bin lorry in Seend could prevent him from reaching his destination in time. But, if memory served, that was a regular Tuesday stumbling block, so he should be fine.

"I'll see you this afternoon," he said as he walked to the lift. "Try to make good use of the time. Just because we're between cases, it doesn't mean you can sit and chat. Give your CV's a spring-clean, and check which blanks you can fill to smooth the path for your next promotion."

When the lift doors closed behind him, everyone started speaking at once.

Downstairs, Gus smiled as he left the lift, started the Focus, and eased into traffic on Church Street. That put the cat among the pigeons. He hoped he had a few more cases in him, but you never could tell. As Neil had said, being forewarned was always wise.

At London Road, he parked as close to the main building as possible, strode up the steps to the front door, and signed in. Gus glanced at the clock as he climbed the stairs to the mezzanine. He had three minutes to kill. Where were Vera and Kassie?

Gus could hear Kassie's voice in the distance. She must be doing the refreshment round with her trolley and was currently behind a closed door. Kassie's voice wasn't troubled by such trifles.

"Well done, you made it in time," said Vera, who suddenly appeared at his shoulder. "Geoff's still in his office. Kenneth's alone if you want a head start."

"No, I'll wait for Geoff," said Gus. "I can hide behind him when the bullets start flying."

"Get on with you. Kenneth's a pussycat," said Vera.

Geoff Mercer appeared at the end of his dark corridor. He spotted Gus and waited while he crossed the admin area to join him.

"All set?" asked Geoff.

"As ready as I'll ever be," said Gus. "When were you going to tell me about Rick Chalmers?"

"That appointment isn't general knowledge yet," said Geoff. "I would have told you as soon as it was appropriate. You're developing a better intelligence network than the legend that was Terry Davis. How on earth did you hear about Rick?"

"Neil saw him on Saturday night," said Gus. "Rick had had a few, so loose lips. Then, yesterday, Neil rang his mate Jake Latimer at Gablecross for confirmation."

"Did Jake tell him his partner, Janina, is pregnant?" asked Geoff. "By the look on your face, he didn't. Good to know I've got some secrets left. Not that her condition had anything to do with Jake getting the promotion. Anna Cromwell headhunted him. She was adamant Jake was the right man for the job. Of course, we would have liked to keep him here in Wiltshire, but when the opportunities arise for our people to move up the ladder, you can't blame them for grabbing their chance."

"A moving target is harder to hit," said Gus. "I should have remembered that. I stayed at Bourne Hill for far too long. Anyway, time to join the boss and let battle commence."

Geoff tapped on the door and waited for gruff permission to enter.

"Good morning, Sir," said Gus. "I trust you had a good weekend?"

Kenneth Truelove turned away from the window overlooking the overflow car park and returned to his desk.

"I had a lot on my mind, Freeman. No thanks to you. My Sunday church visit seems to come around far quicker than it used to when I was younger."

"Confirmation you're getting on in years, Sir," said Geoff. "It happens to all of us."

"Look on the bright side, Sir," said Gus. "Surely you have less to confess now that time flies past so quickly?"

Kenneth sighed.

"We had a brief get-together following your efforts on the Fennell and Roker murders," he said. "As usual, you created as many problems as you solved. Because you were conducting interviews at the custody suite on Thursday and Friday last week, I didn't get the chance to pass on the good news. As you know, Sam Webber and Ian Hood were collected from the Black Horse in Chippenham about an hour after you and DI Packenham arrested Becky Hood. While you were on holiday, the CPS took their sweet time studying the evidence and finally agreed to pursue the charges we indicated. Why it took them so long, heaven knows. Hood and Webber will face charges of bringing drugs into the country, distributing them across a significant part of Wiltshire, plus dealing direct to a discreet clientele within a five-mile radius of their home town. Becky Hood's solicitor indicated his client was willing to provide information on the gang's network in return for a lighter sentence. The CPS probably had enough evidence to proceed without a deal, but belt and braces won the day."

"What did they charge her with in the end?" asked Gus.

"Becky Hood didn't intend anyone to come to harm when she set that fire," said Geoff. "However, she had to accept the lesser charge of reckless endangerment."

"The loss of life cemented the charge as Category One," said Kenneth. "There's a change to the law in the pipeline, and by the time Becky Hood gets to court, she could be looking at a minimum of a four-year sentence. If she gets a hard-line judge, that term could double."

"Perhaps Helen's sister knew more about the gang's business than it appeared when we spoke to her," said Gus. "If so, the added benefits her evidence might bring could help her cause."

"Her husband and Sam Webber will be lucky to escape a life sentence," said Kenneth.

"I won't be shedding any tears," said Gus.

"I hesitate to ask what's in the folders you're holding on your lap, Freeman," said Kenneth.

"The larger of the two contains the secondary element of the Fennell and Roker murders, Sir," said Gus. "You were aware of the headlines before our holiday. However, we didn't have all the information to hand until we returned. My team has included updates from DI Jill Crooks and DS Kurt Burgess. There was a downside to letting the case run away from us, but the overall results speak for themselves. Several unsavoury criminals have been arrested and will be charged."

"Several others have disappeared, fate unknown," said Kenneth.

"I would ask you to refer to my earlier comment regarding Hook and Webber, Sir," said Gus. "The other file contains everything we thought relevant from our trip to Bradford-on-Avon."

"Do you have any doubts about who killed Tammie Kenyon and Imogen Henderson?" asked Kenneth.

"None whatsoever, Sir," said Gus. "Sam Bean was responsible."

"Tricky business," said Kenneth. "That defence has been used before. Did you know?"

"Not in the UK, Sir," said Geoff Mercer.

"I fear it will stir up a hornet's nest when the press gets hold of it," said Kenneth.

"When you read DI Packenham's report, I think you'll agree we've gone as far as we can," said Gus. "It's down to the doctors, shrinks and CPS now."

"You never close a case with a clean finish and a neat bow, Freeman," said Kenneth.

"I can offer something that might cheer you up, Sir," said Geoff. "A detective from Polebarn Road phoned me just before I left the office. They caught an amorous golfer at Cumberwell. He was up to his old tricks again early on Sunday morning. While Sam Bean planned his attacks precisely, the golfer's attacks were random. He tried his luck when he spotted a lone female by the edge of the woods. Little did he know she was a rugby-playing police constable named Jenny Collins. She pinned him to the ground and called it in. Blessing worked with her brother, George, a few weeks ago. It was DC Collins who rang me with the news. The culprit admitted five other offences, one of which was Tony Wyvern's daughter, Nicole, back in May 2016."

"We try our best," said Gus. "Despite Tony Wyvern's daughter being attacked close to where the murders occurred, it was clear to me the events were unconnected."

"It was too close to home, if you see what I mean," said Geoff.

"Quite," said Kenneth. "What is that racket outside?"

"The arrival of our early lunch," said Gus. "I suggest Kassie Trotter calls the maintenance section, if you have one, to service her trolley. That rattle and squeak sound ominous."

"I blame you, Mercer," said the Chief Constable. "They're not designed to take the extra weight of the cakes young Kassie ferries from room to room."

With that, the door opened, and Kassie only remembered to knock after dragging her trolley inside.

"Sorry," she said, grinning from ear to ear. "My trolley's on its last legs."

"Get yourself a new, more robust model," said Kenneth. "Anything for a quiet life."

"You're the best, Mr Truelove," said Kassie. "Everything you ordered is here somewhere. Give me a minute while I sort it out. What would you say to a pineapple upside-down cake?"

"Where have you been for the past thirty years?" asked Gus.

"Retro's all the rage, Mr Freeman, didn't you know?" said Kassie. "Can I tempt you with a slice?"

"We'll all have a slice, Kassie," said Kenneth. "Try not to make too much noise when you leave."

"That's me told," said Kassie as she finished placing food and drink on the table. "Did you have a number in mind for what I can spend on my new wheels, Mr Truelove?"

"Just make sure Vera checks it over," said Kenneth. "If she's happy, I'm happy."

Geoff Mercer held the door while Kassie struggled outside. Gus listened as the squeal of the protesting wheel faded in the distance and then switched his attention to his chicken wrap.

Ten minutes later, their casual lunchtime conversation was at an end. Kenneth opened the top drawer of his desk and removed a folder.

"Warminster," he said. "What do you know, Freeman?"

"It's an ancient market town with a nearby garrison, Sir," said Gus. "We've been close to the place several times since I returned to work. Oscar Wallington lived on the outskirts, and Warminster is on the edge of Salisbury Plain, so it's no surprise there's been a strong military connection for donkey's years. Other than that, if it weren't for the Lions of Longleat on its doorstep and the UFO sightings half a century ago, Warminster is fairly unremarkable as far as I can tell."

"Until five years ago, I would have agreed with you, Freeman," said Kenneth. "As with so many rural towns, there's a darker side. On Sunday, the eleventh of August in 2013, Millie Clark, a twenty-two-year-old girl, was beaten and stabbed to death in Christ Church churchyard in the south of the town. Her body was found the following morning by Mrs Brenda Petty, a seventy-one-year-old widow visiting her husband's grave. She discovered Millie slumped against a willow tree close to Keith's tombstone. Mrs Petty placed the flowers she had brought on her husband's grave and sought help."

"She didn't have a mobile phone, I suppose," said Geoff.

"Perhaps she didn't think she'd need one, Geoff," said Gus.

"Mrs Petty spotted a beer delivery in progress at the Fox & Hounds public house on Deverill Road, next to the churchyard," said Kenneth. "She crossed the road and asked the drayman to phone the police. Uniformed officers secured the scene, and the churchyard was off-limits to the public until the following day. A pathologist and forensic team were summoned from Trowbridge. Meanwhile, DS Robin Hamer and DC Georgia Keen were returning from making enquiries into vandalism at the local skate park. A call from the police station on Station Road redirected them to Christ Church. They arrived at the scene ten minutes after the uniformed officers."

"How long did they have to wait for the cavalry?" asked Gus.

"Forty-five minutes after Polebarn Road received the

initial call," said Kenneth. "Henry Ash, the pathologist, told DS Hamer he thought the victim had been held from behind while she was stabbed from the front."

"So, two assailants, possibly more," said Gus. "What about the weapon?"

"The knife was found in a receptacle for discarded flowers and grave decorations."

"A facility with a water supply, I suppose?" said Gus.

The Chief Constable nodded.

"Although the handle and blade had been washed clean," said Kenneth, "traces of the victim's blood remained. The length and profile of the blade matched the stab wounds. However, they couldn't recover fingerprints or DNA that might have belonged to the killer."

"You haven't mentioned a senior officer yet, Sir," Gus said. "Who ran the operation?"

"Detective Inspector Tom Brewer," said Kenneth. "Tom retired at the end of 2015, lucky devil."

"Didn't you know him, Sir?" asked Geoff. "The name rings a bell."

"We worked together at Warminster in the late Eighties when we were both making our way up the ladder. Tom was a decent, honest copper who made it clear he wasn't keen on reaching the heady heights. There are times when I don't blame him."

"Perhaps you could tell me about Warminster and its police station then, Sir?" asked Gus.

"The police station and six police houses were built in the early Thirties," said Kenneth. "During the war, the station gained additional personnel and acted as a gathering point for Wiltshire Police sent to Southampton to assist during the Blitz. At one time, the police houses were filled with officers, but by the Eighties, officers like myself and

Tom Brewer bought their own properties. Just after I left to move to Devizes, the houses were converted to offices and were used by Social Services. Since the turn of the century, Wiltshire Police have shared the premises with the Warminster ambulance service. Plans are in the pipeline for a smaller station closer to the town centre. If you want to know what type of investigation Tom Brewer ran, I can assure you it would have been methodical and by the book. A glance at this folder indicates the forensic team logged a higher-than-average number of hours and gathered over three hundred exhibits. Tom had seven detectives at his disposal throughout the first few weeks of the search for Millie's killers."

"All to no avail, by the sound of things," said Gus. "So, what went wrong?"

Chapter Two

"WHAT DO you remember of Nathan Harvey and Craig Coombs?" asked Kenneth.

"Never heard of them," said Gus.

"I have," said Geoff Mercer. "I recall that Tom Brewer established a connection between those two and Millie Clark. Harvey and Coombs ran a notorious drug gang operating in Bristol. 2013 was a busy year in that part of the country. There were numerous drug busts and convictions. I recall Border Force collared a man at Bristol International airport with two suitcases of drugs when he arrived from Spain. In another instance, a drug lord was ordered to hand over a house and a luxury yacht as part of a confiscation order due to his cannabis dealing. So we were on a roll for a while."

"Who was driving that campaign?" asked Gus.

"The Police and Crime Commissioner," said Kenneth. "The initiative highlighted those areas where drug dealing was more persistent than others. As a result, there were many outcomes for the offences they exposed. Some offenders were charged and went to trial, while others accepted fines for minor offences."

"Which areas were worst affected?" asked Gus.

"Patchway, Cribbs Causeway, St George, St Paul's, Barton Hill, Broadmead, Hartcliffe and Withywood, " said Kenneth.

"The PCC's approach focused on prevention and education with drug users," said Kenneth. "He believed our priority was to help the users and tackle those who sell drugs because they were the ones causing the issues."

"You can't argue with the approach," said Geoff. "The initiative resulted in enhanced communication, education, early intervention and harm-reduction opportunities and pathways. Or at least that was what the reports said at the time."

"Well, it would, wouldn't it? However, as soon as the spotlight moved to another hotspot, the status quo was reinstated," said Gus. "So, who was Millie Clark, and how did she get involved with a couple of lowlifes like Harvey and Coombs?"

"Millie Clark was born and raised in Keble Avenue, Withywood," said Kenneth. "Millie left school at sixteen with virtually no qualifications. From there, she got involved in drugs and became addicted. Her mother did her best to get help, but she had her own troubles. Jeanette had had her first child when she was still at school, the father moved out when Millie was seven, and there were two younger children aged six and four to look after. The father of those children, Tyler Rowe, was a member of the same gang as Nathan Harvey and Craig Coombs."

"Was Millie still using when she died?" asked Gus.

"Tom Brewer reckoned she was spending around one

hundred to one hundred and fifty pounds a week on her habit."

"Was Millie in full-time employment in Bristol?" asked Gus.

"Millie had a young daughter of her own, Amy, but she managed to get part-time work in a nail bar," said Kenneth. "Her habit meant she needed to resort to petty crime to supplement her benefit and a meagre wage."

"What did that petty crime involve? Shoplifting, purse-snatching?" asked Gus.

"Mainly theft and burglaries in Hartcliffe and the surrounding districts," said Kenneth. "Anywhere except Withywood."

"Standard operating procedure," said Gus. "You don't dirty your own doorstep."

"Quite," said Kenneth. "It was by taking part in one burglary that she paved the way for her brutal killing. That's where the connection to Harvey and Coombs was made. Millie was with friends who broke into his home and stole several items, including a luxury watch. They had no idea who they'd crossed."

"It sounds like we might spend more time in Bristol than in Warminster," said Gus. "What happened?"

"Late in the evening of the sixteenth of June, Millie agreed to act as lookout while her boyfriend, Fergus Munro, and his mate Justin Cannings burgled a house belonging to Nathan Harvey," said Kenneth. "As well as stealing personal belongings, the thieves set fire to furniture and flooded the kitchen and utility room. After using his contacts to find out who had been responsible, Harvey's gang rampaged through Bristol a week later, hellbent on revenge. Among the gang was Cameron Keel, a thug obsessed with black culture with a string of previous convictions. Keel called his flatmate, Ivan Thatcher, who had previous convictions for assault and actual bodily harm. Keel and Thatcher ran a large-scale operation growing super-strong 'skunk' cannabis in Shortwood Road, Hartcliffe. An operation which was overseen by the gang leaders Harvey and Coombs. Nathan Harvey's younger brother, Micah, was also part of the gang looking for the perpetrators."

"So, Harvey didn't report the break-in," said Gus, "but became both judge and jury, handing out punishment for disrespecting his gaff."

"The gang couldn't find Fergus Munro that night. He had already been arrested for another robbery in Bishopsworth. So, the thugs tracked down Justin Cannings. He was beaten and stabbed in both legs with a screwdriver. A friend, Viv Whitaker, who was found with Cannings, was stabbed in the face, beaten with a hammer, and repeatedly kicked in the head. The gang then moved on to track down Millie Clark. They couldn't trace Millie's address but made their way to her aunt's home on Keble Avenue, Withywood. Monique Clark said threats were made to her niece's life. Millie Clark was arrested for her part in the Bishopsworth burglary a couple of days later. Detectives asked magistrates to remand her in custody, but she was granted bail to look after her eleven-month-old daughter, Amy."

"Was Justin Cannings involved in the Bishopsworth burglary, too?" asked Gus.

"He was," said Kenneth. "They had to arrest him in his hospital bed and wait for doctors to declare him fit enough to be released before taking him into custody. Cannings told police he wanted to continue breathing, so he wouldn't tell them who had attacked him. The same went for Whitaker, who had been admitted to the hospital simultaneously. It didn't take long for Bristol Police to put two and two together. They soon discovered that Munro, Cannings, and Clark had worked in concert on a string of local burglaries, and Viv Whitaker was just in the wrong place at the wrong time."

"When did Millie move to Warminster?" asked Gus.

"Millie was constantly in fear of the gang who terrorised the whole neighbourhood in their search for her," said Kenneth. "Her mother, Jeanette, tried to get her out of danger by moving to Warminster in the second week of July. Four weeks later, and only six weeks after the burglary, Millie was spotted by Micah Harvey. He had tracked the Clark family down and spotted her outside Boots Pharmacy on The Avenue in Warminster. He took her back to Weymouth Street and called his brother. Nathan Harvey called Craig Coombs, Cameron Keel, and Ivan Thatcher. The evening began with a shouting match; at one point, according to Micah Harvey, a knife was held to Millie's throat, and she agreed to pay for damage caused by the burglary at the rate of ten pounds per week from her unemployment benefits. Around midnight screaming was heard in the Christ Church graveyard, a short distance from Weymouth Street."

"At the first trial, the jury heard it was Harvey and Coombs who committed the murder, a charge they always denied," said Geoff. "Tom Brewer led a joint investigation where he and his team liaised with detectives from Bristol Police as they slotted pieces of the jigsaw together."

"A task they performed whilst battling against a frightened community in Bristol, too scared to talk," said Kenneth.. "An eyewitness near the Boots pharmacy in Warminster remembered seeing a young girl matching Millie's description getting into a red Mercedes in the afternoon of the eleventh of August. Police checks revealed

Micah Harvey drove a red Mercedes, and officers were soon on the trail back to Hartcliffe and Withywood. Micah Harvey and the other four men were later arrested and charged with murder."

"The first trial?" asked Gus.

"Bristol Crown Court in November 2014," said Geoff Mercer. "That was when Harvey and Coombs claimed Millie left the flat that evening with Keel and Thatcher, who later returned saying they had done as Harvey asked. In turn, Keel and Thatcher claimed Millie had left with Harvey and Coombs. Both men said they believed Nathan Harvey killed Millie Clark and then went into hiding. Micah Harvey was found guilty of unlawful imprisonment but was cleared of murder. However, Nathan Harvey and Craig Combs were found guilty of murder. They launched an immediate appeal claiming the judge had misdirected the jury."

"There doesn't seem to be much doubt about the verdict from where I'm sitting," said Gus.

"Patience is a virtue, Freeman," said the Chief Constable. "The Court of Appeal ordered a retrial which began at Bristol Crown Court in April 2016. The jury heard most of the evidence from the first trial, but there was one important difference. For legal reasons, neither Keel nor Thatcher gave evidence at the retrial, taking out pieces of a prosecution jigsaw puzzle built on circumstantial evidence. As a result, lawyers for Harvey and Coombs successfully argued there was no case to answer, and the judge directed that both men be acquitted of murder because of insufficient evidence."

"You can imagine the furore after the events that followed the Court of Appeal decision," said Geoff. "Jeanette Clark was spitting feathers when Harvey and

Coombs, convicted, and jailed for life at Crown Court just a year earlier, were cleared after the retrial. She said she was disgusted with how things had turned out. It destroyed her faith in the police and the justice system. Her daughter was stabbed to death two years previously, and no one had been made to pay. Jeanette demanded to know who killed her daughter and wanted them behind bars. She told reporters she wouldn't rest until they were."

"What did Tom Brewer have to say on the matter?" asked Gus.

"Tom was retired by the second trial but felt duty-bound to attend. I have his statement to the press in front of me," said Kenneth. "He said the police had thoroughly investigated Millie's tragic murder. In November 2014, four defendants stood trial for her murder, for which two were convicted. Through no fault of the prosecution, a retrial was ordered by the Court of Appeal. During the retrial, there was insufficient evidence to proceed with the case, and both defendants were found not guilty. The last two-and-a-half years had been challenging for the family, and his feelings went out to them. The murder file remained open, and if anyone had information about Millie's murder who hadn't already come forward, he urged them to do so."

"The fact we're taking another look at the case two years later suggests nobody came forward with fresh infor-mation," said Gus.

"That's about the size of it," said Geoff Mercer.

"Where are all the people you've mentioned so far, Sir?" asked Gus.

"The Grim Reaper hasn't caught up with anyone yet, Freeman," said Kenneth. "Several aren't performing the same roles as they were at the time of the murder. Henry

Ash, the pathologist, for example, retired to a bungalow at the seaside in December 2016."

"Please tell me it wasn't near Burnham-on-Sea," said Gus.

"No," said Kenneth, "I'm sure you're aware the south coast gets better weather. Henry Ash lives in Exmouth, Devon."

"You said Tom Brewer retired a few months before the second trial," Gus said. "Has he stayed local?"

"Tom's wife hasn't enjoyed good health for several years," said Kenneth. "I can't see him leaving Heytesbury while she's alive."

"Heytesbury's a village, roughly the same size as Urchfont, three miles southeast of Warminster, Gus," said Geoff.

"I'm aware of that, Geoff," said Gus. "Thanks to DC Umeh, I spent a rather tense night close by in the deserted village of Imber. Heytesbury was home to the man who wrote that the dead were more real than the living – because they were complete."

"Siegfried Sassoon," said the Chief Constable.

"Well done, Sir," said Gus. "The World War One poet lived in the village for over thirty years."

"Something I read at school all those years ago must have stuck," said Kenneth. "Perhaps if Nathan Harvey and his colleagues had paid attention at school, they might have made a more positive contribution to society."

"They would have to have attended school for that to happen, Sir," said Geoff.

"Can we interview them in prison then, Sir?" asked Gus.

"Ever the optimist," said Kenneth. "Nobody would testify against the thugs who attacked them after the burglaries. Micah Harvey served his sentence for unlawful imprisonment and immediately returned to work for his brother."

"Harvey and Coombs have spent the past couple of years trying to convince fellow Bristolians they're genuine businessmen," said Geoff. "Suited and booted whenever they appear in public and carrying the trappings of a successful entrepreneur. Flash cars, jewellery, and arm candy half their age. Keel and Thatcher haven't been so lucky. You can arrange to visit Cameron Keel at his address in HMP Winchester. Ivan Thatcher went to HMP Birmingham. It was only a matter of time before the law caught up with them on other charges."

"That's a start," said Gus. "But why would Harvey and his cronies agree to talk to us? They'll stick two fingers up at us unless we uncover fresh evidence that gives us cause for an official interview. Or at least their lawyers will do it for them. The two thugs currently in prison are a different kettle of fish. So an hour of light relief from the monotony could be very welcome."

"Keel and Thatcher were little more than hired muscle, Gus," said Geoff. "They're not going to point a finger towards their former bosses. At the first trial, they were persuaded by their legal teams to accuse each other of being responsible for Millie's death. There was always a chance all four would get off using that defence."

"They stressed to the jury a guilty verdict was only possible if the prosecution had proved their case beyond a reasonable doubt," said Kenneth. "Juries can be difficult to predict. They sometimes do the exact opposite of what the evidence suggests, even when the judge points them in the right direction. However, the jury found Keel and Thatcher's claims more convincing on this occasion, putting Harvey and Coombs in the frame for the murder."

"It didn't take long for the defence to appeal," said Geoff, "and at the second trial, the judge looked at the concrete evidence the prosecution was left with once Keel and Thatcher refused to testify, and although I bet he thought he was setting two killers free, the law didn't leave him with any options."

"We'll do what we can," said Gus. "Several others could shed light on matters in the months leading up to the murder. Millie's mother has custody of little Amy, I imagine? Does she still live in Warminster?"

"Jeannette left the flat on Weymouth Street months after the murder," said Kenneth. "Her sister, Monique, a single woman, decided to move away from Bristol because of aggravation following the first trial. They are raising Amy and her other two children in Zeals, a village close to the border with Dorset and Somerset."

"We've been in that neck of the woods, too," said Gus. "Property can be expensive in pretty villages."

"Zeals has its share of social housing, Gus," said Geoff Mercer.

"The Clarks rent a semi-detached house from the council," said Kenneth. "Not exactly a country cottage with roses round the door, but a far better environment for Millie's daughter to grow up in than her late mother endured. Jeanette's kids benefit too. Conditions weren't ideal for all of them squeezed into that flat in town."

"What happened to Jeannette's boyfriend?" asked Gus. "He worked for Harvey and Coombs in some capacity, didn't he?"

"Tyler Rowe," said Kenneth. "The father of her two children. He seemed to come and go as he pleased while they lived on Keble Avenue. To call him a partner would be stretching the definition of the term. I get the impression from Jeanette's statements that she left Bristol for Millie's safety. Tyler Rowe wasn't consulted, as far as I can tell. Perhaps the decision was taken during one of the spells when he wasn't living under her roof. However, he did get a mention when the Clark family lived in the Weymouth Street flat."

"So, he tracked her down," said Gus. "I wonder why it took so long for Micah Harvey to do the same. Rowe couldn't have told his bosses he knew where Millie and her mother had gone. It might be worth having a word with Mr Rowe. Where would we find him?"

"Bishopsworth," said Kenneth. "A five-minute drive from his old stamping ground in Keble Avenue. Tyler Rowe lives above an Indian takeaway on Broomhill Road."

"Probably a daft question," said Gus. "Is he gainfully employed?"

"Bristol police describe him as a ducker and diver," said Geoff. "He's fathered seven children they know about, with five different women, and ducks his financial commitments. Whenever he spots an unfamiliar face on the pavement below his flat, he dives through the rear window, drops onto the lid of the huge wheelie bin at the back of the takeaway, and disappears to another bolthole somewhere in the city. We've no idea what he does to earn a crust, but since Millie's murder, he's distanced himself from Harvey and Coombs."

"I bet he's not exactly going straight," said Kenneth. "Mind you, if Harvey and Coombs knew Tyler Rowe had kept information on Jeanette's whereabouts from them, they would have punished him at the time."

"You never know," said Gus. "Tyler Rowe might be prepared to tell us enough about his former employers to compensate for our inability to get close to them."

"Who haven't I mentioned?" asked Kenneth. "Brenda Petty, the lady who had the misfortune to find Millie's body in the churchyard, still lives at the same address. Hamer and Keen, the local police officers first on the scene, can be contacted through Polebarn Road. But, unfortunately, they haven't moved on to better things."

"Nobody's mentioned Millie's boyfriend," said Gus.

"Fergus Munro, Amy's father," said Geoff. "Another dubious character who drifted into Millie's life through drugs. Munro got her pregnant and wasn't inclined to follow her to Warminster. When you speak with Jeannette Clark, I expect she'll confirm that Munro has never been in touch to ask after his daughter."

"Munro avoided the beating his accomplice Justin Cannings received," said Kenneth. "He was fortunate to be on remand for another burglary. He received a custodial sentence at HMP Erlestoke, and on his release, Munro started an apprenticeship with a firm in Gloucester. Young Fergus has cleaned up his act, it appears, and he's now married with a six-month-old son."

"My new Focus could do with several extended runs," said Gus. "We'll leave no stone unturned. Your friend, Tom Brewer, handled our part in the investigations, Sir. Who did he liaise with from Bristol?"

"The details are in the files, Freeman," said Kenneth. "I'll leave your team to chase them down for background. I can't see those detectives offering much else, even though the victim hadn't long left the city. My counterpart was Barry Knee. But, unfortunately, he took early retirement before the second trial."

"Was that significant, Sir?" asked Gus.

"I don't believe so," said Kenneth. "Four years in this

role was probably as much pressure as he could take. I know how he felt."

"There were claims of a cover-up by Wiltshire Police regarding vital evidence of phone calls made by Craig Coombs from the flat on Weymouth Street," said Geoff Mercer. "These calls were logged on the same day Micah Harvey was seen in Warminster in his red Mercedes."

"Twelve hours before Millie Clark died," said Gus.

"Flats in the town centre were being used for a wide range of criminal activities," said Geoff. "It was claimed Wiltshire Police were complicit in allowing these activities to continue."

"We turned a blind eye to what, prostitution, domestic slavery?" asked Gus.

"A campaign for a full investigation by the Police Complaints Authority was launched after posters appeared calling for justice for Millie Clark," said Kenneth. "The campaign also listed the names of various police officers who they claimed were guilty of varying degrees of incompetence."

"The claims of incompetence ranged from failing to investigate the background of key witnesses to failing to respond to information about the whereabouts of the accused," said Geoff. "The campaign claimed to have uncovered evidence linking Millie's murder to the people behind whatever was going on in those flats and that the claim was not properly investigated."

"An eyewitness to the illegal activities, Sid Selman, claimed the police would not take a statement and refused copies of tapes and other photographic evidence he'd gathered," said Kenneth. "If that was true and the evidence suppressed was an important factor in the murder case, then one or more officers might have been party to a conspiracy to pervert the course of justice."

"What did you make of it, Sir?" asked Gus. "I don't recall ever hearing anything relating to this conspiracy business. So either it was rubbish, or the matter was swept under the carpet by one of your predecessors."

"I was an Assistant Chief Constable at the time, Freeman," said Kenneth. "I'd like to think I would have been aware of what was happening across my patch. Even if I was more involved with matters at this end of the county."

"Who was this Sid Selman, and what happened to him?" asked Gus.

"He was little more than an elderly freelance hack," said Geoff Mercer. "No doubt, he would describe himself as an investigative reporter uncovering another national scandal in the rural countryside."

"You didn't attach much credence to his claims then?" asked Gus.

"Selman claimed our officers harassed and intimidated him," said Geoff. "If he'd co-operated with us, we could have examined the evidence he had, but he didn't trust us to do the right thing."

"That gives me a picture of who and what he was," said Gus. "Where can I get hold of him?"

"Not a clue," said Geoff. "Tom Brewer's replacement would have questioned the officers who dealt with him. But, as nothing came of the allegations, I presume they were happy nobody had misbehaved."

"Who did replace DI Brewer, Sir?" asked Gus.

"I was racking my brains while you were chatting," Kenneth said. "DI Clare Edwards, that's the name. She came to us from Hertfordshire with a glowing reputation.

Wiltshire was a brief stopover on her way to Assistant Chief Constable in Norfolk."

"Norfolk?" asked Gus.

"They have phones, Freeman," said Kenneth. "You don't need to drive halfway across the country. If you think it necessary to speak with ACC Edwards, might I suggest you get DI Packenham to make the call? They speak the same language."

"This case has the makings of a tangled web," said Gus. "One thing struck me, Sir. Since all the suspects came from Bristol, what did the media make of it? The Bristol Post has a reputation for developing journalistic talent."

"This was the only editorial snippet in the headlines, Freeman," said Kenneth. "You can tell it was published in the aftermath of the two trials."

The Chief Constable handed a single sheet of paper to Gus.

"A glimpse of the West Country's seamy underbelly emerged last week as campaigners offered a twenty-thousand pounds reward to find the killers of a twenty-two-year-old girl sucked into a world of drugs and depravity," Gus read aloud. "The case of Millie Clark focused attention on the increasing problems of Bristol and its crumbling estates a short distance from the homes of the rich and famous. Against a backdrop of a dramatic increase in burglaries, muggings and shootings, detectives in Warminster, Wiltshire, trying to find Clark's killers, told of fly-posters calling for justice for a woman whose life was ruined by drugs."

"Powerful stuff," said Geoff Mercer. "The Bristol media recognised the victim's problems began in their city. But, on the other hand, they didn't appear to investigate whether the claims emblazoned across those fly-posters had any merit."

"I can't recall seeing a lengthy investigation by reporters from our local newspapers either," said Gus. "Surely, the national press would have sniffed it out if something was found?"

"Perhaps the campaigners were right, and the matter was swept under the carpet," said Kenneth. "I hope you'll give me some warning if your enquiries disturb a hornet's nest, Freeman."

"My priority is always to seek the truth in the case I'm investigating, Sir. Nothing more, and nothing less. I'm looking for Millie's killer. Everything I've heard suggests we'll find them among our names in that folder. If my team need a reminder of why we do what we do, they can read the rest of this article."

Little Amy Clark went to bed on her fourth birthday last night and blew a kiss to her murdered mother. 'Good night, mummy,' she said. 'God bless. I love you, and I hope Jesus is looking after you.' It is a ritual she performs every night at her home in the village of Zeals, near Warminster. The four-year-old was just a baby when her mother was stabbed to death in a churchyard in the town. Amy, now adopted by Millie's mother, Jeanette, takes flowers and leaves them alongside the wooden cross near the tree where her mother died. A tree that is now a shrine.

Jeanette says Amy knows what happened and will learn more as she grows: 'I've kept every cutting from the Wiltshire Times to show her. I don't know how it will affect her later, but I'm determined she sees everything. Amy talks a lot about Millie. She tells her friends mummy lives with Jesus. She wants to be like her friends who have mummies at home.'

Jeanette is angry and bitter. She stopped taking her children to school recently because she was fed up with people asking about the trials and upsetting her. Jeanette believes Millie would still be alive if the police had acted differently when the whole thing started. Officers were called to her sister's former home in Withywood when a gang burst in looking for Millie regarding a burglary in Hartcliffe. No charges were laid, and two months later, Millie was murdered forty miles away in Warminster. Jeanette, 43, said: 'I have lost my daughter, and Amy has lost her mother. Her killer or killers are still out there.'

Kenneth Truelove stood and walked to the window.

"The folder on my desk has everything you need, Freeman," he said. "I know I can rely on you to do your best."

Gus returned the single sheet to the open folder, closed it, and tucked it under his arm.

"We'll get started straight away, Sir," he said.

Geoff Mercer joined Gus as they left the Chief Constable to his thoughts.

"He's worried we'll find something, isn't he?" said Gus when they were outside, behind the closed door.

"Honestly? I don't think there's anything to find," said Geoff. "You know what he's like when it's children involved. Concentrate on finding the killer, and I'll have a dig around on the so-called conspiracy. If there's a grain of truth in rumours of a cover-up, no matter how deep they think they've buried it, I'll find it."

"Thanks, Geoff," said Gus. "We've got enough names in the frame without adding more."

Gus gave Vera and Kassie a wave as he reached the top of the stairs, then made his way outside to the Focus. As he drove slowly towards the exit, he glanced towards Kenneth's window. His boss was still staring into the middle distance. The trials and tribulations of a senior position had never appealed to Gus, and he was ever thankful that he'd never experienced them.

Chapter Three

THIRTY-FIVE MINUTES LATER, Gus turned into the Church Street car park behind the Old Police Station. He eased his Focus into the space beside Amazing Grace's Smart car and switched off the engine. Where on earth were they going to start with this new case?

Gus collected the Millie Clark folder from the passenger seat and called the lift. As the doors opened seconds later onto the first-floor office, he felt five pairs of eyes turn his way.

"Bristol and Warminster," he said before Neil had a chance to welcome him back.

"Sounds like an old building society taken over by one of the nationals," said Alex.

"We're going to need a bigger map," said Blessing.

Neil hummed the theme tune to Jaws.

"Stop it, Neil," said Grace. "Gus needs a cup of coffee. I sense we have a tough week ahead."

"In that case, we'll all have one," said Lydia. "Come on, Neil, we'll do the honours."

As Lydia and Neil headed for the restroom, Gus dropped the large folder on Alex's desk and flopped into his chair.

"Which parts of the city do we need street maps for, guv?" asked Alex.

"Bishopsworth, Hartcliffe, and Withywood, for starters," said Gus.

"The BS13 postal district then," said Alex. "Which includes Headley Park and Bedminster Down."

"I bow to your superior knowledge, Alex," said Gus.

"What about the Wiltshire maps, guv?" asked Alex.

"Warminster and surrounding district," said Gus. "Oh, and make sure the villages of Heytesbury and Zeals on the county borders are included."

"Anywhere else?" asked Alex.

"We'll be making trips to Exmouth and Gloucester, but we can rely on our satnavs to provide the details we need. So I don't envisage those places will need more than a flying visit."

Neil and Lydia returned with coffee and green tea.

"Did anyone fancy a Hobnob?" asked Neil. "I checked the opened packet we've got in the cupboard, and ideally, they should have been eaten by the end of September."

Silence reigned.

"Ah well, waste not, want not," said Neil. "I'll buy a new packet of Bourbons at the weekend. They're the best variety for dunking, and they last longer."

"Not around here," said Lydia.

"Dunking," said Grace. "That's gross."

"It works fine with normal tea and coffee," said Neil, nodding towards Grace's green tea.

Gus drank his black coffee while Neil and Grace

37

engaged in friendly banter. Everyone deserved a moment's relaxation before tackling their next cold case.

"Right, if you're ready," he said five minutes later. "Millie Clark was found stabbed to death in a graveyard in Warminster in August 2013. Despite a huge police investigation and two Crown Court trials, no one has been found guilty of her murder. Campaigners believed this was because the local force failed to investigate the crime properly. They wanted a full investigation by the Police Complaints Authority. They distributed a list of officers accused of varying degrees of incompetence, from allegedly failing to investigate the background of key witnesses to failing to respond to information about the accused's whereabouts. The campaigners reckoned they had uncovered evidence which linked the murder to another gang operating in the town. A claim that has never been properly investigated. Well, we can put that to bed right now. DS Mercer is undertaking a comprehensive review of how the investigation was handled while we concentrate on finding Millie's killer or killers. Millie only lived near Warminster town centre for a few short weeks with her mother, so it's unlikely either woman was aware of the alleged criminal activities in the area."

"What do we do if one of our interviewees goes off-piste, guv?" asked Lydia.

"I hope I can rely on you to steer them back on track, Lydia," said Gus. "Just make sure you don't lose sight of the desired result of our cold case review. DS Mercer is perfectly capable of coping with conspiracy theories and matters that attract the attention of Internal Affairs."

"That's why they pay him the big bucks, Lydia," said Neil. "We just want to learn who killed Millie Clark and why."

"You said we were looking for her killer, or killers, guv," said Blessing. "What do we know about events leading up to the murder?"

"I was coming to that," said Gus. "I just wanted to set the ground rules first."

"Got it, guv," said Blessing.

"I always thought Warminster was a quiet sort of place, guv," said Neil. "It must have been more lively fifty years ago when the Army had a larger presence in the town. I read that the armoured cavalry, the Royal Dragoon Guards, was moving to the barracks eighteen months from now. But there will be far fewer soldiers due to the latest cuts."

"As the Chief Constable reminded me earlier, Neil. Many rural towns have a darker side," said Gus. "For Blessing's benefit, plus the rest of you, I'll run through the events of the night of Sunday the eleventh of August in 2013 as we know them."

Gus rescued the crime scene photos from the folder and fixed them to the nearest whiteboard.

"Millie Clark, a twenty-two-year-old girl, was beaten and stabbed to death in Christ Church churchyard in the south of the town. Mrs Brenda Petty, a widow, visiting her husband's grave early on Monday morning, found her body. Millie was slumped against a willow tree close to Keith Petty's headstone. Mrs Petty spotted a drayman outside the Fox & Hounds public house on Deverill Road, next to the churchyard. He was finishing a beer delivery when Mrs Petty ran across the road to ask him to phone the police."

"Does Warminster have a full-time police station, guv?" asked Alex.

"The town is like many others around the country, Alex," said Grace. "With falling crime figures, the focus switched to local policing teams dedicated to serving the community. Teams made up of officers based in the town, supported by additional specialist officers from the wider area. In this case, Polebarn Road, Trowbridge."

"The Chief Constable told me the current team work out of old premises on Station Road," said Gus. "They'll move to a smaller building closer to the town centre in a year or so. As for personnel, I'd expect them to have an inspector, perhaps two sergeants, two constables, and half a dozen PCSOs. Their team will work closely with the local authority, local organisations, and residents to find long-term solutions to local problems. Of course, when the balloon goes up, as it did five years ago, the cavalry would have had to come from Trowbridge."

"DI Cook would have been working at Polebarn Road then," said Neil.

"John Cook wasn't required on this occasion, Neil, thank goodness," said Gus. "DI Tom Brewer had been in Warminster for several years. He worked alongside our current Chief Constable for a while, but I'm getting ahead of myself. The drayman dialled 999, and three uniformed officers from Station Road responded and secured the scene. The churchyard was off-limits to the public until the following day. A pathologist and forensic team were summoned from Trowbridge. In the meantime, DS Robin Hamer and DC Georgia Keen were returning to Polebarn Road from the other side of Warminster when they were redirected to Christ Church. They reached the churchyard ten minutes after the constable and two PCSOs."

"I imagine it's unusual to see many people in the churchyard at that time of day," said Neil.

"It got a lot busier forty-five minutes after Polebarn Road received the initial call," said Gus. "The pathologist was first to arrive. Henry Ash was an experienced practitioner, not prone to making a wrong call. There was little doubt about the cause of death, as seen from the crime scene photos. Someone gave her a beating and stabbed Millie Clark five times in the chest with a knife."

"A lot of blood, guv," said Blessing.

"It was a savage attack, Blessing," said Gus. "I think we can all agree on that."

"She didn't stand a chance," said Lydia.

"Henry Ash told DS Hamer he thought the victim had been held from behind while she was stabbed from the front," said Gus. "We can see the bruising on the upper arms."

"Which came first, guv," asked Alex. "The stabbing or the beating?"

"The beating, surely?" said Neil. "Why, though?"

"I'll come to that, Neil," said Gus. "For now, let's concentrate on the photos."

"We're looking for at least two assailants, possibly more," said Neil.

"What about a weapon?" asked Alex. "Did the police find one?"

"They did," said Gus. "A knife with a serrated blade, matching the depth and shape of the wounds on the victim's chest, was found near the entrance to the churchyard. The knife had been hidden amongst dead flowers and other items in a large, galvanised steel receptacle beside a stone sink. The killer had attempted to clean the handle and blade under the tap, but the forensic team still managed to find traces of the victim's blood."

"So, they could confirm it was the murder weapon," said Lydia.

"Indeed, but they couldn't recover fingerprints or DNA belonging to the killer or perhaps the person who disposed of the knife."

"When did DI Brewer get to the churchyard, Gus?" asked Grace.

"Thirty minutes after the cavalry arrived from Trowbridge," said Gus. "You must have worked out by now that Tom Brewer was an experienced detective. Our boss assured me his investigation would have been by the book, and every angle would have been explored."

"Rumours of a conspiracy theory don't fit with that approach, guv," said Alex.

"We've parked that subject, Alex," said Gus. "DS Mercer will deal with it. Just focus on the evidence."

"Got it, guv."

"When did DI Brewer retire, Gus?" asked Grace.

"At the end of 2015," said Gus. "He still lives in Warminster. His wife doesn't enjoy the best of health. Remember that when we go to interview him."

Grace nodded and made a note of it.

"There will be plenty of opportunity to delve into the murder file tomorrow," said Gus. "You'll find Tom Brewer wasn't short of resources in his endeavours. He had seven detectives at his disposal for more than a month. The forensic crews collected a higher than the average number of exhibits from several properties in Warminster and Bristol. However, this complex case defied Tom and his colleagues to the end."

"He retired over two-and-a-half years after the murder, guv," said Blessing. "You said there were two trials."

"The first was in November 2014," said Gus. "The second was in April 2016."

"DI Brewer was retired by then," said Blessing. "So,

Millie Clark's murder was one of those you've mentioned before, guv. Instead of a tick, a cross in his career stayed with him and kept him awake at night."

Gus shivered.

"It happens to the best of us, Blessing," he said. "However, we haven't finished with the crime scene photos yet. Tomorrow morning I'll explain why Millie Clark was in Warminster and why someone attacked her."

"Sorry, guv," said Blessing. "My father always said I wanted to run before I could walk."

"Are we looking at the beating now, guv?" asked Neil.

"Tell me what you can see, Neil," said Gus.

"Someone pinned the victim's arms to her side and punched her several times."

"Millie Clark suffered a broken nose," said Alex, reading from the folder, "plus a minor fracture of the mandibular bone. In addition, the pathologist noted cuts and abrasions to the cheekbones."

"They beat her and then stabbed her," said Lydia.

"That was the conclusion Henry Ash came to," said Alex. "When we learn why Millie was attacked, perhaps we'll understand why someone went to such lengths."

"Time to call Divya at the Hub, Alex," said Gus. "I suggest we spend the final hour of the day preparing our digital files for the case. Get a good night's sleep, everyone. We have a busy day ahead tomorrow."

At five o'clock, Gus followed the others to the lift and travelled down with Blessing and Amazing Grace.

"Not long now, Grace," he said as they stopped by their cars.

"No, I'm moving to join Blessing at the farm at the weekend," she replied. "I'm looking forward to it."

"See you tomorrow," said Gus.

43

He waited for Grace to reverse her Smart car out of her parking space and join the queue of vehicles making their way onto Church Street. Then he watched in his rear-view mirror until the rush was over before easing the Focus into the line of traffic, eager to get out of town. A mad five minutes every weekday. Sometimes Gus wondered why the same people seemed so keen to do it again the next day. As sure as eggs were eggs, there would be just as many cars trying to get into this small car park in the morning.

The drive home to Urchfont was uneventful. Suzie's Golf was already parked under the rambling roses, and when Gus stepped into the hallway, he could hear her singing in the kitchen.

"Someone's had a good day," he said as he poked his head around the kitchen door.

"You think?" she replied. "I'm fairly certain my next job is your doing, but Geoff Mercer swears it wasn't."

"I gather you drew the short straw. Geoff's got you working on the 2016 conspiracy theory," said Gus.

"I'm the best person for the job, according to Geoff," said Suzie.

"Nobody can argue with that," said Gus. "You've handled several initiatives and minor projects with aplomb over the past six months. It's about time you got something that might make the top brass sit up and notice. I was puzzled by your choice of a song, though."

"Everyone likes to think they're popular among their colleagues," said Suzie. "An inquiry into fellow officers accused of perverting the course of justice won't win me any new friends, and it could lose me a few old ones. It's a long time since we listened to an Animals track, but We've Gotta Get Out Of This Place seemed appropriate."

"Well, I hope it won't be the last thing you ever do," said Gus.

"So do I," said Suzie. "But these cases can drag on, can't they? It could well be my last stint before having the baby. I reckon that's why Geoff chose me. If things blow up in our faces, he'll retire early and suggest it might be better if my maternity leave was made permanent."

"Fear not," said Gus. "Approach the task with the same vigour as you are that piece of boneless meat, and you'll both come up smelling of roses."

"Our beef escalope will cook in minutes," said Suzie. "If you want to help, you can knock up a green salad while I finish the preparation."

"I'll shower and change first," said Gus. "See you in six minutes. Are we short of time tonight? Did we have something planned I've forgotten about?"

"No, we're good," said Suzie. "There's a new thriller on TV later. I thought we could watch it together."

"Mmm, that will make a change," said Gus.

He escaped to the bathroom before Suzie could find something to throw.

Tuesday, 30 October 2018

"ANOTHER DAY DAWNS," said Suzie as she slid as elegantly as she could from under the covers.

"Did I miss much last night?" asked Gus.

"You lasted longer than usual," said Suzie. "You fell asleep during the final commercial break. The recap at the start of next Monday's second episode will allow you to catch up. No need to fret."

Suzie disappeared into the bathroom. Gus got up, and as he walked to the kitchen, he wondered what Suzie would like for breakfast today. He needn't have worried. She'd brought the waffle maker forward on the work surface and added a post-it note. 'Chocolate waffles are thought to reduce the risk of pre-eclampsia', Gus thought he'd stick to toast and honey.

They made it outside to the cars by half-past eight.

"Good luck with your new case," said Suzie.

"You too," said Gus. "My turn to cook tonight. What do you fancy?"

"Surprise me," said Suzie. "Instead of watching TV tonight, perhaps we can compare our progress. However, I may not be able to share some things with you. I'll need to check with Geoff."

"I won't have much to tell you anyway," Gus said. "Today, we'll mostly be running through the background of the case and scheduling meetings for later in the week."

"I'll check the TV schedules on my phone when I get five minutes," said Suzie. "Love you."

With that, the VW Golf was already halfway through the gateway and into the lane. Gus made a sedate start in the Focus and caught up with Suzie at the first set of traffic lights. It never pays to be too hasty.

Suzie peeled off towards London Road with a wave, and Gus followed a milk float as it trundled along Bath Road out of town. He wondered whether people who lived in this part of the town realised they owed Albert T Marshall a massive vote of thanks.

As he turned into Church Street, Gus recognised several cars and their drivers from sixteen hours ago. They *were* creatures of habit like him. He spotted Blessing Umeh, checking she was correctly aligned for a slow reverse into her parking space. Neil Davis was two cars in front of Gus, waiting patiently in line. The red Mini next to Blessing's Micra showed that Alex and Lydia were already upstairs. Grace's colourful Smart car appeared in his rear-view mirror. All was right with the world for now.

Everyone was eager to get started when they arrived in the first-floor office.

"Divya will deliver the maps, in person, by coffee time," said Alex.

"From my experience of the techies in the Hub, that could be in the next five minutes," said Gus.

"I reminded them during my review that a healthy work ethic was required if they didn't want empty workstations around them," said Grace.

"You're all heart, ma'am," said Neil. "Right, guv, who was Millie Clark, and what did she do to deserve getting knocked about and stabbed?"

Gus found the relevant headline report.

"If you're sitting comfortably, then I'll begin. It's a familiar modern tale. Millie Clark was born and raised in Keble Avenue, Withywood. She left school at sixteen, got involved in drugs, and became addicted. Millie still lived with her mother, Jeanette, but her father moved out when Millie was seven."

"Was Millie in touch with her father, guv?" asked Lydia.

"I wouldn't think so," said Alex. "I've found another report in the murder file folder. It looks to have been prepared by detectives in Bristol in 1998. Police were called to a domestic incident at the address on Keble Avenue. Jeanette Clark had thrown her partner out of the house because she suspected he was abusing Millie. Her partner had disappeared when uniformed officers arrived, and Jeanette Clark wouldn't give his name."

"Not a great start in life for a young girl, was it?" said Grace.

"Jeanette was fifteen when she had Millie," said Gus. "After the break-up with Millie's father, she met Tyler Rowe. He moved in, and he and Jeanette had two children; the boy was six, and the girl was four when Millie died in 2013."

"What do we know about this stepfather, or whatever he was, guv?" asked Alex.

"Not an upstanding member of the community, that's for sure," said Gus. "Tyler Rowe was a member of the same gang as Nathan Harvey and Craig Coombs. Harvey and Coombs ran a notorious drug gang operating in Bristol. Rowe wasn't counted among the most valuable crew members. However, he was one of many dealers Harvey and Coombs had on their books."

"I presume Millie Clark was a customer," said Lydia. "Even if the two bosses didn't sell her the drugs she craved. Was Tyler Rowe her supplier?

"That's not clear from the murder file," said Alex. "We can ask Jeanette Clark."

"How was Millie paying for her regular fix?" asked Neil.

"I've told you Millie was twenty-two when she died," said Gus. "She'd met Fergus Munro, an unemployed layabout from Bishopsworth when she was twenty, and although they never lived under the same roof, they had a daughter, Amy, who was eleven months old when Millie died."

"It gets worse," said Blessing. "That poor little mite."

"Because her mother had two young children to cope with, I don't suppose Millie could expect too much help from Jeanette. As a result, she found it difficult to find full-time employment," said Gus. "How much involvement

Fergus Malone had in caring for his daughter, we don't know. We do know that Millie worked part-time in a nail bar in Withywood."

"I don't suppose the benefits she could legally claim, plus a few hours at minimum wage, were sufficient to cover all her expenses," said Grace.

"Exactly," said Gus. "Millie's habit meant she needed to resort to petty crime to supplement her income. DI Brewer thought Millie spent at least one hundred pounds a week on her habit."

"What about Munro, the boyfriend?" asked Neil. "How did he fill his day?"

"In the same way many other addicts do, Neil," said Gus. "They tend to resort to petty crime. A spot of shoplifting or snatching a purse from an old-age-pensioner during the day. Mugging an unwary adult on a quiet street, stealing their cash and mobile phone in the evening."

"No wonder they never have time to go to work," said Neil.

"Where did Munro operate?" asked Lydia.

"Mainly in Hartcliffe and the surrounding districts," said Gus. "Young Fergus steered clear of committing crimes on his local patch. Millie Clark accompanied her boyfriend on many of these escapades, and when easy money was hard to find, they progressed to breaking and entering. It was her role in one burglary that led to her murder. That's where the direct connection to Nathan Harvey comes in, rather than the indirect connection from Tyler Rowe. Millie and Fergus, plus another layabout, broke into Harvey's home. Obviously, they had no idea who they'd crossed."

"When was this?" asked Blessing.

"On the sixteenth of June," said Gus. "Millie had

agreed to act as lookout while her boyfriend, and his mate Justin Cannings, burgled the house."

"So, Millie didn't enter the house," said Blessing.

"Not on this occasion," said Gus. "As I said, the two men inside were unaware they were stealing from one of the most notorious men in Bristol. Nathan Harvey owned several properties in the city, and the nature of his chosen profession meant he didn't encourage uninvited visitors. His neighbours were unlikely to be asked to put his bins out if he was on holiday, nor was anyone invited around for coffee. People came and went, mostly under cover of darkness, and those who lived on the street soon learned to keep quiet and steer clear."

"Were Bristol Police aware of what was going on at the address?" asked Lydia.

"According to evidence supplied to DI Tom Brewer, the house was Harvey's main dwelling place," said Alex. "His home from home, if you wish."

"He and his close friend, Craig Coombs, had their fingers in several lucrative pies," said Gus. "They brought drugs into the city in large quantities and had an operation in Hartcliffe, where gang members Cameron Keel and Ivan Thatcher grew skunk cannabis."

"Another profitable side-line," said Neil.

"What did Munro and his pal get away with in the burglary, guv?" asked Lydia.

"As well as stealing personal belongings and jewellery, the thieves set fire to furniture and flooded the kitchen and utility room," said Gus. "After using his contacts to find out who had been responsible, Harvey sent his thugs through Bristol a week later searching for the burglars. Among the gang members was Cameron Keel, a thug obsessed with black culture with a string of previous convictions. Keel called his flatmate, Ivan Thatcher, who had previous convictions for assault and actual bodily harm, to join them. Nathan Harvey's younger brother, Micah, was also part of the gang looking for the perpetrators."

"So, Nathan Harvey didn't report the break-in to the police," asked Blessing,

"No," said Gus. "He's always considered himself above the law and punished those who crossed him. The gang couldn't find Fergus Munro that night. He had already been arrested for an earlier robbery in Bishopsworth. So, the thugs tracked down Justin Cannings. He was beaten and stabbed in both legs with a screwdriver. An innocent victim, Viv Whitaker, watching TV with Cannings in his flat, was stabbed in the face, beaten with a hammer, and repeatedly kicked in the head. The gang then moved on to track down Millie Clark. Justin Cannings didn't know Millie's address, but he did know where her aunt, Monique, lived. The thugs visited Monique Clark's house and banged on the door, telling her to pass a message to Millie's mum Jeanette. They told Monique to tell her they would kill her daughter."

"I can imagine Harvey wasn't a happy bunny, guv," said Neil. "Men like him react badly to someone disrespecting them."

"Not that they deserve any respect," said Grace.

"Millie Clark had sold several items stolen from the house in Court Farm Road over the previous weeks to get her regular fix," said Gus. "Bristol Police were already hot on the trail of Fergus Malone and Justin Cannings for the burglary in Bishopsworth. It was only a matter of time before all three were arrested. They weren't the cleverest of thieves. Forensic evidence was abundant at several addresses they'd targeted, which put them clearly in the frame. Millie hadn't been at her own home or her aunt's house before the police arrested her. Since the furore following the Court Farm Road burglary, Millie had been living in a squat in Withywood. Following the gang's visit to her aunt's home, Millie was arrested for her part in the Bishopsworth burglary. The police wanted to keep Millie in custody, but the magistrate gave her bail because she had Amy, her daughter, to look after. So Millie was released."

"If only they'd kept her on remand," said Blessing.

"Was Justin Cannings arrested for the Bishopsworth burglary too, guv?" asked Neil.

"Bristol Police had to arrest him in his hospital bed," said Gus. "Then they waited for doctors to declare him fit enough to be released before taking him into custody. Cannings told police he would die if he talked. The same went for Whitaker, who had been admitted to the hospital that night. It didn't take long for Bristol Police to put two and two together. They soon realised that Munro, Cannings, and Clark had worked in concert on a string of local burglaries, and Viv Whitaker was just in the wrong place at the wrong time."

"Poor devil," said Alex.

"What happened next, guv?" asked Blessing.

"Millie was constantly afraid of the gang who terrorised her aunt," said Gus. "She knew they wouldn't let it go. Everyone involved in the burglary had to suffer. Her mother tried to get her out of danger by moving to Warminster in the second week of July. Four weeks later, and eight weeks after the burglary, Millie was found by Micah Harvey. He had tracked the Clark family down and spotted Millie outside Boots Pharmacy on The Avenue in Warminster. He took her to the flat on Weymouth Street and called his brother."

"So, Justin Cannings was badly injured," said Blessing.

"But Fergus Malone was in custody before the gang caught up with him. That doesn't seem right. Why did Millie have to die?"

"Fergus received his punishment in prison," said Alex. "When you all get to see the murder file in its entirety, you'll be able to read the account of what happened to Millie's boyfriend while on remand."

Chapter Four

ALEX WAS ABOUT to continue when his phone rang.

"Divya Yadav is downstairs with our maps, guv," he said.

"A good time to take a drinks break," said Gus. "Who's turn is it to do the honours?"

"I'll go," offered Blessing. "Could someone join me in the restroom once we learn what Divya wants to drink?"

"Will do, Blessing," said Neil.

Alex took the lift to fetch Divya from the ground floor, and soon the pair arrived in the office carrying a selection of cardboard tubes.

"These should give you plenty to be getting on with, Alex," said Divya. "Hello, everyone."

"It's been a while," said Neil.

"Either you haven't had a team-building night at the Waggon & Horses in Harrington End, or you've stopped inviting me."

"Don't be silly," said Neil. "You're our twelfth man, Divya. Would you like a coffee?"

"White, without, please, Neil," she replied.

"Another sporting analogy that doesn't match current thinking, Neil," said Gus. "I'm sure I saw girls playing cricket on TV last summer. I think they'd resent a player omitted from the side to be referred to in that fashion."

"How long have I got, guv?" asked Neil as he made his way to the restroom to join Blessing.

"Until we've finished our drinks," said Gus.

Blessing and Neil soon returned with everyone's orders.

"Right," said Neil, blowing on his cup of white with one sugar. "Teams are selected several days before a match, but it's not until thirty minutes before the start of play that a decision is made on the final make-up of the side. Weather conditions might have changed or are about to."

"In this country, we can get all four seasons in one day anyway," said Gus.

"It's also the first time either side gets to see the pitch that's been prepared," said Neil. "That can influence the captain's decision on who to leave out."

"Why select twelve people if you only need eleven?" asked Blessing. "It would save a lot of trouble."

"Too easy, Blessing," said Gus.

"My husband loves his cricket," said Divya. "Which isn't uncommon for an Indian. I asked him what position he played before we married. He said he batted at six, which seemed late in the day, and fielded at third man or long leg. I gave up trying to understand the game."

"Third man will have to go," said Gus. "Wherever they stand, they'll need a new name for that position before long."

"Cricket uses terms called short leg and long leg, guv," said Alex. "If they account for both tall people and short, that should avoid some of the inclusivity problems."

Gus drained his cup of the last of his black coffee.

"Game over. Back to the grindstone," said Gus.

"I'll get out of your hair," said Divya. "Many thanks for the coffee. Just give me a shout if you need the Hub to perform any searches or provide statistical information. Don't forget we're a resource you can use whenever you wish."

"The Chief Constable reminds me almost every time I speak with him, Divya," said Gus. "We haven't forgotten. As Neil said, when we have another success to celebrate, you're more than welcome to join us at the pub. Bring Arjun along if he's available. He can talk cricket with Neil while we have fun discussing something we all understand."

Divya laughed. Lydia escorted her downstairs in the lift, and when the hub's whizz kid was safely off the premises, she returned to the fray.

"So, what happened after Micah Harvey rang his brother, guv?" she asked.

"Nathan Harvey called Craig Coombs, Cameron Keel, and Ivan Thatcher," said Gus. "They were said to have parked near Chinn's Court shopping precinct on Weymouth Street and walked to Jeanette Clark's flat. Jeanette and her young children had gone swimming at the local sports centre. Millie had been dragged to the flat and held against her will by Micah Harvey. When the gang arrived, the evening began with an argument where Millie came face-to-face with the homeowner she helped to rob. Millie pleaded with Nathan Harvey not to hurt her and was said to have offered to pay back the money from her benefits at the rate of ten pounds per week."

"I can imagine that went down well," said Neil.

"Like a lead balloon," said Alex.

"According to Micah Harvey, Millie sat on a sofa while

Craig Coombs held a knife to her throat," said Gus. "Later, she was taken to the churchyard, and someone stabbed her to death. Witnesses said they heard screams from the churchyard at about a quarter to one in the morning. However, neighbours from Weymouth Street said they heard nothing while the gang and Millie walked the short distance to Christ Church. After Millie was found dead, her photograph and description were published in national newspapers and on local television. DI Tom Brewer led a joint investigation with detectives from Bristol Police as they pieced together the evidence."

"There wasn't much evidence at the churchyard," said Alex. "How did they trace things back to Harvey and his crew in Bristol?"

"An eyewitness near the Boots pharmacy in Warminster remembered seeing a young girl matching Millie's description getting into a red Mercedes in the afternoon of the eleventh of August. Police checks revealed Micah Harvey drove a red Mercedes, and officers were soon on the trail back to Hartcliffe and Withywood. Micah Harvey and the other four men were later arrested and charged with murder. It proved to be a tough ask getting anyone in the Bristol community to speak out against the gang members. After hearing what happened to Viv Whitaker, who had no connection to the burglary, they feared reprisals if Harvey and his gang learned they had spoken to the police."

"When did the case eventually get to court, guv?" asked Lydia.

"That was at Bristol Crown Court in November 2014," said Gus. "Harvey and Coombs claimed that Millie left the flat that night with Keel and Thatcher. Keel and Thatcher claimed Millie had left with Harvey and Coombs. Keel and Thatcher said they believed Harvey and Coombs killed

Millie Clark and went into hiding. Micah Harvey was found guilty of unlawful imprisonment but cleared of murder. Nathan Harvey and Craig Combs were found guilty of murder. Both men denied murdering Millie Clark and launched an immediate appeal claiming the judge had misdirected the jury."

"Were all four men represented by the same lawyers, guv?" asked Blessing.

"No, Blessing," said Gus. "Whether by accident or design, the strategy deployed by the defence teams proved pivotal. Harvey and Coombs engaged the services of Stuart Coles, a barrister from a renowned London firm. Kevin Escott, who worked in a Bristol office, represented Keel and Thatcher. Micah Harvey had a colleague of Stuart Coles in his corner, a lady called Kathy Hardman."

"So, the four main gang members were in two camps, with one pair blaming the other for the murder," said Grace.

"None of them denied being in the churchyard," said Neil. "Despite nobody hearing or seeing what was going on."

"The only people in the churchyard were in court, except for Millie Clark," said Lydia.

"Why didn't Jeanette Clark interrupt proceedings at the flat?" asked Grace. "Surely, she would have got home from the sports centre by late afternoon or early evening?"

"Don't forget, it was the school holidays," said Gus. "Their financial state meant trips abroad, or even to the seaside, were out of the question. Instead, Jeanette was going to her sister's Withywood address by train, so the three kids could stay overnight. Jeanette's two kids would have been able to play with some of their old friends on Keble Avenue before returning on the train to Warminster the following evening. After Millie's body was discovered, police called at the flat on Weymouth Road. There was nobody home, so DI Brewer called Bristol Police for assistance. Local uniformed officers were familiar with the sisters' previous history. They soon found Jeanette Clark at her sister's house and informed her of Millie's death. The police drove Jeanette and the three children back to Warminster just after lunch."

"Police had the evidence from the phone call made by Micah to his brother," said Grace. "So, Nathan couldn't deny any knowledge of the events leading to the murder. Nathan Harvey had also called Craig Coombs, which scuppered his chances. Then, there were phone calls to Cameron Keel and Ivan Thatcher telling them their services were required. It was pointless claiming they weren't in Warminster. They chose to blame one another, but the prosecution's argument was strong enough to persuade the jury to convict Harvey and Coombs."

"Nobody spoke out about the gang's methods of discovering who had burgled the house in Hartcliffe," said Blessing.

"What are you getting at, Blessing?" asked Gus.

"The court case seemed to centre on Micah Harvey spotting Millie Clark and what happened in the churchyard at Christ Church at around one o'clock the next morning," said Blessing. "What about the gang's activities in Bristol? What about the assaults that took place in the weeks after the burglary? The gang had threatened to kill Millie, according to her aunt."

"The only thing the jury had to decide was who was guilty of killing Millie Clark," said Alex. "Harvey and Coombs weren't charged with offences related to their drug business, grievous bodily harm, or attempted murder."

"The Crown Prosecution Service decide which cases to pursue," said Gus. "They tend to go hard on cases with a higher chance of success. For example, in November 2014, they believed, based on the evidence collected by DI Brewer and his team, that the killer was among the men who dragged Millie Clark to the churchyard."

"Micah Harvey was there too, wasn't he?" asked Lydia.

"There was never any suggestion by either of the other four men in their evidence in court that Micah Harvey went to the churchyard," said Alex. "Harvey and Coombs claimed Keel and Thatcher took Millie away. They claimed the opposite."

"Again, the CPS considered they had a cast-iron case against Micah for unlawful imprisonment," said Gus. "Adding a charge where the outcome could be more of a lottery was considered unwise. That's the way of things in the modern world."

"So, the jury decided Harvey and Coombs murdered Millie," said Lydia. "That knife you mentioned, guv? The one Craig Coombs had in the flat. Was that the murder weapon?"

"Impossible to tell, Lydia," said Gus. "It's not unusual for people like Harvey and Coombs to have weapons at their disposal. Remember that Keel and Thatcher were just heavies, according to the police. However, they were among the group's enforcers, so, no doubt, they were armed too. Therefore, in the churchyard that night, it was possible there were five weapons if everyone from the flat went along. Even though Micah Harvey was reckoned to be a mere bystander, anyone engaged in that level of criminality might have felt the need for protection."

"The gang members didn't always carry knives, guv," said Blessing. "Not all of them. Someone stabbed Justin

Cannings with a screwdriver, and Viv Whitaker was beaten with a hammer."

"Perhaps other gang members were involved when they rampaged through the BS13 postcode district searching for the burglars, Blessing," said Neil. "You're talking a lot of streets, hundreds of houses, and a dozen apartment blocks for a handful of men to cover. I bet they went mob-handed to put the fear of God into the community. That approach would have suited Harvey and Coombs, as they wanted to make sure nobody crossed them again."

"So Micah was found guilty of keeping Millie in the flat against her will," said Lydia. "What sentence did he receive?"

"Six years," said Gus, "of which I believe he served a little over three. Micah Harvey was on remand from the middle of August 2013 until November 2014. That would have come into play when the decision was taken."

"Harvey and Coombs were found guilty and jailed for life, and yet they appealed almost before the ink was dry," said Neil. "Was that a knee-jerk reaction, or did they seriously believe they could change the verdict with a different jury?"

"I can see why you referred to their defensive strategy as pivotal, guv," said Blessing. "Do you think they planned it that way? Was that London lawyer Coles one of those you read about in the newspapers?"

"The criminals' friend, d'you mean, Blessing?" asked Neil. "A lawyer more used to the Central Criminal Court than working in the sticks in Bristol. He probably ran rings around the prosecution."

"Do I believe the gang got together and decided they could have two bites at the cherry with three different people representing them?" asked Gus. "No, I don't. It's far more likely Nathan Harvey and Craig Coombs could afford the best and paid for it. Cameron Keel and Ivan Thatcher were obliged to take the economy version. Either way, Harvey and Coombs would want the distinction between management and staff to be crystal clear in that courtroom. There could be no doubt over Micah Harvey's guilt. Therefore, anyone Stuart Coles brought with him on the train from Paddington to Temple Meads would suffice."

"How long did it take the jury to reach their verdict, guv?" asked Neil.

"I can't recall reading that level of detail yet, Neil," said Gus. "The Chief Constable likes to give me the headlines. Otherwise, we'd be tied up all day."

"I've found a note on the subject in the murder file, guv," said Alex. "After receiving their final directions from the judge, the jury was taken to a private room to consider whether or not the defendants were guilty. They notified the court bailiff they wanted to return to the courtroom after two hours."

"Isn't that quick, guv?" asked Blessing. "There couldn't have been much doubt in their minds."

"Henry Fonda wasn't among the jurors, Blessing," said Neil.

"Who?" asked Blessing.

Gus groaned. It was easy to forget that Blessing was so young.

Amazing Grace came to his rescue.

"Juries are never under time pressure to reach a verdict, Blessing. They're told not to speak to one another about the case until they reach the jury room. The verdict is a decision for all of them to make together in that private space. It takes as long as it takes."

"The last thing the judge told them was that they had

heard all the evidence in the case, and there would be no more evidence presented to them," said Alex.

"That's normal. It's a straightforward enough procedure," said Gus. "When the jury reached the verdict, the court clerk asked the foreman whether they had reached a verdict upon which they were all agreed."

"In this instance, the answer was no," said Alex.

"I hadn't realised that was the case," said Gus, sitting up straight in his chair. "I presume the Chief Constable didn't consider it a highlight. DS Mercer didn't mention it either."

"A different set of rules applied when that happened," said Grace. "When the jury first retires, they get told only a unanimous verdict can be accepted. If they reach an impasse but believe a majority verdict is possible, they return to the court for further instructions. The judge, in certain circumstances, can accept a majority verdict."

"So, the judge gave them licence to return a majority verdict," said Blessing.

"That's right," said Alex. "The jury returned, discussed the case further, and then took a vote. They returned within the hour to return a majority guilty verdict by ten votes to two."

"Why did Stuart Coles believe there were grounds for an immediate appeal?" asked Lydia.

"The Juries Act 1974 requires at least two hours to pass between a jury retiring and a majority direction being given," said Grace. "In practice, it is rare for a judge to give a majority direction after such a short period. Much depends on the complexity of the case and the issues involved."

"It doesn't appear from this note that the judge gave the legal teams a chance to agree or disagree, guv," said Alex. "Stuart Coles complained that the time it took to transfer the jury from the court to the jury room and back again should have been included in the calculations. Instead, the judge had taken matters into his own hands and gave the majority verdict direction too soon. That was the first item listed on the grounds for appeal, which Coles submitted."

"A moot point," said Gus. "But that can be all you need to overturn a verdict. I would have pursued a different option if I'd been in the two defence counsels' shoes. There had to be reasonable doubt over which of the five men known to be present in the churchyard struck the mortal blows. Instead, for some reason, they went with it wasn't my clients, your honour, it was the other lot."

"There was no difference in effect between a unanimous and a majority guilty verdict, Gus," said Grace. "Sorry, I know I don't need to tell you that, but Blessing might not realise both verdicts meant the defendants were found guilty, and there could be no reduction in the sentence just because a conviction was by a majority."

"I've got a lot to learn," said Blessing.

"These are details a young Detective Constable like you will come to appreciate in time," said Gus. "Articles on the arcane workings of the criminal justice system aren't necessarily prime reading for police officers of higher rank either. I found out the hard way how inflexible the courts can sometimes be. I worked on more cases than I care to remember where I believed I had provided enough evidence for a suspect to be sent to prison, only to have the case thrown out on a technicality."

"Did the fact it was a majority verdict influence the appeal, guv?" asked Neil.

"A majority verdict alone doesn't provide grounds for appeal, Neil," said Gus. "The defendant will still be sentenced. Sentencing can take place either immediately or at a later date if further information is required. When that happens is entirely down to the judge. The jury has discharged its duty."

"A custodial sentence was inevitable in this case," said Grace, "and the judge didn't consider it necessary to adjourn the case for reports. As murder is such a serious crime, the approach to sentencing for this offence is set out in law. The judge must impose a life sentence and follow guidance on the minimum amount of time the offender must be in prison before being considered for release."

"The harm caused by any offence that results in a death is immeasurable," said Lydia. "It's impossible to set a term that equates to the value of the life lost."

"I couldn't have put it better, Lydia," said Gus. "It's unusual, but some offenders have received a whole life tariff, meaning they would spend the rest of their lives in prison. We have around seventy-five prisoners serving whole life sentences in prisons in England and Wales. In a case such as the murder of Millie Clark, where an offender brought a knife to the scene and used it to commit murder, the starting point was twenty-five years. The judge was also bound to consider any aggravating or mitigating factors that may have amended the minimum term."

"There were no mitigating factors to reduce the minimum term," said Alex. "The judge noted two aggravating factors. The accused inflicted physical and mental suffering on Millie Clark before she died and used duress and threats to enable the offence to take place. As a result, the judge increased the minimum term to thirty years."

"Given the ages of the two men involved, that *was* a life sentence," said Neil.

"So, Harvey and Coombs faced thirty years in prison," said Lydia. "But their defence team must have submitted an appeal almost before the two men reached a cell. Where did they take them?"

"HMP Long Lartin in Worcestershire," said Alex. "Sixty-five miles from Bristol. They would have been there in ninety minutes via the M5."

"The wheels of justice can move extremely slowly," said Gus. "Think what happened to Micah Harvey. He was on remand for over a year before his day in court. When he was eligible to approach the Parole Board for early release, his time served stood him in good stead. On the other hand, Harvey and Coombs were on remand in the Category A prison until April 2016. That was sixteen months after the first trial ended in November 2014. Sixteen months during which they always maintained they were innocent."

"My heart bleeds," said Neil. "Ten out of twelve would have been good enough for me."

"It could just as easily have been the other two accused, Neil," said Alex. "Why have a dog and bark yourself?"

"Exactly," said Gus. "Keel and Thatcher were employed as enforcers. Both had a list of convictions for violence. Harvey and Coombs weren't without a stain on their characters, but they were drug dealers, not street fighters."

"So, after due consideration, the Court of Appeal ordered a retrial," said Grace.

"You can imagine the reaction to that decision," said Alex. "Jeanette Clark had sat in the Bristol Crown Court just over a year earlier when Harvey and Coombs were convicted of her daughter's murder. She couldn't believe they thought the case should be heard again. However, she never missed an opportunity to get her point across to reporters from the local press."

"The second trial was held again at Bristol Crown Court," said Gus. "Most of the evidence from the first trial was heard by the new jury, but with one important difference. Cameron Keel and Ivan Thatcher declined to give evidence. Without their evidence, the prosecution's case was much weaker. There was no evidence regarding what had happened in the churchyard and nothing to prove who held the murder weapon. Stuart Coles successfully argued there was no case to answer, and the judge directed both men be acquitted of murder because of insufficient evidence."

"Did someone get to Keel and Thatcher, guv?" asked Neil.

"Who was running the gang's affairs while Harvey and Coombs were on remand?" asked Blessing.

"Keel and Thatcher were responsible for the skunk cannabis operation, guv," said Lydia. "Because they were cleared at the first trial, did they pick up from where they left off?"

"Surely, those operations were shut down by Bristol Police?" said Neil.

"These are questions we need to ask over the coming days," said Gus. "Whether everyone involved will be keen to provide answers is debatable. The Chief Constable told me that Nathan Harvey and Craig Coombs had spent the past couple of years conning their fellow Bristolians into believing they were genuine businessmen. As successful entrepreneurs, they drive expensive cars and are regularly seen in the company of beautiful young women. Those two have nothing to gain by speaking with the police. The first word we would hear if we approached them for a friendly chat would be, lawyer. No, we must uncover fresh evidence before moving in their direction."

"Micah Harvey is out of prison now, Gus," said Grace.

"He went straight back to work for his brother," said

Gus. "Whether Nathan and Craig were able to steer the ship from their prison cells near Evesham, I don't know."

"Perhaps there are gang members Bristol Police are aware of that we could question, guv," said Alex.

"If they weren't in the churchyard in Warminster, it's hard to see how they could provide anything other than hearsay evidence, Alex," said Gus. "As it happens, we can talk to Keel and Thatcher at our leisure. Cameron Keel is incarcerated in HMP Winchester, and Ivan Thatcher in HMP Birmingham. The law caught up with them in the summer of 2015. I don't know how much they might be prepared to reveal, but when you're banged up for long periods during the day, even a conversation with a detective can prove irresistible."

"They weren't so keen to go to court nine months after the first trial, guv," said Neil.

"Keel and Thatcher were hired muscle, Neil," said Gus. "They had pointed a finger towards their bosses at the suggestion of their legal representative, Kevin Escott. He persuaded them to accuse Harvey and Coombs of being responsible for Millie's death. That may have been a ploy devised by Stuart Coles and gratefully accepted by Kevin Escott. For his part, Coles would have stressed to the jury that a guilty verdict was only possible if the prosecution had proved their case beyond a reasonable doubt."

"It was certainly the only option they had available, which might result in all four men being found not guilty," said Grace.

"DS Mercer believed the judge was aware he might be setting two killers free after the retrial," said Gus. "In fact, I expect he wondered the same thing after the first trial."

"How did Jeanette Clark react when Harvey and Coombs were released?" asked Lydia.

"I can answer that," said Alex turning over another sheet of paper in the murder file. "She said she was disgusted with how things had turned out, and her faith in the police and the justice system had been destroyed. Her daughter was stabbed to death two years previously, and no one had been made to pay. Jeanette demanded to know who killed her daughter and wanted them behind bars. She told reporters she wouldn't rest until they were."

"After all the work he and his team had put into the case, DI Brewer must have been upset," said Blessing.

"Tom Brewer attended the retrial in Bristol, although he was already retired," said Gus. "As far as he was concerned, the police had thoroughly investigated Millie's murder. The Court of Appeal ordered a retrial without fault attached to the investigators or the prosecution. Tom Brewer hadn't foreseen the possibility of Cameron Keel and Ivan Thatcher not appearing at the retrial. However, he accepted that without their evidence, the judge had no alternative but to find both defendants not guilty. He stressed that Millie's killer was still at large, and the murder file remained open. If anyone had information about Millie's murder who hadn't already come forward, he urged them to do so."

"Five years after the murder, here we are," said Grace. "Where do we start?"

Chapter Five

"I'D LIKE to throw that question back to you," said Gus, looking at the rest of the team. "We've handled enough of these cases for you to have gathered a few ideas on how to proceed."

"We can request to speak with Cameron Keel and Ivan Thatcher, guv," said Neil.

"Then pray they accept," said Gus.

"What did you say happened to DI Brewer, guv?" asked Lydia.

"He lives in Heytesbury, a few miles out of Warminster," said Gus. "DI Packenham has already noted that Tom's wife is sick. We must tread carefully when interviewing her husband, but getting background, not in the murder file, is vital."

"I'll start making our list of interviewees, guv," said Alex.

"We could interview the pathologist, guv," said Neil. "Was he certain the wounds came from a single blade? Could two people have owned a similar weapon?"

"What made you think of that, Neil?" asked Alex.

"Gus told us that, at first, all five men were charged with Millie's murder. However, the CPS kept the murder charge on the books for Micah Harvey, even though they were certain they had him bang to rights for unlawful imprisonment. Gus told us at the first trial, Micah had been found guilty of false imprisonment but cleared of murder. That reinforces the idea DI Brewer believed there were several weapons in Christ Church graveyard that night."

"Fair enough," said Alex. "But we can't be sure whether Micah was ever there."

"Nor can we be sure whether the other four were all there simultaneously," said Grace.

"There had to be at least two people to explain what the pathologist reported," said Lydia.

"I want to know why we keep referring to four of the accused in pairs, guv," said Blessing. "It's always Harvey and Coombs or Keel and Thatcher. How do we know they weren't acting together?"

"Oh, heck," said Gus. "That's a can of worms I wouldn't want to open. It's my understanding the accused were responsible for selecting their legal representation. We discussed that earlier. The second trial preceded the Supreme Court decision on joint enterprise by a couple of months."

"When two or more people are named on the same indictment, they are known as the co-accused, Blessing," said Grace. "It's quite common for several people to get charged with the same crime if it arises from the same facts, as in this case. You're suggesting all five men were equally criminally liable for aiding and abetting the killer. Regardless of whether they were present when the killer stabbed Millie."

"Surely, there was evidence that each of those men knew what would happen in the churchyard," said Lydia. "If someone held Millie while she was beaten and stabbed, they assisted in the commission of the crime somehow, didn't they?"

"Maybe a trip to the seaside to speak with Henry Ash *is* in order," said Gus. "Add him to your list, Alex."

"No worries, guv," said Alex. "Did Jeanette Clark stay in Warminster?"

"Who was awarded custody of Millie's little girl, Amy?" asked Lydia.

"One at a time. Millie's mother has custody of Amy," said Gus. "Jeannette left the flat on Weymouth Street a few months after the murder. She lives with her sister, Monique, these days. Monique had no ties to keep her in Withywood. She couldn't leave the house without someone asking her about the trial and the retrial and telling her how sorry they were about Millie. It seems you can suffer from a surfeit of sympathy."

"Where did they move to, guv?" asked Alex.

"The sisters are raising Amy and Jeanette's other two children in Zeals, a village close to the border with Dorset and Somerset. They rent a modest semi-detached from the council."

"What happened to Jeannette's boyfriend?" asked Neil.

"Tyler Rowe," asked Gus, "the father of her two children? A serial philanderer, by all accounts. I got the impression that commitment was lacking in the relationship. He turned up at Jeanette's home in Keble Avenue when it suited him."

"Why do women fall for that type?" asked Blessing.

"Heaven only knows," said Grace.

"Jeanette had left Withywood because of the harassment the family faced from Harvey and Coombs," said Gus. "She feared for Millie's safety as well as her own. Tyler Rowe wasn't consulted, as far as we can tell. So perhaps she made her escape when he wasn't sleeping in her bed in Keble Avenue."

"Did Rowe find out where Jeanette had gone, guv?" asked Lydia.

"There was a mention of his name in evidence provided to DI Brewer," said Gus. "At some point during the four weeks that the Clark family lived in the flat before the murder, Tyler Rowe may have been present. How long for we need to find out."

"The boyfriend could have found Jeanette before Micah Harvey did then, guv," said Neil. "I wonder how long it was he had that information? Why didn't Rowe make a call to his bosses? Maybe he thought more of Jeanette than the police thought. Where is he now, do we know?"

"Bishopsworth," said Gus. "A five-minute drive from Keble Avenue. Living in a flat above an Indian takeaway on Broomhill Road."

"The sort of accommodation Rick Chalmers would enjoy, guv," said Neil.

"Positives and negatives, Neil," said Gus. "Just like anywhere else."

"What does Rowe do for a living, guv?" asked Blessing. "Does he still work for the drug dealers?"

"It's unlikely he's got an honest job, but since the first trial, he's distanced himself from the gang," said Gus. "Bristol Police told Tom Brewer that Rowe had fathered several children and failed to support them. The latest number is seven, with five different women. Two of those children are living in Zeals with Jeanette and Monique

Clark. But, whether Tyler Rowe knows or cares is unknown."

"If Harvey and Coombs knew Tyler Rowe failed to pass on information about Millie and her new address, he would have received a visit from the heavy mob," said Alex. "What do you think? Is he worth tracking down?"

"Tyler Rowe will have inside knowledge of the gang that could prove useful," said Gus. "He was only one of the minions, but a few minutes of conversation from him could be far more than Harvey and Coombs will ever be prepared to give us."

"Can we discount the lady who found the body, guv?" asked Alex.

"I can't see what Brenda Petty can add to the statement we already have, Alex," said Gus. "The same goes for DS Hamer and DC Keen, the first detectives on the scene."

"That leaves Fergus Munro, Millie's boyfriend, guv," said Alex.

"He was Amy's father, wasn't he?" asked Blessing.

"Munro got Millie pregnant," said Lydia. "He persuaded her to go on a thieving spree to help pay for their drugs. I wouldn't be surprised if Munro got her into drugs in the first place."

"Fergus couldn't follow Millie to Warminster," said Gus. "He was on remand when the gang searched for the three people who broke into the property in Hartcliffe. We need to ask Jeanette Clark whether Fergus Munro ever got in touch after he left prison. From what we know of his character, it's unlikely."

"Did Cannings and Munro receive custodial sentences, guv?" asked Neil.

"They did, Neil," said Gus. "Munro initially avoided the beating Justin Cannings received in Bristol, as we know.

Cannings joined him at HMP Erlestoke after he'd been released from the hospital. We can track down Justin Cannings for background. Was what happened to Fergus Munro a few weeks into his sentence a random attack? Or did the order come from Nathan Harvey? The Wiltshire prison is less than forty miles from Bristol. It's not inconceivable that Erlestoke held young villains from Bristol among their five-hundred prison population. Fergus Munro was attacked by as many as six inmates and beaten black and blue. Munro suffered two black eyes, several broken ribs, and a broken hand. He did little to protect himself as he feared there would be consequences if Harvey and Coombs heard he fought back. When he was found unconscious in the prison shower block, he was taken to the Great Western Hospital in Swindon. Doctors felt it necessary to give him a head scan, but he escaped without a skull fracture or any lasting damage."

"The attack on Munro is consistent with the trend over the past decade, Gus," said Grace. "Violence in prisons is spiralling out of control, with prisoner-on-prisoner assaults increasing by fifty percent. Serious assaults have more than doubled in the same period. It could just have been the way he looked at another prisoner. Someone off his head on drugs."

"I've read the figures, Grace," said Gus. "They make grim reading. I know Fergus Munro wasn't alone and that one in five prisoners gets assaulted. The Ministry of Justice has admitted that the levels of violence must be tackled. Safety in prisons is fundamental to the proper functioning of our justice system. Prisons are supposed to be places of rehabilitation. However, this assault wasn't caused by the availability of drugs circulating within a prison such as Erlestoke. It's far more likely Munro was targeted from the outside. Nathan Harvey had to ensure he punished everyone who disrespected him."

"With so much time locked away, prisoners do turn to drugs to provide an escape, Gus," said Grace. "More specifically, the legal highs banned in 2016 had a dramatic and destabilising effect. The effects of those drugs could be unpredictable and extreme. Their use was linked to attacks on other prisoners and staff, self-inflicted deaths, serious illness, and life-changing self-harm. The Prisons and Probation Ombudsman identified almost forty deaths in prisons two years before the attack on Fergus Munro. All those deaths could be linked to the use of legal highs. The situation showed no improvement in the next twelve months, so the death toll rose. No doubt, there are alternative highs in the prison system today. Prison staff have to be on their guard every minute."

"I think I've used this phrase before, Grace," said Gus. "I'll bow to your superior knowledge."

"During my spell at Portishead, I was allowed to visit HMP Ashfield, near Bristol. I met prisoners who had self-segregated to escape the violence caused by these substances. I talked with members of staff who described the terrifying effects they can have on those who take them. Staff told me how they struggled to get prisoners safely to and from education, training, and other activities. The implications on a reform programme based on enhancing the role of education in rehabilitation were obvious."

"Well, further background to the justice system will improve our team's understanding of the issues. One new fact every day is the high road to success, as one of my old teachers used to tell me. In this instance, I'm convinced Munro was punished for his part in the Court Farm Road burglary. Pure and simple."

"Are both Cannings and Munro still in prison, guv?" asked Neil.

"The Chief Constable failed to mention what happened to Justin Cannings," said Gus. "As for Fergus Munro, he started an apprenticeship with a firm in Gloucester after he left HMP Erlestoke. That suggested Fergus had cleaned up his act. Perhaps his time in the Great Western Hospital in Swindon gave him time to consider his future. I understand he's now married with a six-month-old son."

"I'm still searching for a note on the whereabouts of Justin Cannings, guv," said Alex. "It must be hidden away in this murder file somewhere. I *have* found comments made by Pippa Malone, Fergus's wife, after his release. Firstly, she was upset about the violence, of course, and stated Fergus's only priority after the attack was getting home safe. The next quote from her was six weeks later when she complained her husband wasn't getting the support he needed from the authorities."

"A lack of support after leaving prison is a common complaint throughout the system," said Grace. "Many prisoners also say they don't get access to the right programmes inside to address their offending behaviour. Instead of getting help, as many as forty percent of prisoners spent less than two hours a day out of their cell. Excessive time locked in a cell can often lead to a deterioration in mental health."

"Pippa Munro also said Fergus wasn't the same man she had met on a night out in Bristol," said Alex. "This was days before he was arrested for the burglaries."

"When he was supposedly Millie Clark's boyfriend," said Lydia. "His daughter was only nine months old, and he was seeing someone else."

"Pippa said since he came out of prison, Fergus suffered mood swings," said Alex. "For days, he would wander around like a lost sheep, and suddenly, something would irritate him, and he'd go ballistic."

"Did he have a quick temper before he went to prison?" asked Grace.

"He was an addict, ma'am," said Neil. "They don't tend to be the most even-tempered of people."

"The symptoms Pippa describes would match several of those for an addict," said Lydia. "Anxiety, depression, and angry outbursts are typical effects of long-term use. The murder file suggested Fergus was turning his life around, guv. Did he get help after he recovered from the attack? Or was it the help of a good woman that did the trick after he left Erlestoke?"

"We can speak with Fergus and Pippa later in the week," said Gus. "Fergus is still working in Gloucester. How long his apprenticeship was for, I don't know. But, if he's still capable of going from nought to sixty in a blink of an eye, it might indicate he's not entirely out of the woods."

"A not unfamiliar event, Gus," said Grace. "Almost half of addicts relapse after battling to get clean."

"I still haven't found anything relating to Justin Cannings, guv," said Alex.

"What about the detectives who worked on those burglaries, guv?" asked Blessing. "Could they point us towards Justin Cannings?"

"That's possible, Blessing," said Gus. "Their names must be in that file somewhere, Alex. Items such as Pippa Munro's updates have been added since the retrial. Tom Brewer said the file remained open. Although nobody has come forward with anything crucial, at least a few scraps have been added."

"The burglaries were handled by DI Mick Budd and DS Lizzie Gale, guv," said Alex.

"Add them to the list, Alex," said Gus.

"I know we mustn't concern ourselves about the claims of a cover-up," said Grace. "But do we know how many calls Craig Coombs made from the flat in Weymouth Street?"

"His service provider provided his mobile phone logs," said Alex. "Coombs made three phone calls between the hours we believe he was in Warminster. The first was at four o'clock. The second call was just before seven, and the last was at ten minutes to eleven."

"Who did he call, and what was said?" asked Grace. "Do we know?"

"Those conversations could have gone to a burner phone," said Neil.

"We wouldn't be able to trace those, would we, guv?" asked Blessing.

"I'll come to that in a moment, Blessing," said Gus. "Once Coombs was arrested for an indictable offence, DI Brewer had the power to seize any phones Coombs had in his possession."

"Where was he arrested, guv?" asked Neil.

"I bet he was arrested with Nathan Harvey," whispered Blessing.

"I'm more interested to learn why he was arrested," said Lydia.

"If you were going to travel to Heytesbury with me, you might find out, Lydia," said Gus. "As it is, you'll have to wait until Grace and I get back."

"We've already heard an outline of how the investigation went, Lydia," said Grace. "A few steps were missed when the Chief Constable briefed Gus, but DI Brewer gathered evidence and put together a compelling case."

"Tom Brewer spoke with everyone we've mentioned

today," said Gus. "He soon learned what had happened in Bristol before Millie Clark moved to Warminster. Witnesses put Micah Harvey in the town on the afternoon she died. He was seen accosting Millie and dragging her to the flat. The phone call to his brother was logged, as was Nathan's call to Craig Coombs. We know Keel and Thatcher also received a phone call. Once the times of those calls were known, Tom Brewer was able to work out how long the four men would have taken to drive to Warminster. Eyewitnesses saw their car parked in the car park a hundred yards from the flat. The sightings matched DI Brewer's timeline. Monique Clark's statement showed that Harvey and Coombs had threatened to kill her niece before Jeanette left Withywood. Neighbours in Weymouth Street heard the shouting match during the evening as Millie pleaded for her life. Nobody heard Millie and her captors leaving the flat, but they did hear screams at around one in the morning from near Christ Church. Tom Brewer couldn't know for certain who had taken Millie to the churchyard, but Henry Ash's post-mortem results showed at least two men were with Millie. So, Tom Brewer went to Bristol Police, asked for their help finding the suspects he had identified, and the five men were taken into custody."

"The details of those arrests are in the murder file, guv," said Alex. "Nathan Harvey was arrested at his home in Court Farm Road. Uniformed officers caught Craig Coombs in nearby Park Wood Close. Coombs had half a dozen security cameras at his property, and he was out of his patio doors and over the back fence before Tom Brewer's colleagues reached his front doorstep. A foot chase followed, but Coombs carried too much weight to be an athlete. Cameron Keel and Ivan Thatcher kept clear of their cannabis farm in Shortwood Road, Hartcliffe. Word that the police were swooping on gang members reached them within minutes. They made the five-mile drive to Temple Meads station and would have been en route to Paddington, London, or New Street, Birmingham if staff monitoring traffic cameras in the city centre hadn't spotted Keel's erratic driving. Instead, uniformed officers greeted the pair when they approached the ticket office at Temple Meads."

"What about Micah Harvey?" asked Neil.

"Micah still lived with his Mum in one of Nathan's properties on Huntingham Road in Withywood. Tom Brewer arrested him while his Bristol colleagues were chasing Keel and Thatcher. Everyone was picked up within a three-hour window."

"That makes more sense now that I've followed every step, guv," said Lydia.

"It fits with what we know, Lydia," said Gus. "I wouldn't assume we've got all the steps yet, let alone all the players. We've been caught out before."

"You were going to explain the phones, guv," said Blessing.

"Essentially, police can search premises in the process of using their power of entry to arrest a suspect," said Gus. "So, with the correctly worded warrants Tom Brewer, or his Bristol counterparts, were entitled to secure various devices the gang members used to communicate. They could also enter premises without a warrant connected to a person under arrest for an indictable offence. Which was useful when they learned that Micah Harvey didn't have a place of his own."

"That was covered under the Police and Criminal Evidence Act, guv," said Blessing. "I knew that bit. What

I'm not clear on is whether a burner phone is as secure as Neil thinks."

"I can help with that, Blessing," said Alex. "I attended a course while I was at Gablecross before my accident. Generally, a burner phone number *can* be traced. All mobile phones and burner apps go through a service provider. Your identity can be tracked via call logs, data usage, location, and text messages. The police can compel companies to provide this information. Since the service provider is involved in every phone call, text, and data link, unsecured call logs and account information reveal subscriber identities. Individuals give up their rights to the data collected when they activate any mobile phone service."

"The whole idea of burner phones back when they were actual throwaway phones was that they couldn't be traced back to the user," said Grace. "People would buy a temporary phone, use a temporary phone number, and get rid of the phone when it no longer served their purpose."

"If we dig out the content of Craig Coombs's phone calls, we might get an insight into what was planned for Millie Clark and who was responsible," said Gus. "On the other hand, the calls could have been unrelated. The wheels of the drug business were still turning in relentless fashion 24/7 back in Bristol. Millie Clark was just a side issue to Harvey and Coombs. A side issue that needed to be dealt with. As far as text messages either of the men might have sent relating to their criminal activities, it's likely they were encrypted."

"We could get times and dates of when they were sent, but not the content," said Neil. "Every villain is in a WhatsApp group these days. It stands to reason."

"Anyone else we should consider approaching for an interview?" asked Gus.

"Who replaced DI Brewer, guv?" asked Neil. "They must have handled the case after he retired. They could have been responsible for those later additions Alex read out if they're still around. Perhaps they could expand the footnotes."

"The new DI was a rising star who transferred to Wiltshire from Hertfordshire," said Gus. "We'll find Clare Edwards in Norfolk these days, where she's an Assistant Chief Constable. She sounds like someone you might enjoy calling, Grace."

"If you don't mind giving me pointers on what to ask her, Gus, it will be my pleasure. I do know a little about the area, after all. So we'll have some common ground."

"We'll get our heads together in the morning to work out our strategy for every person we intend to contact," said Gus. "For the rest of today, I suggest you all make yourselves familiar with the contents of the murder file."

"I'll get the street maps on the walls, guv," said Alex. "We've already got the crime scene photos separated from the folder to pin to the whiteboard."

"What was it Sherlock Holme's used to say?" asked Gus.

"This feels like a three-pipe problem, guv?" said Neil.

"I thought that was it," said Gus. "Useless for me, as I don't smoke. Plus, I'm cutting back on the hard stuff. So, I can't opt for a three-tumbler problem."

"My father says he finds it best to sleep on a problem, guv," said Blessing. "It's never worked for me, though."

"We already have the killer among the names in that murder file, Blessing," said Gus. "If we ask the right questions of the right people, I'm sure the truth will come out."

Nobody argued with Gus, regardless of whether they agreed with him. Finally, at five o'clock, the office emptied, and Gus drove home to Urchfont. Suzie's Golf was already parked in its usual spot outside the bungalow.

Gus drew alongside, switched off his engine and went indoors. He went straight to the kitchen. He was in charge tonight, and the sooner he started, the sooner they could sit together in the lounge and relax.

"Everything okay?" asked Suzie. "I was reading in the lounge when you came in."

"A long day, with painfully slow progress," said Gus.

"Me too," said Suzie. "Don't forget. We're not discussing our cases tonight. Geoff Mercer didn't quite get me to sign the Official Secrets Act, but 'hush-hush, whisper who dares' comes to mind."

"Lovely," said Gus. "Did you ever meet Clare Edwards when she worked at Warminster?"

"I was too junior for her to deign to engage in meaningful conversation, Gus," said Suzie. "You know what these high-fliers are like. Clare barked a couple of orders in my direction, but that was it. Was she involved in the case you're working on?"

"She took over from Tom Brewer when he retired at the end of 2015. Tom attended a retrial ordered in our murder case, which took place the following April. DI Edwards would have handled matters for three months before attending Crown Court in Bristol, then kept tabs on things as the murder faded from memory until she got her next promotion."

"That sounds as if you believe she missed something," said Suzie.

"I have no idea," said Gus puffing out his cheeks. "Unless someone *did* drop the ball somewhere along the way, I'm struggling to see how we can resolve the major sticking point."

"We're not supposed to be discussing this," said Suzie.

"Fair enough," said Gus. "I'll take Kelechi Umeh's advice and sleep on it."

"I haven't spoken to Blessing for a while," said Suzie. "I wonder what Kelechi thinks of the new Vice-Chancellor. He used to be Professor of Physics at Bath twenty years ago, and after the salary furore over the past couple of years, the post is a bit of a poisoned chalice."

"Kelechi struck me as the sort to protest if his department was facing budget cuts while the bosses were raking it in," said Gus. "It's a familiar story, I'm afraid. Well, you've successfully deflected me from thoughts of my case. Back to our meal, I remember you suggested I surprise you with our meal tonight. I've decided I'm desperate for a Chinese. Which of the three takeaway numbers do you want me to call?"

"Surprise me," said Suzie.

Wednesday, 31 October 2018

GUS WAS in the shower before Suzie was fully awake. Then, as he crossed the hallway to the kitchen, he heard the rattle of pans.

"I'm starving," she said. "We've got plenty of eggs. I'm having two poached eggs on toast. Will you join me?"

"Sounds good to me," said Gus. "I thought after that veggie chow mein last night you would have been happy with a croissant."

"What were you thinking? Ordering all those extra side dishes?"

"I needed the boxes," said Gus. "With every box I

opened, I put another suspect under the microscope. I weighed up the contents of their particular box and tried to determine whether they were guilty."

"You said you were going to sleep on it," said Suzie.

"I did. After I'd checked every box," said Gus. "I slept like a baby. I must thank Kelechi the next time I see him."

"And have you worked out who did it?" asked Suzie.

"It wasn't the egg fried rice, of that I'm certain," said Gus. "All the other suspects are still in the game."

"Will you be good company tonight when we meet the Reverend and her fiancé?"

"Aren't I always, darling?" said Gus, buttering four slices of toast.

Suzie placed two hard-poached eggs on Gus's two slices of toast, keeping the two runny ones for herself.

"Oops," she said with a grin.

At eight thirty-five, they were outside the bungalow sharing a kiss before leaving for work.

"See you tonight," said Suzie. "Don't work too hard."

"I'll do my best," said Gus. "Love you."

Suzie jumped into the driving seat of her Golf and set off towards the gateway. Gus had always thought the Le Mans start was overrated. He took his time getting ready, and as he suspected, despite only pootling along the lane, his Focus was stopped directly behind Suzie at the first set of traffic lights again.

They exchanged waves at the same point as yesterday. Suzie drove to London Road to do battle with officers who had disabused their position of trust. Gus made for the Old Police Station office to begin the search for a killer in earnest.

Chapter Six

GUS SPOTTED Neil Davis pulling into the car park ahead of him and watched as his colleague reversed into the space to the left of Lydia Logan Barre's red Mini. Gus parked his Focus on the other side of Lydia, leaving Blessing the option of whichever end space she thought least dangerous. Grace would have to take what was left.

Those two would arrive together in a few weeks, and there would always be a spare space. Gus realised he would need to ask Geoff Mercer to acquire a traffic cone to prevent a cheeky local from claiming squatters' rights. However, it would be cheaper than letting the Crime Review Team have a Detective Sergeant to replace Luke Sherman.

As Gus walked towards the lift, two more cars entered the car park. A Nissan Micra led the way, followed by a Smart car that Gus would never grow to love. He stood with his hand poised over the button.

"Going up?" he asked.

"Two more for the first floor, please," said Grace.

"Good morning, guv," said Blessing. "Another warm day, with barely a cloud in the sky. We mustn't grumble for the time of year."

"Positively, balmy, Blessing," said Gus as they waited for the lift.

"Hallowe'en," said Grace. "All Hallow's Eve when the souls of the dead return to their homes. Will you be warding off evil spirits in Urchfont tonight?"

"I was hoping for a quiet evening in the Lamb," said Gus. "We're meeting friends for a regular midweek meal and lively conversation. But, instead, I suppose the pub will be filled with idiots in masks who can't hold their drinks. Thank goodness it's only one night a year."

"It's very popular in the States, guv," said Blessing.

"If only they'd kept it there, Blessing," said Gus.

"I didn't have you down as a spoilsport, Gus," said Grace.

"It's that time of the year, Grace," said Gus. "Less than a week separates two occasions when people celebrate events without knowing their meaning. Bonfire Night might have been relevant at one time. Now Hallowe'en and November the fifth are just commercialized dates in the calendar where big business squeeze as much money out of families as possible. Christmas is around the corner. How can people afford it all?"

The lift doors opened, and they entered the office.

"Morning, guv," said Neil. "Today, you should wish us happy haunting rather than happy hunting when we leave for an interview."

"Don't make it worse, Neil," said Grace.

"What have I done now?" asked Neil.

"Right, Alex," said Gus. "Who's first in the firing line?"

"Not me, I hope," Neil whispered to Grace as she sat behind her desk.

"Tom Brewer can see you whenever you wish, guv," said Alex. "He will be at home all day."

"Give Tom a callback, Alex," said Gus. "Grace and I can be in Heytesbury in about half an hour. What have you got lined up for the rest of you?"

"Henry Ash, the pathologist. He says he's home by mid-morning after walking the dogs and fetching his copy of The Times from the newsagents. Lydia can drive us to Exmouth if that's okay?"

Gus checked what Lydia was wearing this morning. As long as Henry Ash didn't have a heart condition, it should be safe enough. Nobody should have legs that long.

"That's fine," he said. "What about Neil and Blessing?"

"I thought they could visit Monique and Jeanette Clark," said Alex.

"Will they both be at home?" asked Gus. "Do either of them work?"

"Do you think we should speak with them separately?" asked Neil.

"I do, Neil," said Gus. "Jeanette might not open up about her relationship with Millie's father or Tyler Rowe if her older sister is in the room. Also, her relationship with Millie may not have been as rosy as she painted after the murder. Death has a strange effect on people and their memories."

"Monique could have her secrets too, guv," said Blessing.

"It could be difficult to find sufficient privacy in their semi-detached house," said Gus. "We should invite them to attend the police station in Warminster, one at a time. See what you can arrange, Neil. If there isn't a room they can make available, be creative. Look for somewhere where both women will feel at ease. We need them to tell us a lot more than they gave to Tom Brewer and his team five years ago."

"Got it, guv," said Neil. "Leave it to the A-team."

"In your dreams, Neil," whispered Grace.

"Don't get comfortable, Grace," said Gus. "We're on our way. Alex will have warned Tom Brewer to expect us well before we reach Heytesbury."

Grace gathered her things and chased after Gus. He was already striding towards the lift.

"Alex hasn't mentioned anything about the tougher calls he had to make, Gus," said Grace as they travelled down in the lift.

"No news is good news, Grace," Gus replied.

Gus eased the Focus from the parking space. Blessing had parked so close to him that Grace could not open the passenger door. They joined the morning traffic on Church Street when she was seated and belted.

"I prefer the A350 through Trowbridge and then join the B3414 to drive into Warminster before finding the A36 to reach the village," he said. "Suzie would drive across Salisbury Plain if she was heading out that way from London Road. A more picturesque journey, perhaps, but this is more practical."

"By driving through the town, we can get a feel for the place," said Grace. "Neither of us has spent much time there."

"Exactly," said Gus. "I like to learn how places in the murder file relate to one another, distances, and whether the places are smart and well-kept or downmarket and scruffy."

"A comparison that applies equally to the people and the buildings," said Grace.

"People often use the word neighbourhood without

considering that it's not just an area where people live and interact with one another," said Gus. "They tend to have their own identity based on who lives there and nearby places. Residents may have similar types of families, incomes, and education levels. You will find restaurants, bookstores, and parks nearby with better neighbourhoods. While at the other end of the scale, you find takeaways, pound shops, and abandoned supermarket trolleys."

Grace laughed.

"Are you sure you didn't get out of bed on the wrong side? Nobody's safe this morning."

"I say what I see, Grace," said Gus. "We're on the outskirts of Trowbridge now, a classic example. The boundaries are blurred between one neighbourhood and another. It's hard to tell where one starts and another ends. Major streets often act as logical boundaries, but people can often define a neighbourhood by its characteristics. Residents in the houses on our left generally have similar social characteristics. For example, they share a sense of public order."

"Move two streets across on our right, and suddenly you're in an area rife with school truancy, anti-social behaviour, and sexual assaults. If we asked Polebarn Road for a hotspot that attracts the most attention for their officers, then a street over there would be in the top three."

"We're halfway to Warminster now. It doesn't display the same demographics as Bristol," said Gus. "The city port has always attracted immigrants across the centuries. St Paul's was where the Windrush generation settled. Sometimes, the dominant ethnicity in a neighbourhood defines its character. People cluster near others with the same cultural heritage."

"When they do band together," said Grace. "It strengthens their sense of community and preserves cultural traditions. Residents benefit from nearby relatives, a common language, and stores and services geared to their needs. In addition, they are close to important institutions, such as churches and clubs."

"That's why St Paul's has become such a vibrant, colourful neighbourhood," said Gus. "It has problems, but a few miles away, there are streets lined with despair. One in four children in Bristol lives in poverty, as do one in five older people. Jeanette Clark raised Millie in one of those neighbourhoods. Monique couldn't escape to somewhere better, like Redlands, where a three-bedroomed home sets you back a million pounds, and the streets are neat and without litter. There's hardly any graffiti, and crime rates are as low as expected."

"A stone's throw away in relative terms?" asked Grace.

"A little over five miles," said Gus. "The inequality between neighbourhoods is stark. So you can understand why Jeanette fled to Wiltshire in general and Warminster in particular. It has a few rough edges but is a big step up from where they were."

"The flat on Weymouth Street certainly didn't sound ideal," said Grace.

"I imagine Jeanette got what she could at short notice," said Gus. "Escape was her priority. She wanted to save her daughter's life."

"Jeanette moved to Zeals months after leaving Bristol," said Grace.

"Can you blame her?" asked Gus. "Weymouth Street didn't hold happy memories. She wouldn't enjoy hearing the bells at Christ Church every Sunday reminding her that her daughter died just a five-minute walk away."

"Why Zeals, though?" asked Grace.

"It certainly helped that Monique wanted to move in

with her," said Gus. "The countryside would have been attractive to both women. No doubt, the children appreciate the fresh air and smaller schools too. Zeals is one of those villages that's an anomaly. You might imagine it follows the pattern of many other rural villages. A place packed with retired rich people: bankers, factory managers, and shop-keepers. In fact, Zeals has a younger population than the vast majority of rural communities. On the flip side, more people claim Universal Credit in Zeals than elsewhere in the county."

"So, unemployment levels are high," said Grace. "What about crime?"

"Lower than most, and it has excellent links for those who need to commute. Any chance you'll change your mind and move there?"

"I'll pass, Gus," said Grace. "Worton Farm will be my home until my next promotion. I shall inevitably be in a different part of the country when that comes."

"I hope we don't lose you just yet, Grace," said Gus. "You've still got plenty to learn."

Grace gave him a sidelong glance.

"I can never tell when you're serious, Gus Freeman."

"My point, exactly," said Gus. "Give me your first impressions of Warminster. Oh, and keep an eye out for the turning to Heytesbury once we hit the A36. I've been on that road twice in my life, and I was deep in thought on both occasions. Don't worry. I wasn't driving."

"Lydia was driving, I presume?" asked Grace.

"Perhaps. If she was, I was deep in thought with my eyes closed."

"No comment," said Grace. "Well, I'm impressed by the approach to the town centre. A pleasant mix of country cottages on the outskirts, terraced housing from the Victorian age, and the occasional imposing Georgian building as we move towards the centre. It lives up to its description of being a friendly market town. I wish there weren't so many roundabouts. Oh, look, there's the turning for Christ Church."

"Forget it for now, Grace. We don't want to keep Tom Brewer waiting too long. Maybe we'll tour the town on our way back to the office."

"We stay on the B3414 to the A36 junction at Norton Bavant. It won't be long now."

"He's another star from the silent era that people have long forgotten," said Gus.

"Sorry? You've lost me," said Grace.

"No matter. Another couple of miles, and we'll be knocking on the door of Primrose Cottage."

Gus joined the stream of traffic on the busy A36, and at yet another roundabout, he saw the Heytesbury exit.

"A lot of red brick houses and whitewashed cottages," said Grace. "The thing I notice most is the amount of space. They never built houses right on the edge of the road in the old days, did they?"

"They never imagined everyone having a car either," said Gus as he left the High Street and guided the Focus down a leafy lane. He prayed nothing was coming in the opposite direction.

"Here we are," said Grace. "Primrose Cottage. Yours for half a million."

"Idyllic," said Gus. "I hope Tom doesn't mind me parking on his driveway. If I left it on the highway, I'd get done for obstruction."

"I know," said Grace. "The tree branches were brushing the roof of your car on both sides."

They walked towards the cottage. Tom Brewer opened the front door and greeted them.

"You must be Gus Freeman and DI Packenham," he said. "Welcome to our humble abode."

Grace produced her ID while Gus fumbled in his jacket pocket for confirmation he was a consultant.

"I'm Grace, Mr Brewer," she said. "Let's dispense with formalities. May I call you Tom?"

"Of course," said Tom. "You're very young to be a Detective Inspector. It took us far longer in our day."

"We understand you worked with Kenneth Truelove," said Grace.

"I haven't seen Ken in ages," said Tom. "Come on through to the kitchen. Cynthia's nodded off again in the lounge. I don't want to disturb her; she had another restless night."

"Kenneth told me your wife was unwell," said Gus. "It must be hard."

"Dementia," said Tom. "The decline has been gradual and started a year after I retired. We had planned so much. Finally, after decades of me having to pull out of all sorts of things because of a case, we could go anywhere we chose. A cruise around the Med and a trip to Scotland for the Northern Lights were all we managed. Are you married, Gus?"

"I lost my wife six months after I retired," said Gus. "I was sat in Swindon Crown Court during the day, then in town having a few beers in the evening with my old team. We celebrated after watching a gang get sent down for armed robberies—my last case. When I got home, I found Tess on the kitchen floor. It was a brain aneurysm. The doctors said she was dead before she hit the floor."

"It's tough either way, isn't it?" said Tom. "You had no

warning, no time to prepare for the end. I have no idea how long Cynthia will stay with me. I'm losing a little of her every day, but I'll care for her. It's what we signed up for, isn't it? In sickness and in health. Let me get you a coffee, tea, or soft drink; what is it to be?"

"Black coffee for me," said Gus.

"A soft drink for me, Tom," said Grace.

"Cynthia enjoys barley water," said Tom.

"That's fine," said Grace.

Gus and Grace sat at the kitchen table while Tom fixed the drinks.

"Right," he said. "First things first. How are Ken and his wife? I must admit I was surprised when he stepped up to Chief Constable. I appreciate the circumstances were less than ideal. Although I've been out of the game for almost three years, I still have friends in the force."

"In that case, you'll be aware Wiltshire had a rapid turnover in the top job," said Gus. "The PCC believed a period of stability was in order. Kenneth's wife wanted him to retire, but when Kenneth suggested a year to eighteen months as Chief Constable wouldn't harm her street cred, she postponed her Mediterranean cruises."

"Don't get me wrong," said Tom. "I wasn't suggesting Ken wasn't up to the task. Far from it, he's always been a policeman's policeman. I'm sure he's the steady hand on the tiller the county requires until the storm passes. We thoroughly enjoyed our time, learning on the job and working together in Warminster. Sorry, Grace, I expect that sounds like an old-fashioned approach. We weren't university educated, unlike you and your contemporaries. We came up through the ranks, where promotion depended on dead men's shoes. There were no fast-tracked graduates, of either sex, in our day."

"Times change, Tom," said Grace.

"When Kenneth persuaded me to come out of retirement, he accepted I was a dinosaur," said Gus. "He warned me the knives would be out the second I made a mistake, but he had the confidence to give me the resources to tackle the cold cases he had in his desk drawer."

"You've been successful," said Tom. "I told you; the grapevine is still in good working order. I'm sure you want to ask me questions about the next case on your list. Fire away."

"When did you get the call?" asked Grace.

"We lived in town at the time," said Tom. "A detached house, only a two-minute drive from my old stamping ground in Station Road. I had arrived in the office, ready to start work at nine. There were a handful of ongoing cases my team was dealing with. My colleague DS Andrea Howell and I were running through the list when someone stuck their head around the door. The desk sergeant had received a report of a dead body in the churchyard at Christ Church. His first reaction was it was a wind-up, but he'd sent a PCSO to check. Soon, he had confirmation of a dead body above the ground, which looked like a stabbing. I told the desk sergeant to alert Polebarn Road, so they could arrange for the pathologist to attend, plus a forensics team. We sent two more uniforms to secure the scene, keep the public away, and await further instructions. Andrea and I were all set to drive over to Christ Church, but one of the incidents we were checking on was vandalism at the skate park. She reminded me that two of our bright young things were already close by. Andrea contacted DS Robin Hamer and told him to get to the churchyard with DC Georgia Keen, pronto."

"You didn't think it warranted your presence?" asked Grace.

"We rarely got a murder in Warminster, Grace," said Tom. "Ken Truelove and I never handled one during the years we worked together. Anyway, although the PCSO was adamant the girl was dead, it was the first time she'd seen a dead body, and until we had confirmation it wasn't a drug overdose, an accidental death, or suicide, I felt DS Hamer could handle things. Because our station had been reduced to a community policing operation, if anything major happened, we always had to wait for specialist support to drive over from Trowbridge before making any progress. So I left Andrea checking the paperwork on our caseload and drove down to Deverill Road about an hour after the desk received the initial call."

"Did you speak with Mrs Petty?" asked Grace.

"I had a brief chat," said Tom. "She visited her husband's grave regularly. I can't recall the exact details, but his death was fairly recent. It wasn't unusual for her to put flowers on his grave early in the morning. She gathered them from their garden and popped into the churchyard on her way into town to do her daily shopping. Mrs Petty told me she dropped the flowers onto the grave and ran towards the gateway when she saw the body. There was nobody else in the vicinity that early in the morning."

"She saw a delivery driver on the opposite side of the road," said Grace.

"That's right. He spoke to the desk sergeant. Unfortunately, because the woman was distressed, the message wasn't as clear as it might have been, which caused the sergeant to wonder if someone was pulling his leg. Also, I believe the chap from the brewery was Latvian, and his English wasn't great, which added to the confusion."

"What was happening around you while you spoke to Brenda Petty?" asked Gus.

"By the time I had arrived, Henry Ash, the pathologist, was on site, the uniforms had all but done their job, and the Crime Scene Investigators were crawling over the church-yard searching for clues."

"Who did you speak to next?" asked Grace.

"I asked Robin Hamer for an update," said Tom. "He told me when the two uniformed officers arrived, they found Mrs Petty comforting the young PCSO rather than the other way around. Robin and Georgia reached the churchyard perhaps ten minutes after the constable and the other PCSO."

"We understood the people from Polebarn Road arrived forty-five minutes after the initial call," said Gus. "Those timings don't seem to gel. I thought your detectives arrived before the cavalry."

"We were slow off the mark, Gus," said Tom. "The desk sergeant sent the female PCSO to check the call was genuine. When she called in to say she was standing next to a willow tree, looking at a bloodstained body, and trying to hold onto her breakfast, he rapidly contacted Trowbridge. Henry Ash lived on this side of Bratton, so he drove straight to Christ Church after receiving the call. Henry could have got there in ten minutes if he pushed it. So, he was on the scene before Robin and Georgia drove across from the skate park on the other side of town. Henry hadn't been there long, but he was happy to share his initial thoughts."

"Which were?" asked Gus.

"The deceased was a female in her early twenties. Death was caused by five stab wounds she had received to the upper chest. Henry noted that the deceased showed evidence of regular drug use. Both her arms were bruised between the elbow and the shoulder. Someone had punched her in the face, possibly breaking the nose. Further examination would be required to determine whether there were any fractures to the eye socket or the cheekbone. Henry considered the deceased had suffered a severe beating and was then stabbed to death. The victim was fully clothed, and there was no indication of sexual assault."

"What did he say about the bruising to the upper arms?" asked Grace.

"Henry thought someone had restrained the victim from behind while the person in front of her had carried out the beating. The stabbing could have occurred at the culmination of this attack. Another person present could have stabbed her on the ground after she collapsed due to her injuries. You know how it goes. Henry qualified everything by saying that he couldn't confirm the time of death, nor anything else he'd mentioned until he'd completed the autopsy."

"The autopsy report didn't include anything that wasn't covered by his initial thoughts," said Gus.

"Except the time of death," said Tom. "Henry recorded TOD as being between midnight and two in the morning. By the time we received the autopsy report, we'd learned quite a bit about Millie Clark. His findings matched our timeline and the background we'd uncovered."

"Were you there when the forensic people found the murder weapon?" asked Grace.

"I'd returned to the office," said Tom. "The forensic crew concentrated on the area closest to the willow tree and the pathways that led from the two entrances. The victim wasn't wearing a coat, nor did she take a mobile phone with her as far as we could tell."

"Did that turn up later?" asked Gus.

"Forensics found it in the flat in Weymouth Street, where she lived with her mother," said Tom. "However, Henry found a small purse, cum card holder, in the front left-hand pocket of Millie's jeans. We soon had a surname and an initial to work with and filled in the gaps after two or three phone calls. One person who helped us was the Bristol nail bar manager. Millie had worked for her part-time before the family moved to Warminster. She was able to give us Millie's mother's name. I called Bristol Police for assistance. They had chapter and verse on Jeanette, Monique, Millie, and several other villains they were linked with. That got the ball rolling. The detective I spoke to, DI Budd, drove to Withywood, spoke to Jeanette Clark, and informed her of her daughter's death. DI Budd arranged for a Detective Sergeant to drive the family back to Warminster. I spoke to Jeanette Clark at her home in Weymouth Street later on Monday afternoon."

"We'll come back to that conversation," said Gus. "Let's return to the murder weapon."

"I received a call from DS Hamer that one of the forensic crew had discovered a serrated blade hidden under a scattering of dead flowers and foliage in a container close to the gate."

"Which gate was that?" asked Gus.

"The one that led onto Deverill Road," said Tom. "The blade had been washed clean under the nearby tap. Forensics found traces of the victim's blood when they returned the blade to the lab, but there were no usable prints on the handle. Millie's attackers must have worn gloves. The lab didn't get DNA evidence from the weapon, Millie's clothing, or the rubbish container. They also checked the tap, the sink and the two gateways they had to negotiate. At the autopsy, Henry Ash could confirm that the blade forensics discovered was consistent with having caused the wounds on the victim's body. "

"Did you ever consider there might have been two knives?" asked Grace.

"Nobody ever suggested that possibility," said Tom, looking puzzled.

"When did you start to form a theory on a motive for Millie's murder?" asked Grace.

"Well, my initial phone call to Bristol Police lit the fire," said Tom. "Although now I think about it, the lady I spoke to earlier hinted at an altercation with some unsavoury characters."

"Was that the nail bar manager?" asked Gus.

"That's her," said Tom. "Jenny Dodimead. She told me Millie hung around with a waste of space called Fergus Munro. I was keen to interview him. It's usually someone closely connected to the victim that's responsible. Then Ms Dodimead mentioned the trouble with Nathan Harvey that precipitated Millie's move to Warminster."

"Armed with the victim's name, and a bit of background, you called Bristol Police," said Gus. "Were they surprised to learn of Millie's death?"

"DI Budd was shocked," said Tom. "He told me everything they had on the gang Harvey and Coombs ran. He described the burglaries he and his colleague, DS Gale, were tackling and painted an overall picture of the events of the previous months. My working theory soon evolved into Harvey pursuing the people responsible for damaging his property in Court Farm Road, Hartcliffe. But, no matter where they went, they had to be seen to suffer. Otherwise, he would appear weak."

"Millie was on the list of people known to have been involved in the burglary," said Grace. "But did she even go inside? Her role was as a lookout. Her boyfriend would have been the logical target."

"Fergus Munro was on remand," said Tom. "They'd punished Justin Cannings. Harvey's brother, Micah, was doing the hard yards searching for Millie while Nathan stayed in Bristol, counting his drug money. Mick Budd didn't think things were meant to end in murder, but as he told me if you resort to violence, there's always a risk. The other gang members, Keel and Thatcher, were both capable of dishing out a severe beating. Mick Budd said he would have only been mildly surprised if they had taken the next step."

"Yet Monique Clark said when the gang members were banging on her door, they told her to tell Jeanette they were going to kill her daughter, " said Grace.

"Monique couldn't identify the people outside her house," said Tom. "It will come as no surprise that neither of the men we arrested admitted they were anywhere near Withywood on the night in question."

"Did you find any eyewitnesses?" asked Gus.

"Nobody saw a thing," said Tom. "Harvey and Coombs were feared throughout the southern half of the city. Their customers couldn't afford to antagonise them if they wanted continued access to drugs. Mick Budd reckoned the last time anyone spoke to the police about dealers brazenly standing on street corners, their house was firebombed. A neighbour rescued the elderly lady and her dogs, but the property was gutted."

Tom Brewer collected two empty cups and glass and moved them to the worktop beside the kitchen sink. Grace heard sounds from the lounge.

"I think Cynthia may have woken, Tom," she said.

Tom left the kitchen and walked along the hallway. He opened the lounge door, turned, and called out.

"Cynthia's on the floor," he said. "I think she must have tripped on the carpet in front of the fireplace. It looks as if she banged her head on the coffee table."

Grace ran into the lounge and took charge.

Cynthia was trying to sit up. There was swelling over her right eye but no broken skin. Grace could see Cynthia's eyes darting from her to Gus. She didn't know where she was or who these strange people were.

"Tom?" she cried.

"It's okay, Mrs Brewer," said Grace. "You've had a fall. Let's get you back in your chair, and Tom will fetch you a cup of tea."

"I hope you have some sugar, Tom," whispered Gus. "Would you like me to phone your doctor?"

"Fat chance anyone would make a home visit," said Tom. "Either I'll have to drive her to the nearest A&E Department, or we sit and wait for an ambulance."

"I think it best if someone sees her, Tom," said Grace. "I'll make the call and casually mention my rank. They might get here quicker. We can always come back another time to carry on our conversation. Gus wants to take a walk around Warminster, anyway. Cynthia's your priority now."

Tom Brewer looked at his wife and nodded.

"I'll give your office a ring in the morning with an update," he said.

Gus tutted as Grace spoke to the call handler.

"They're on their way, Tom," said Grace. "Fifteen minutes tops."

"I can't thank you enough, Grace," said Tom as he showed them to the front door.

"I thought Suzie was investigating officers who abused

their position," said Gus as they walked to the car. "I'm not sure I would have got away with that."

"Tom deserved a good turn, Gus," said Grace. "He was very helpful."

"What did you spot?" asked Gus.

"The same as you," said Grace. "Don't play cards for money. You sat up straight as soon as Tom mentioned Deverill Road."

"We're on our way there now," replied Gus. "Let's check which entrance they dragged Millie through."

"It could be important," said Grace. "Let's not jump to conclusions, though. If there's only one water supply, the killer *had* to go to that part of the churchyard to wash the knife. His accomplice could still have left through the other exit."

Chapter Seven

GUS NEGOTIATED the tight turn needed to rejoin the leafy lane with ease. He congratulated himself on making a good choice when he finally replaced his old Focus. The drive to the main road held the same potential danger of meeting another car, or worse still, a tractor and trailer. However, he needn't have worried. They were soon on the main road and heading for the town centre.

"Keep an eye out for a signpost for that Chinn's Court car park," said Gus. "We'll use the same start point as our Bristol gang."

"The shopping precinct is just on our left, Gus," said Grace. "The car park must be at the rear. Here's the turning for Weymouth Street."

Gus slowed as he entered Weymouth Street looking for places from the murder file.

"How far would The Avenue be from this junction?"

"A five-minute walk," said Grace. "Micah Harvey took her home, and we know what happened next. Here's the car park; there's a space in the far right corner."

"For your tiny car, maybe," said Gus. "I'll wait for this lady to finish putting her shopping in the boot of the Range Rover. Even Blessing could park in that wider bay."

Gus waited patiently for the woman to reverse out of the space and drive towards the exit. He parked the Focus without incident, and they set off on their walking tour of the town.

"We carry on down Weymouth Street to Upper Market Street," said Grace. "There's a walled extension to Christ Church and an entrance to the old churchyard."

"A pleasant journey at this time of day," Gus said as they walked side-by-side on the left-hand pavement. "Not so appealing at midnight. However, this end of the street is a built-up area with houses and shops on either side. I'm surprised nobody saw or heard anything. Especially on a Sunday night when, by and large, there would be less background noise."

"Jeanette's first-floor flat was above two commercial premises on our right, Gus," said Grace. "The murder file stated that whoever dragged Millie to the churchyard would have taken around five minutes to reach the spot where her body was discovered."

"That building over the road with a DHS delivery van parked outside looks favourite, doesn't it? But, of course, we can't learn anything from pestering whoever lives in the flats now, so let's keep walking."

"The roads in the town vary quite a bit," said Grace. "Have you noticed?"

"In width, you mean. Yes, some streets remind me of Marlborough, but it's just the result of the town's gradual growth over the centuries. The old town here still has narrow lanes leading off the main thoroughfare, but where new housing and retail outlets have expanded the boundaries, you get a more regulated pattern of street and avenue, punctuated by mini-roundabouts."

"We'll need to cross over soon," said Grace. "The pavement continues on the right-hand side the further we get from the town centre."

"People drive in from the suburbs these days, Grace," said Gus. "They don't encourage residents to keep fit by walking, do they?"

"It's cyclists using the pavements that annoy me," said Grace.

Gus couldn't recall the last time he'd seen The Reverend anywhere near a pavement. He looked towards the car park and the building containing Jeanette Clark's former flat.

"I'm leaning towards discounting the theory that the gang dragged, or frog-marched, their victim along this road, Grace," said Gus. "If only we get the chance to interrogate Harvey and the others," he sighed. "Doesn't it make more sense they dragged Millie to the car park we've just left and then drove her to the churchyard? Then, there would be far less chance of being seen."

"An interesting observation," said Grace. "There's a gap between those two cars approaching us, Gus, and nothing behind us for a hundred yards. So let's dash for it."

Grace made the narrow pavement on the opposite side with impressive speed. Gus decided that for him, fast enough was fast enough. The second car didn't even come close to hitting him.

"We'll need to go single-file the further along the street we go, Gus," said Grace. "The pavement is narrower at this point."

"Lead on, McDuff," said Gus. "It lends weight to my argument that Harvey and his colleagues didn't walk crocodile fashion, like a class of schoolchildren on their way to the local swimming baths."

"It would be possible if only two people went to the churchyard with Millie, as they attested at the first trial," said Grace. "The streets would have been deserted. It would be dangerous for you to walk alongside me this morning, but feasible for someone to grab Millie's arm at midnight."

"I suppose you're right," said Gus. "It's such a nuisance not knowing how many people we're dealing with."

"That was their best line of defence, Gus," said Grace. "The more doubt they put in the jury's minds over who was in the churchyard, the better. It backfired at the first trial, but the retrial corrected the error as far as Harvey and Coombs were concerned. They always maintained their innocence."

"Well, they would, wouldn't they," said Gus. "We'll need to cross over again in a minute. I can see the church tower above the trees."

Grace waited on the edge of the pavement for a gap in traffic.

"We could be here a while, Gus," she said. "It's lunchtime."

"A subtle hint," said Gus.

"I owe you a snack," said Grace. "You paid when we were in Burnham-on-Sea."

"We can wait a little longer. So here we go," said Gus. He darted between cars slowed by a queue overtaking another DHS delivery van parked opposite the Fox & Hounds pub.

"Cheeky," said Grace as she joined Gus at the entrance to the churchyard.

"This is the only pathway on this side of the church,"

said Gus. "Our rubbish bin and sink should be just inside on our right."

They stood and surveyed the spot where forensics had found the serrated blade.

"Nothing much has changed," said Grace. "A new tap, by the looks of it. Forensics looked for prints at the entrance, didn't they? I imagined wrought iron gates and plenty of surfaces to swab. But unfortunately, the churchyard doesn't appear to have any gates. Just old wooden posts where gates used to hang. I wonder when they were removed?"

Gus shrugged and moved away. He was keen to find how far it was from this sink to the willow tree. He counted the paces while Grace chuntered about sunken gravestones and wondered who cut the grass.

"Thirty yards," he said.

"Sorry?" asked Grace.

"I was counting," said Gus. "We're thirty yards from the entrance. I looked for where the nearest streetlights were on my way in, and that gateway would be well-lit at night. I wonder when the streetlights go out?"

"In most areas, they're off between one and six in the morning between March and October," said Grace.

"So, anyone leaving by that gateway between one and two o'clock would be in darkness."

Gus stood beside the willow tree and gazed in every direction.

"Unless some idiot reversed the murder scene photos, Millie's body was hidden from view to anyone walking past that gateway between midnight and one o'clock."

"There's sufficient room between the tree and those laurel bushes on the boundary edge for several people to have stood unseen," said Grace.

"They used the Upper Market Street entrance and

walked to the furthest corner from the road," said Gus. "Would you say we're closer to that gateway than the first?"

"Yes, Gus," said Grace. "It feels more like twenty yards to me."

"We'll check on our way out," said Gus. "Come on. There's nothing more to see here."

"Did you notice the flowers, Gus?" asked Grace.

"There were flowers everywhere I looked," said Gus. "Except by the tree. Maybe Jeanette hasn't been able to bring little Amy in from Zeals this week."

"I think it must have been Keith Petty's birthday at the weekend. Brenda left a bunch of assorted flowers and a small card. Unfortunately, the blooms are starting to fade. No doubt she'll drop in again later in the week."

They reached the gateway into Upper Market Street.

"Twenty yards, give or take," said Gus.

He paused to study the wide entrance to the street.

"Plenty of room for a car to park on the opposite side of the road. It wouldn't have attracted attention by that high hedge."

"You won't let it go, will you," said Grace. "This gateway has no actual gate either. So where are we off to next?"

"If you haven't tired yourself too much, we'll head for The Avenue. It sounds like a good spot for a coffee shop or something similar."

When they reached The Avenue, Gus scratched his head.

"I can see how an eyewitness saw Millie get snatched by Micah Harvey," he said. "This must be a busy corner every day of the week. I expected a row of shops, not a surgery, public toilets, a supermarket, and a large car park."

"Perhaps Millie was collecting a prescription from the pharmacy," said Grace.

"We could check, but to what end?" said Gus. He sighed. "I'm looking forward to that snack now," he said. "It must be the fresh air and exercise."

"There's a place with great reviews in Market Place," said Grace checking her smartphone. "We can cut through North Row and be there in five minutes."

"Happy days," said Gus.

"What shall we do this afternoon, Gus?" asked Grace as they followed the shortcut indicated on her phone.

"We won't hear from Tom Brewer until tomorrow," said Gus. "The others should be back by two o'clock. So, we'll have lunch here and then drive back to the office. Once we've collated all our various bits of information and assessed what they've added to our investigation, we can update the Freeman Files before going home. But, of course, the schedule for tomorrow will depend on Cynthia Brewer's health and what Alex can arrange for the names we still have on our list."

Grace opened the door to the establishment claiming to be a local chain serving gourmet global coffees, juices & snacks in a relaxed space. She spotted a staff member and indicated she was looking for a table for two. When they reached an empty table close to the counter, the young girl asked whether this would be too noisy for her father.

"This isn't my father," said Grace indignantly.

Gus tried not to laugh.

"She'll be even more confused when you pay the bill," said Gus. "I'm not your father, nor your sugar daddy. They'll gossip about us in the kitchen all afternoon, trying to fathom our relationship."

Grace grimaced and picked up a menu.

"Things are improving," she said. "They offer a good selection of vegan snacks and a Chinese green tea that will suit me. Shall I order for you? A bacon bap and a black coffee?"

"You know me so well," said Gus.

A different staff member delivered the drinks. She gave Gus the once over. He wasn't sure whether she thought he was punching above his weight or jealous of Grace.

The snacks were just what the doctor ordered. Not healthwise in Gus's case, but more than enough to get them through the rest of the working day. Two young faces watched as they made their way to the exit after Grace had paid the bill. Gus held the door open for Grace and winked at the young girl who had studied him from head to toe.

They walked to the Chinn's Court car park in silence. Once Gus had started the car and moved to the exit, he realised that Grace was near tears.

"Anything you want to share?" he asked.

"I've never visited anywhere alone with my father," she said. "We've never had that sort of relationship."

"Things went south when you joined the police, I believe," said Gus.

"I was supposed to have a career in law. Like my older brothers, I was expected to follow in my father's footsteps. We've hardly spoken since."

"There's still time, Grace," said Gus.

Thirty minutes later, Gus was turning into Church Street. The others had arrived ahead of them.

"Do you think we've got any closer to finding our killer today, Gus?" asked Grace as they headed to the lift.

"Two steps forward, three steps back," said Gus. "I know. It's a phrase that makes little sense in this situation, but every time I think I see a chink of light, another curtain gets drawn to plunge me into the dark again."

When they entered the office, everyone was hard at work updating their files. Gus paused by his desk, waiting for the inevitable quip from Neil. Silence reigned.

"Right," said Gus, "who wants to go first? Alex and Lydia? How was Henry Ash?"

"Elderly," said Lydia.

"Henry lives alone in Mount Pleasant Avenue, Exmouth, guv," said Alex. "In a modern bungalow with a sea view on a clear day. He's fit for his age and can thank the dogs for that. Henry walks them when he collects his daily paper from newsagents on the Esplanade. That has to be a good half-hour walk each way. Henry reckons he does it in all winds and weather."

"What was he able to remember about the Millie Clark case?" asked Grace.

"Henry had looked out the notes he'd made before we arrived," said Lydia. "He was all set, with paperwork laid out on the table in his lounge."

"I asked him when he first received the summons to Warminster, guv," said Alex. "He said he answered a call from Polebarn Road at twenty-five past nine. They gave him directions to the churchyard, and he jumped into his car and floored it. That was Henry's expression, guv."

"Tom Brewer reckoned Henry could have made the journey in ten minutes if he broke the speed limit," said Gus.

"Henry claimed he did it in eight minutes, guv," said Lydia. "He parked on Deverill Road, and once he donned his protective clothing, he walked across the panels placed on the ground by the uniformed officers to view the body. They were going about their business, looking after the lady who alerted the police, taping everything in sight, and making sure no more visitors came in to trample on any evidence."

"Henry soon confirmed they were dealing with an unexplained death of a female in her early twenties," said Alex. "He counted five stab wounds to her upper chest and believed the blood volume surrounding the body showed she wouldn't have survived long after the blow to the heart. Henry noted scarring on the victim's lower arms, showing evidence of regular drug use. There was substantial bruising between the elbow and the shoulder on both arms, suggesting someone had stood behind the victim, holding her, while someone hit her. Her attacker had punched her in the face, possibly breaking her nose, and her left eye socket and cheekbone could have been fractured. Everything he saw pointed to the victim having suffered a severe beating, followed by the stabbing. The victim was fully clothed, and there was no indication of sexual assault."

"Henry told us he couldn't be certain whether the same person who hit her was the person who stabbed her," said Lydia. "Both attackers were right-handed. He was confident about that, but the ferociousness of the stabbing was at odds with the damage caused by the punches."

"The lack of forensic evidence indicated that they wore gloves," said Neil. "But from what we know about the attacks on those guys in Bristol, the gang members weren't afraid of using screwdrivers or hammers to inflict pain."

"Henry referred to his autopsy report, then guv," said Alex. "He stated that time of death was between midnight and two."

"Who else did Henry mention?" asked Gus.

"He told us that two young detectives arrived not long after him," said Lydia.

"DS Hamer and DC Keen," said Grace. "They were redirected to Christ Church from the skate park."

"Henry told DS Hamer as much as he could," said Alex. "With the proviso that the autopsy could alter everything."

"In the end, nothing changed," said Gus.

"No, guv," said Lydia. "Henry said the forensic crew from Trowbridge were still setting up their equipment when the detectives arrived. The crew began collecting evidence as Henry was updating DS Hamer."

"DI Brewer was the next to arrive, guv," said Alex. "He had a quiet word with Brenda Petty, put an arm around the shoulder of a PCSO, and asked his detective to fill him in on the details. Henry said he couldn't do any more at that stage, so he liaised with the uniformed officers and the crime scene manager about removing the body to the morgue. Then he changed out of his protective gear and headed home."

"Henry left before they found the knife," said Grace.

"The knife travelled to the lab along with all the other evidence they gathered," said Lydia. "The serrated blade then accompanied Millie Clark's body to the autopsy room, where Henry could compare the blade to the wounds. He was convinced the blade found in the rubbish container at Christ Church was the murder weapon."

"What did you make of Henry Ash?" asked Gus.

"Everything Henry told us was in line with what we read in the murder file, guv," said Alex. "I thought a few timing references might have been scrambled, but that was understandable. A crime scene can get chaotic if someone doesn't grab hold of it and get things organised from the get-go."

"That ties in with what we learned from Tom Brewer,"

said Gus. "He admitted that the guy delivering beer to the Fox & Hounds had been a foreigner. The driver knew enough English to realise Mrs Petty needed him to make an emergency call, but when the desk sergeant heard the driver's version of what the old lady had discovered, he thought it was a wind-up. Initially, he sent a young PCSO along to see what was what. She was green as grass and had never seen a dead body before. As a result, there was a delay before the right people were dispatched from the police station and then from Polebarn Road. Tom Brewer was lax in not getting to the churchyard more quickly with his experienced Detective Sergeant. He drove there alone, under the impression DS Hamer could cope."

"I can't see how Henry Ash's role in the morning's affairs could be criticised, guv," said Lydia.

"He didn't query whether there was more than one weapon," Neil reminded her.

"That's not what we should concentrate on, Neil," said Gus.

"Sorry, guv. I just think it unlikely there was a single person in that gang not carrying a weapon of some sort. It's natural for criminals in the drug game. After they get dressed in the morning, they look for their bling, mobile phone, burner phone, car keys and knife. The further you go up the chain of command, the more likely that knife is replaced with a gun."

"Neil's right, guv," said Alex. "So, if that's not relevant in this case, what should Tom Brewer and his colleagues have concentrated on from Henry Ash's findings?"

"On Monday morning, Tom Brewer didn't know about Nathan Harvey and the others. But, as the day unfolded, he gained insight into Millie's background. The deeper he dug into the violent campaign Harvey and Coombs carried out after the burglary should have made him question the events that followed."

"You're talking about Henry Ash's comment to DS Hamer, aren't you, Gus," said Grace. "He said the ferocity of the stabbing was at odds with the injuries caused by the punches."

"Surely, that suggests there were two attackers in front of Millie, guv," said Blessing. "One big man could easily restrain a slip of a girl like Millie Clark from behind."

"Which means both versions provided at the first trial were incorrect," said Neil. "Both pairs swore they stayed in the flat while the other took Millie to the churchyard and killed her."

"Grace and I have made the journey from the Weymouth Street flat to the churchyard," said Gus. "I know Harvey and the others felt safe rampaging around parts of Bristol where they held sway, but this was their first time in Warminster. Residents in a rural town were more likely to call the police if they spotted something suspicious late on Sunday night. The way the street and its pavements are laid out also means a direct walk to Christ Church without raising the alarm feels out of the question."

"Gus believes the gang moved Millie to the churchyard by car," said Grace. "They were parked close enough to the flat for someone to have soon fetched the car. They took Millie downstairs from the flat, bundled her inside a car, and could have been opposite the entrance to the churchyard in two minutes with no one being the wiser."

"That makes sense," said Blessing. "But at the first trial, it was alleged two men stayed in the flat while two men left with Millie. Nobody mentioned Micah Harvey. Did he stay, or did he go? Which pair would he have been most likely to go with? His brother and Craig Coombs, surely? The evidence collected by the pathologist proves there were more people with Millie than came out in court. If it were three men, it could have been Nathan, Craig, and Micah."

"Go on, Blessing," said Gus. "What do you think happened next?"

"Craig Coombs restrained Millie," said Blessing. "Nathan was the one who felt most aggrieved by the burglary; it was his house, after all, So it was he who hit Millie around the face. What if it was Micah who carried things too far? Maybe Nathan grew tired and offered Micah the chance to punish Millie. Micah produced the knife, lost his temper, and went crazy."

"Surely, Craig Coombs would have released Millie, pushed her away," said Neil. "He and Nathan would have wanted to stop Micah from being a fool. The last thing they wanted was a dead body on their hands. Although the guys they attacked in Bristol suffered painful injuries, they were still breathing."

"We need to check whether Micah Harvey is right-handed," said Lydia.

"Micah didn't have anything on his record to indicate he was violent," said Alex. "He was a lover, not a fighter, according to his defence solicitor, Kathy Hardman."

"How did she know?" asked Lydia.

"Perks of the job, perhaps," said Neil. "Maybe she thought she'd look good in a red Mercedes."

"Time to get back on track, Neil," said Grace.

"Yes, ma'am," said Neil.

Gus stood and walked to the crime scene photographs.

"I said to Grace earlier that we keep thinking we've made progress in this case," he said. "Then something knocks us back to the beginning. Until we know how many people left the flat that night to travel to the churchyard, I don't believe we'll ever solve Millie's murder."

"You didn't think my theory had merit then, guv?" asked Blessing.

"It's one way of interpreting the facts we have so far, Blessing," said Gus. "Something in my gut tells me the punishments handed out by the gang were meant to be proportional to the damage done to Nathan Harvey's property. Several of you have overlooked the importance of a comment in Henry Ash's report. He said he couldn't be sure whether the stabbing was part of the same attack. Millie could have been semi-conscious after the blows to her nose and cheekbone. Millie was short in stature and weighed less than fifty kilos. Her lifestyle wasn't conducive to keeping fit and healthy. After the beating from whoever dished it out, she could have slumped to the floor in a daze. Maybe it was then that someone stabbed her."

"Henry Ash didn't record blood spatter in the churchyard," said Grace. "Everything lay beside and beneath her body where she was discovered, next to the willow tree."

"In that case, we're back to square one," said Alex. "Only two people could have been with her: one holding, one hitting. When Millie collapsed, the one doing the restraining pulled the knife and stabbed her to death. It was a different level of ferocity to the punches, which suggests the first attacker didn't kill her."

"We're going around in circles, guv," said Lydia. "What did you learn from Tom Brewer?"

Grace explained what had happened at Primrose Cottage in Heytesbury. She told the team they hoped to continue hearing Tom Brewer's account of the Bristol end of the case tomorrow.

"We'll keep interviewing as many people as will accept

our invitation," said Gus. "Neil and Blessing haven't told us what they learned from Jeanette and Monique yet."

"Nothing much, guv," said Neil. "I did as you suggested and called to ask whether we could see them in Zeals alone. Monique wasn't keen on getting involved. She wants to put the whole episode behind her. Jeanette was distracted by her youngest child. She was off school with a tummy upset. Jeanette was happy to meet us once the child was better, but she and Monique don't spend much time apart. It would be impossible to have a meaningful conversation with either of them at home."

"We were creative, guv," said Blessing. "My parents visited the National Trust place at Stourhead a few weeks ago. Jacky Ferris told my mother the gardens were beautiful. The café restaurant is just two miles from Zeals. We're collecting Jeanette at ten o'clock in the morning."

"Well done," said Gus. "What about Monique?"

"Jeanette said she would ask her to look after her daughter if she wasn't well enough to return to school, guv," said Neil.

"That's good to know, Neil. But I meant, when are we going to speak to her? If Monique doesn't cooperate, we'll have to ask her to attend Warminster police station."

"Got it, guv," said Neil. "I'll give Monique another try. Once we've spoken to her sister, perhaps she'll agree to meet. If only to see if she can find out what Jeanette told us."

"That's more like it," said Gus. "Alex, did you manage to arrange any more interviews?"

"I was in the middle of that when you got back to the office, guv," said Alex. "We can talk with Fergus Munro and his wife, Pippa, tomorrow afternoon. Also, DI Mick Budd and DS Lizzie Gale can be available for an hour tomorrow morning at the Trinity Road police station."

"You and I can get together in a few minutes to agree on what you need to ask them," said Gus. "Neil and Blessing will be in deepest, darkest Wiltshire, and Grace and I are dependent upon a phone call from Tom Brewer. So, you and Lydia are in the chair for those two visits."

"Bristol in the morning and Gloucester in the after-noon," said Lydia. "Do we get expenses for lunch, guv?"

Grace was already flicking through her phone.

"I can recommend a place on Northgate Street in Gloucester, Lydia," she said. "Gus and I paid a visit to one of their branches today. Although Gus didn't tell me I could put in a claim for expenses."

"You can try," said Gus. "Alex, if Cynthia Brewer hasn't recovered, is there anyone I can call this afternoon to fill the gap in our timetable?"

"I forgot to mention this," said Alex. "When I spoke to DI Budd about tomorrow's meeting, he told me what happened to Justin Cannings. After his release from Erlestoke, he tried to stay on the straight and narrow."

"So, where is he now?" asked Gus.

"HMP Erlestoke, guv," said Alex. "He lapsed."

"Can we make the short trip to speak with him?" asked Gus.

"We'll have to be quick, guv. Canning's is getting released at nine o'clock on Friday morning."

"Inform the people in charge at Erlestoke that Grace and I will be there sometime tomorrow. Justin Cannings will have to be flexible."

"Got it, guv," said Alex.

"I suggest we wrap up the few pieces of admin we've raised," said Gus, "and then get stuck into updating our digital files. That should keep us busy until going home time."

Gus didn't hear any dissenting voices. He joined Alex in framing a list of questions for Thursday's meetings. Neil phoned Monique, and Jeanette informed him she had caught the bus to Mere. She didn't expect her back before six. Neil thanked Jeanette and reminded her that he and Blessing would pick her up by the Post Office at ten o'clock the following day.

When Gus returned to his desk, Grace came to sit beside him.

"Is this about claiming for expenses?" he asked.

"Of course not," she replied. "I just wanted to ask you not to mention what happened today to the others."

"What, being mistaken for my daughter?" asked Gus.

"Well, indirectly. I reacted badly, and it's never good for a senior officer to show signs of weakness."

"I wouldn't call it weakness, Grace," said Gus. "It's just being human, and I've forgotten it already."

Grace returned to work on her computer; when Gus next looked up, it was five to five.

"That'll do," he said, saving his report and signing out. "Happy haunting tonight, Neil."

"I used to be a werewolf, guv. But I'm alright nowooh," said Neil as he headed for the lift.

Chapter Eight

GUS ARRIVED at the bungalow at a little after half-past five. Suzie had beaten him home again. As he battled with road-works in Seend for the umpteenth time, he mulled over what he and the team had learned today.

Was how Millie Clark reached the churchyard important?

Has anyone ever mentioned how many cars were used by the gang?

Why was Neil so hung up on there being a vast array of weapons on hand?

Why was Monique Clark reticent about talking to them?

When was Alex going to admit that he had got nowhere with getting a response from Nathan Harvey and Craig Coombs?

Gus realised Suzie was tapping on his window.

"Are you staying out here all night?" she asked.

"Sorry," said Gus. "It's been one of those days."

"Come indoors and tell me about it. Or as much as you can."

Gus got out of the Focus and followed Suzie inside.

"Coffee?" she asked.

"I'm not driving to the pub later," said Gus. "A large glass of Malbec might help me unwind."

"I'll bring it through to the lounge," said Suzie. "I'd love to join you, but a coffee will have to do in my condition."

"A girl from a coffee shop in Warminster thought I was Grace's father today."

"Were you hurt?" asked Suzie.

"Not a scratch," said Gus. "It upset Grace. I didn't expect her to be so fragile, given the skirmishes in our first few months together."

"I told you that you'd misjudged her," said Suzie. "Geoff thinks the world of her."

"Perhaps Geoff would like to take on the role of a father figure then," said Gus. "Grace and her father have fallen out."

"It sounds as if there's another reason for the move to Wilton," said Suzie. "Anyway, that's enough about your staff members. What progress did you make on your case?"

"Hard to tell. That was what I was considering outside. Something I thought was important became trivial in a heartbeat, and vice versa. Someone keeps moving the goalposts to use one of Neil's sporting analogies. We visited Tom Brewer in Heytesbury this morning. Unfortunately, his wife had a fall just before lunch, so we had to cut our meeting short. We'll hear in the morning if we can pick up the threads. Did you meet with Geoff on your investigation today?"

"A brief chat over coffee and cake," said Suzie. "Kassie Trotter wanted to show off her new trolley. She must have spent the whole of last night baking. She had enough cakes to show the thing to everyone at London Road."

"I've told you a million times not to exaggerate," said Gus. "Back to the brief chat. What did Geoff have to say?"

"Did you realise that last year there were three thousand allegations of police corruption in this country?" said Suzie.

"It does seem a lot," said Gus. "All thoroughly investigated, I hope?"

"Far from it," said Suzie. "About half were given the correct treatment. I asked Geoff why that was, and he said that for many police officers, corruption was becoming routine. He quoted examples of officers increasingly using their powers to crack down not on criminals but anyone who dared speak out against them."

"When you scratch the surface of any long-standing organisation such as the police, there's always a risk you'll find a rotten patch," said Gus. "I'm far from happy to learn it's got that bad, but I'm not surprised."

"Almost half the officers and staff surveyed by the HMIC and FRS said that if they discovered corruption among their colleagues and reported it, they didn't believe their evidence would be treated in confidence. They feared their career prospects would nosedive."

"You lost me with the initials," said Gus. "Didn't the Inspectorate of Constabulary have statutory responsibility for inspecting our people? So who are the FRS?"

"The Fire & Rescue Services were amalgamated with the Inspectorate last year," said Suzie. "I expect you were on the allotment the day the announcement was made."

"It strikes me that if you can't report dishonesty and malpractice whenever you see it and receive the full support of the force, then this rotten patch will simply flourish and eventually swamp you."

"We're on the same wavelength," said Suzie leaning

forward to kiss Gus on the forehead. "That's almost word-for-word what I said to Geoff."

"What else?" asked Gus.

"That was as far as we got today," said Suzie. "The balloon went up at a mosque in Swindon. Someone broke in last night, smashed a few windows, daubed the walls with racist graffiti, and tried setting fire to several prayer rugs. The offender was arrested and charged before lunch, but Geoff thought he should go to Broad Street to speak to elders at the mosque."

"Community policing at its best," said Gus. "Everyone deserves to know we care."

"What do we need to do before we get ready to go out?" asked Suzie.

"Only a shower and change for me," said Gus. "Unless I've forgotten something."

"We should make sure the bungalow is in darkness before we leave. A few kids from the village could wander along the lane on a trick-or-treat mission. We don't want to encourage them to try their luck."

"I hid behind the settee last year until they gave up, " said Gus. "There were no pumpkins on the porch or anything to suggest I was remotely interested, but they were persistent."

"How did Tess deal with Hallowe'en?" asked Suzie.

"What do you think?" said Gus. "She was a teacher when we worked in Salisbury, and in the last week of October, she would have helped the little ones create grotesque masks, carve pumpkins, and all sorts. So, Tess would stand on the doorstep, waiting for the local kids, from six in the evening. She was in her element."

"That must have annoyed you," said Suzie.

"Not really. I escaped to the pub on the rare occasion I wasn't working."

"Typical," said Suzie. "As you can imagine, the long driveway to my parent's farm meant we never got bothered by visitors on foot. Mum might have wished she could swap the reps from agricultural merchants almost every day of the week for a handful of kids on October the thirty-first. At least she could send them away with a beaming smile and their bag of sweets and a hot sausage roll."

"Will we change our minds when we have a child of our own, do you think?" asked Gus.

"There will be a few years before they're interested in occasions like that," said Suzie. "We can defer any decision for now."

"That works for me," said Gus. "Right, I'm off to have that shower and search for something suitable to wear from my wardrobe."

"I've hung your shirt on the door," said Suzie.

"Do I get a say in what you're wearing tonight?" he asked,

"What do you think? This little bump has reduced my options to A or B. I wore A last Wednesday."

"We'll go shopping at the weekend to hunt for C and D," said Gus. "Rain's forecast, so I can't spend time on my allotment."

"You're all heart," said Suzie.

Twenty minutes later, while Suzie took her turn in the bathroom, Gus went around the bungalow, closing curtains and ensuring the back door was securely locked. It was all very well leaving the place in darkness, so kids were eager to move to the next house in the lane, but there were others loose in the countryside who preferred a pitch-black environment.

When Suzie emerged from the bedroom, looking radiant, she found Gus checking the screens on his security system.

"I don't remember you bothering with those for months," she said.

"The days when a young lady might flash her breasts at my cameras are long gone," he said. "When I rushed to have these installed, I didn't know whether I'd live long enough to pay for them. It seemed vital to do what I could to protect myself. So often, we hear homeowners say that their cameras are just for show. Seeing a place with cameras is enough of a deterrent to make a burglar try somewhere else. I admit that although my cameras are in good working order, I tend to forget to check what's been recorded; in case some tearaway has been looking for a way in."

"We could be missing some fascinating nocturnal activity in our back garden," said Suzie. "If there's not much on TV one night, perhaps we should take a look. For instance, we might be entertained by a vixen and her cubs."

"We might as well keep watching TV," said Gus. "Our recordings would only be hours of inactivity which we would fast-forward, and a few minutes of entertainment."

"Not much to choose between the two. Come on," said Suzie. "Let's get to the pub. Two hours with Brett and Clemency will lift your spirits."

Gus switched off the lights in the lounge, hallway, and porch as they left the bungalow. He paused at the gateway and looked back.

"Why is the only neon streetlight on this stretch of the lane right outside my bungalow?" he moaned. "All my work counts for nothing."

"Oh, I don't know," said Suzie. "Those lights give an

eerie glow that reminds me of a haunted house I saw in a film."

They walked to the pub without seeing any children doing the rounds of trick or treat. Brett and Clemency were already inside the Lamb, sitting at a table close to the back door.

"Good evening, you two," said Brett. "We thought we'd tuck ourselves in a corner this evening. The landlord warned us that although he's not expecting a mad rush, any Hallowe'en revellers will assemble in the bar area. Bert is sitting on his usual stool for now, but he'll be off home soon. He doesn't want to leave Irene alone in the house."

"I'll pop along and have a word," said Gus. "I doubt I'll see him this weekend. The weather forecast doesn't look promising."

"Can you get our drinks, darling?" asked Suzie. "We'll look at the menu while you're gone. Are you happy for me to order?"

"It won't be the first time today that someone's done that," said Gus. He made his way to the bar, nodded a greeting to the landlord, and squeezed past a witch and a warlock to find his old friend.

"Evening, Mr Freeman, Gus," said Bert. "Glad to see you haven't succumbed to wearing fancy dress." He tutted and took a sip of his pint of cider.

"How are things at the allotment, Bert?" asked Gus. "I've been too busy to make more than a fleeting visit."

"The Reverend has had other things on her mind, too," said Bert with a grin. "I haven't spent as long as I'd like there today, as it happens. I went to Devizes to get a sign for the gatepost. I fixed it in place this afternoon."

"You have a house number on the gatepost already, Bert," said Gus. "Were you planning to give the place a name like Primrose Cottage? I went to one of those today; not a primrose in sight."

"I bought a 'Beware of the Dog' sign," said Bert.

"You haven't got a dog," said Gus.

Bert tapped his nose.

"Those little devils from the housing estate don't know that for certain," he said. "Me and Irene don't want to be pestered with callers at our time of life. It will put a few off tonight, but I might get my money's worth over the months ahead. Irene's already put an answer machine on my phone to frustrate cold callers. Unless it's someone we know, we don't answer."

"Did you answer every call that came in before?" asked Gus.

"I couldn't if I was here or at the allotment," said Bert. "But when you're living on your own, there are times when it's good to hear another voice. I admit I was interested in keeping some of them talking, but I always decided to think it over and end the call rather than commit to anything."

"A sensible man; shall I get you another pint, Bert?" said Gus.

"Thank you, Gus, but I'll pass," said Bert. "Irene's expecting me home early tonight."

"Well, have a good evening," said Gus. "I'll see you soon."

"Give my regards to Miss Suzie," said Bert. "Tell Brett not to forget Sunday lunch at our place."

Gus tried to catch the landlord's attention as Bert finished his pint, eased himself down from his stool, and headed for the door. Gus was soon carrying his glass of Malbec and Suzie's lemonade and lime back to their refuge in the far corner.

"Won't have long to wait," said Suzie. "The kitchen isn't busy tonight."

"Bert's on his way home," said Gus. "He said hello, and wanted me to remind you that the two of you are booked for Sunday lunch."

"A family get-together," said Clemency. "Irene wants to cook for us."

"A pleasure we've avoided so far," said Brett.

"I've never heard Bert complain about her cooking," said Gus.

"I don't think Irene gives him much opportunity," said Clemency.

"I was thinking about you today, Reverend," said Gus.

"Really, Gus," said Clemency.

"Have you ever ridden on the pavement?" asked Gus.

"Heavens, no. I wouldn't dream of it," said Clemency.

Two staff members arrived with the food order, and the conversation on two wheels was interrupted. Gus was thankful it seemed forgotten when they had finished their desserts. He and Brett risked walking to the bar to settle the bill.

"If you want a drink on a night like this, you ask for a straw or leave the mask above your nose," said Brett. "Defeats the object, doesn't it?"

"The shock factor is somewhat diminished," said Gus.

"Unless you find you haven't been canoodling with your husband but someone who visited the same fancy dress supplier," said Brett.

"Are you two free on Saturday?" asked Gus.

"As far as I know," said Brett. "Where did you have in mind?"

"We haven't been to the Waggon & Horses at

Harrington End in a while. Parking can be an issue, but the food is excellent."

"Perhaps we'll see you here on Friday night?" said Brett. "We can firm up arrangements then."

Gus and Brett wandered back to the table to find it empty.

"I expect Clemency is outside unlocking our bicycles," said Brett.

He pushed open the pub door, and the sound of voices confirmed both ladies were in the beer garden.

"I thought we'd walk up the lane with them, darling," said Suzie.

"Safety in numbers," said Gus.

They said goodnight to Brett and the Reverend at the gateway. Gus and Suzie made their way to the front door, and Gus took forever to get his key in the lock.

"Hurry up," said Suzie. "I didn't visit the loo before we left the Lamb. I'm bursting."

"Success," said Gus as the door finally opened. Suzie dashed to the bathroom while Gus switched on the light in the hallway. He rescued a scrap of paper hanging from the letterbox.

'U was out. Put a choclet bar thru the door at 57, pls. Ta.'

"Anything interesting?" asked Suzie when she emerged from the bathroom.

"We had a visitor," said Gus, "I'll check my cameras in the morning. I might be able to drop a photograph of the culprit through the door at number 57."

Suzie read the note.

"What about the chocolate?" she asked.

"If they're dim enough to try to extort chocolate from two police officers, they need to learn that crime doesn't pay," said Gus.

Thursday, 1 November 2018

THE JOURNEY from Urchfont into town was much the same as every other day this week. Gus waved goodbye to Suzie and motored steadily out of Devizes before descending into the valley. Maybe revellers had been out in force elsewhere and were having a lie-in. Because there didn't seem to be as much traffic on the roads as usual. For a change, Gus was the first of the team to arrive in the Church Street car park.

He travelled in the lift to the first floor and awaited the arrival of the others.

Amazing Grace exited the lift with Neil Davis at five to nine.

"Good morning," said Gus. "I hope you're fully refreshed."

"Melody's mother spent the evening at our place, guv," said Neil. "I've got another list of jobs they need me to do at the weekend."

"All in a good cause, Neil," said Gus.

"I settled down with a book at about eight o'clock," said Grace. "That was after an hour of answering the door to kids and their parents. I had to send them all away empty-handed. Why would I have supplies of goodies for kids?"

"You'll be the Wicked Witch of Market Lavington," said Neil.

"As if I'd care, even if I was staying," said Grace. "I won't be there next year, thank goodness."

Blessing arrived with Alex and Lydia while Grace and Neil were talking.

"What was all the excitement," asked Blessing.

"You wouldn't have noticed, Blessing," said Gus. "I

expect you had a long chat on the phone with your mother and then had an early night."

"It's a Wednesday night, guv," said Blessing. "Work in the morning, so it's just like school nights used to be."

"We went to the cinema," said Alex. "It was our first opportunity to watch Bohemian Rhapsody, the film that premiered at Wembley Arena last week."

"Awesome," said Lydia.

"What time do we need to leave, Neil?" asked Blessing.

"Fifteen minutes, Blessing," said Neil.

"I'll try a couple of numbers for you, guv," said Alex. "Then Lydia and I will leave for Trinity Road."

"I'd drive to the M4 on the other side of Chippenham from here, Lydia," said Neil. "The M32 will take you almost to the front door."

"Thanks for the tip, Neil," said Lydia. "I love motorway driving."

Gus tutted.

"I'll be careful, guv, honest," she said.

Gus was about to say something when his phone rang. It was Tom Brewer. The conversation was brief.

"Okay, Grace, we're off to Heytesbury. It's déjà vu, all over again."

"Cynthia has recovered then, Gus?" asked Grace.

"Tom said she asked why he'd put the house on the market without discussing it. Cynthia thought we were a couple of estate agents. Other than that, her fall did no lasting damage."

"That's the triple-play," said Neil. "We now have three teams out."

"I have no idea where that comes from, Neil," said Gus.

"It's a rare baseball term, guv," said Neil.

"You never cease to amaze me, Neil. It's time you left."

One by one, the pairings left the office and headed for their scheduled interviews.

Gus and Grace sat in the Focus while Lydia and Neil joined the queue for the exit.

"I'm not sure whether these are early morning shoppers returning home or locals with a parking permit leaving for work," said Gus.

"Does Lydia mind she no longer seems to be partnered with you, Gus?" asked Grace.

"She hasn't said anything. I was trying to get the right balance," said Gus. "I suppose having two DIs in the same team is top-heavy, even if I'm retired and only a consultant. I can still teach you a thing or two, but maybe I should be motivating Lydia to ask for a promotion. The same goes for Blessing."

"You don't think you can do the same for Alex and Neil?"

"Neil's a Steady Eddie," said Gus. "He'll get to the next level at his own speed. Nobody will fast-track him. As for Alex, I think he's ready now, but the top brass seems to have doubts because of his accident. His body took the brunt of the crash, not his brain, but his troubles with his pain meds back in the summer will count against him."

"How do we play things with Tom this morning?" asked Grace.

"I suggest we let him tell us about his meeting with Jeanette on Monday afternoon. Then, we can get him to give us the lowdown on gangland Bristol South. Then, check it with DI Budd and DS Gale's version of events later."

Gus drove past the Warminster turning they'd taken yesterday and joined the A36 at the Cley Hill roundabout. He drew up outside Primrose Cottage ten minutes later.

Gus and Grace walked to the front door. Grace rang the bell.

"Sorry," said Tom Brewer as he opened the door. "I didn't expect you this early. Cynthia's having a lie-in, thanks to whatever the doctor gave her. I took her a cup of tea an hour ago. She drank that, but she nodded off again while I was telling her you were on your way. So let's use the lounge today. It will be more comfortable for you."

Tom led them through into the lounge. Grace looked around the room.

The loose carpet in front of the fireplace had gone.

"I see you noticed, Grace," said Tom. "I've got to be more alert to the dangers surrounding us. You never imagine you might trip over anything when you're young, do you? If you do, you laugh it off because it doesn't cause you to lose your balance."

They sat down, and Tom turned to Gus.

"What did you want to ask about next?" he said,

"Could you run us through what happened after Jeanette arrived back in Warminster, Tom?" said Gus. "I think you said yesterday that DI Budd got a detective to drive her and the kids back from Withywood."

"That's right. As soon as I learned Millie had lived in Withywood until just a month before she died, it was likely the motive for her murder originated there. But, of course, it could have been a random attack, and it wouldn't have mattered where Millie lived or what she had done with her life to that date. Henry Ash hadn't ruled out a random attack, but in the first hour or two, the way Millie died had me asking questions such as: Was it racially motivated? Was it homophobic? Was it gang related? No gangs in Warminster had ever attacked a person just because they were newcomers. We'd had our fair share of Europeans moving into the area over the previous twenty years without any significant bother. So, the microscope turned on the south of Bristol."

"Was Jeanette a local girl?" asked Gus.

"Born and bred," said Tom. "Her family lived in Bishopsworth, a stone's throw from Withywood. Jeanette's ambition was to leave school as soon as possible, get married, and have children. She told me she met an Irish lad one morning while walking to secondary school. Everyone called him Paddy; he was from a Romany family that pitched up in Bishopsworth every year. Paddy was eighteen and handsome. Jeanette was already sexually active, and they started seeing one another. She told me she fell the first time they had sex. The day Jeanette realised her period was late, she was sitting in a classroom waiting for the bell to go for the end of the lesson. As she glanced at the lime-green painted wall beside her, she saw someone had scratched a message – I'm pregnant – Jeanette told me she had found a compass in the desk drawer and scratched – so am I beneath it. She was fifteen years old."

"Paddy," said Grace. "Was that the man that abused Millie?"

"Mick Budd told me when Millie was seven, police were called to Keble Avenue in Withywood. Jeanette suspected Paddy had been grooming their daughter. The pair had a blazing row; punches were thrown, pots and pans too. The argument spilt out onto the pavement, and neighbours called the police, thinking someone was going to get killed. Whether anything had happened or not, Mick Budd couldn't establish."

"I'm surprised, with his background, this Paddy character stuck around," said Gus. "His people like to keep on the move, not put roots down in one place."

"Paddy didn't abandon Jeanette when she told him she was expecting," said Tom. "He got a job, and although he disappeared from time to time when the house's four walls in Withywood became too much, the three of them were still together. However, the thought that Paddy might have designs on her little girl was too much for Jeanette. She wouldn't have Paddy back in the house. He'd done a runner before the uniforms had arrived in Keble Avenue. Jeanette knew his surname but wouldn't tell the police. Neighbours followed suit and reckoned they'd never heard his name; he was just Paddy. Mick Budd looked into the Romany families, that were regular visitors to the area. He might be able to tell you more. We stopped worrying about it because although the alleged abuse could well have influenced the descent into drugs that followed for Millie, there was no sign of Paddy in Bristol after that day."

"So, Millie's life followed a similar pattern to her mother," said Grace. "Secondary school, a boyfriend, and an unwanted pregnancy."

"Millie left school at sixteen," said Tom. "She was a pretty girl and attracted a lot of boys. Precocious was a word that came to mind when I listened to both Jeanette and Monique describe her during the investigation. Fergus Munro wasn't her first boyfriend by any means, and Millie wasn't as young as her mother when she got pregnant."

"No, Amy, her daughter, was less than a year old when Millie died," said Gus.

"Millie had few qualifications, so she drifted from one low-paid job to another. Often she had spells where she was unemployed. Jeanette wouldn't confirm or deny whether Millie was on the game for a while in her late teens. The one job she enjoyed was in the nail bar, working for Jenny Dodimead. However, once she fell for Amy, she was forced to go part-time, which didn't bring in enough money to satisfy her needs. Jeanette couldn't help, as she had two more kids at home."

"Jeanette was in a relationship by this time, wasn't she?" asked Grace, "Tyler Rowe was his name."

"The break up with Paddy was in 1998," said Tom. "Jeanette steered clear of men for several years, but Tyler Rowe must have caught her eye. Heaven knows why. Later, we discovered he was on the fringes of the drug gang, had never held down a proper job, and had a girl in every corner of the city. Nevertheless, he moved in with Jeanette in 2006, and they had a son, Sammy, the following year and a daughter, Shania, two years later."

"How did Tyler get on with Millie?" asked Gus. "She was fifteen and precocious in your estimation when he moved in. Given his reputation, you would have thought Jeanette would have been wary."

"Jeanette told me Millie had started using soon after she left school," said Tom. "Maybe she was suffering from the effects of whatever went on between her and her father. Then, perhaps, she started considering her prospects and realised they were bleak. Drugs were a means of blocking out the harsh realities for a time. Thanks to Nathan Harvey and his gang, they were in abundant supply in Withywood and Hartcliffe."

"Who was Millie's supplier?" asked Grace. "Did Jeanette know?"

"Jeanette and Monique were no angels," said Tom. "It's impossible to miss the stench of cannabis once you recognise it. Her flat in Weymouth Street reeked of it. She swore she never went further than smoking a joint whenever she could afford it, but Jeanette and her sister got their supplies from the same man while they lived in Bristol. That was Tyler Rowe."

"So, Millie met Fergus Munro, another youngster drifting through life in a haze of drugs," said Gus. "Millie was addicted by this time, I presume?"

"She was, Gus," said Tom. "Millie was twenty when she met Fergus at a squat in Bristol, and they were soon sleeping together. She got pregnant, had Amy, and continued living in Keble Avenue with her mother, while Fergus shared a flat close by with many fellow addicts. He had long since turned to crime to supplement his benefits, whether by shoplifting, mugging, or housebreaking. Millie tagged along with Fergus and one of his flatmates, Justin. They were desperate for cash or something they could quickly convert to cash. Proper housebreakers do their research, know who they're targeting, and don't leave evidence behind if at all possible. So Fergus and Justin would get stoned and break into a property on a whim. That's what happened on the night they were in Hartcliffe."

"The sixteenth of June," said Grace.

"The date sounds familiar," said Tom. "Jeanette told me after Millie got home, which wasn't for a day or two, they had stood across the road and admired a brand-new Humvee on the driveway of a detached house. The electronic doors opened on the double garage, and the interior light came on. Justin recognised a Porsche and a BMW parked inside. The owner came out of the house through the garage and drove off in the Humvee. Fergus and Justin couldn't get across the road quick enough before the garage door descended, but they decided there had to be rich pickings inside. They didn't recognise Nathan Harvey and had no idea where he lived. They were out of their heads, broke in, nicked what they could, and then decided to do as much damage as possible. Millie stood outside, keeping lookout, praying the Humvee didn't return. Jeanette said Millie suspected the owner was someone they shouldn't have messed with, but like the others, she had never met Nathan Harvey."

"Mick Budd was already investigating the spate of burglaries Munro and Cannings were carrying out, wasn't he?" asked Gus.

"He was hot on the trail of those two," said Tom. "As I said, they were amateurs. Mick Budd wasn't aware Nathan Harvey was a victim. The break-in was never reported. Harvey owned several properties across the city, so it wasn't certain whether he would return home that night. It was only a few days before his people started going door-to-door in streets and properties they suspected might be home to the people he sought. In the meantime, Mick Budd had arrested Fergus Munro."

"Millie had run to hide in the squat in Withywood where she had met Fergus," said Grace. "Why didn't she return home once she realised he wasn't there?"

"Jeanette said Millie had sold some of the trio's stolen items and used the cash to buy drugs. She was away with the fairies for a few days and probably hadn't noticed."

"When did Jeanette hear Nathan Harvey was searching for Millie and her boyfriend?" asked Grace.

"News spread across the estates of groups of men breaking down doors and terrorising the people inside. Justin Cannings wasn't at the squat but had holed up with another addict, Viv Whitaker. Cannings was stabbed in both thighs with a screwdriver, tortured with cigarette burns, and beaten with a baseball bat. Whitaker's injuries were more severe when the gang burst in. Cannings told them he thought Munro had been arrested as he hadn't seen him since the robbery. Monique's was the only address he could give them with a link to Millie.

"That was when she heard someone outside her flat threaten to kill Millie," said Grace.

"That's right," said Tom. "Millie heard about Justin being attacked and hurried home to her mother's place. The following day, Mick Budd arrested her."

"If only they'd kept her on remand," said Grace.

Chapter Nine

"HINDSIGHT IS A WONDERFUL THING, GRACE," said Tom Brewer.

"How did DI Budd trace Millie Clark?" asked Gus.

"Did Fergus Munro give her up?" asked Grace.

"Unlikely," said Tom. "DI Budd learned of the late-night visits to properties in Withywood and the surrounding districts. Mick wasn't sure why they were happening because he didn't know Harvey's house had been robbed and ransacked. However, the authorities were alerted once the victims turned up in the hospital. Mick visited Justin Cannings to tell him DNA evidence had been collected from properties he had broken into with Fergus Munro. Mick arrested him and took him into custody as soon as the doctors discharged him. I couldn't speak to Cannings at that stage, obviously, but as Millie was arrested the same day, it seems likely Cannings told police Millie Clark was the third person in their outfit. Whether he was hoping to protect her by having her arrested, I don't know."

"Sadly, it only delayed the inevitable," said Grace.

"Mick Budd did recommend Millie should be remanded," said Tom. "The magistrate gave her bail because of Amy. Jeanette told me she looked after the baby more than Millie, anyway, so it wouldn't have been any hardship."

"When did Jeanette hear about the death threat?" asked Gus.

"Monique came to see Jeanette during the evening following the gang's visit to her place. She kept her head down during the day and ensured nobody followed her. Jeanette heard that someone banging on Monique's door had yelled – 'Tell Jeanette. We're going to kill Millie.'"

"They knew each of the women by their first name," said Gus.

"Monique swore to Jeanette she didn't recognise the voice," said Tom. "Monique was asked in court if she had met Nathan Harvey. She said she had never met Harvey or Coombs."

"It must have been a worrying time for all three women," said Grace. "The gang members were hell-bent on punishing the people who robbed the home in Court Farm Road, and although DI Budd had Munro and Cannings on remand, Millie Clark was on bail. So she was vulnerable, and the police had no idea why."

"Jeanette told me Millie wasn't the only one in fear of the gang. Monique feared they would return and torture her for information, as they had with Justin Cannings. Jeanette knew Tyler Rowe would keep his distance too. She would no longer have access to her weed, and Millie would have to continue chasing connections via the squat for supplies. Tyler hadn't always been around for the past few weeks. Jeanette had heard the rumours about other women but had her head in the sand. She didn't want to ask where he'd been and discover that the rumours of other women and several children were true."

"As for Tyler, he wasn't daft enough to antagonise Harvey and Coombs by fraternising with the mother of a girl his bosses wanted to punish," said Grace.

"That was a thought that struck us," said Gus. "If Tyler Rowe knew where Jeanette lived, why didn't he point Nathan Harvey in the right direction?"

"Was he involved in the gangs carrying out the attacks?" asked Grace.

"If he was, it was never mentioned in conversations before the first court case," said Tom. "It's possible Tyler Rowe was so engrossed in what he was doing elsewhere in the city he wasn't aware of the revenge attacks."

"Well, he appears to have missed that Jeanette decided to escape from Withywood and move to Warminster," said Gus. "She was prepared to take anything she could to hole up in until the dust settled."

"Jeanette told me on Monday afternoon that she moved the five of them here in the middle of July," said Tom. "Millie was still anxious but started to relax as the days passed, and they both felt confident nobody had followed them from Bristol. According to Jeanette, Millie had always been quick to make friends, even if they weren't always looking out for her best interests. So, Millie soon established a connection to get them what they needed."

"Did Jeanette give you the dealer's name?" asked Gus.

Tom nodded.

"It was a name I was already familiar with. They're no longer dealing on the streets of Warminster. Someone else has taken over, of course. It never stops. Not my problem these days."

"What could Jeanette tell you about the events of Sunday?" asked Gus.

"Jeanette said she took Sammy, Shania, and Amy to the local sports centre in the afternoon. First, the older kids went swimming. Next, Jeanette played with Amy in the toddler's pool. Then, they caught the train to Bristol and took a bus to Monique's place. They had arranged to spend the night there; Sammy was missing his friends. They were due back on the train in the evening."

"Why didn't Millie go with them?" asked Gus. "Why didn't Amy stay with her?"

"Jeanette said Millie hadn't been well for a couple of days. So Millie was going to pick up some medication and get some sleep. Jeanette said she asked whether something else was troubling her, but Millie told her not to worry."

"Was there anything else, Tom?" asked Gus.

"Not from our conversation on Monday afternoon and evening. I was happy to get out of the flat and drive home. Cynthia suggested I put my clothes in the wash and have a shower. Have you spoken to Mick Budd and the others since you started this review?"

"We have other team members with DI Budd and DS Gale as we speak," said Grace.

"Well, I'm sure they will be able to fill in some of the gaps. I relied on them to have chapter and verse on all the elements that made up the drug gang's affairs. As we joined the dots between the Christ Church churchyard and Court Farm Road, Hartcliffe, it felt that we'd got our men. We could never be sure whether it was Harvey and Coombs or their musclemen, but we should have nailed one pair of villains, all things being equal. Once the lawyers get involved, nothing is cut and dried."

"Eventually, your joint investigation with Mick Budd

and his team bore fruit," said Gus. "I imagine you went to trial with high hopes?"

"High hopes that all the names we had in the hat would be found guilty," said Tom. "The CPS and their barrister reckoned without the strategy the defence adopted. Divide and conquer. The jury, in their wisdom, decided to concentrate on the organ grinders rather than the monkeys. We couldn't be sure whether the killer was Harvey or Coombs. As far as I was concerned, we had done a good job. The Court of Appeal ordered a retrial thanks to the judge making a minor transgression. Perhaps he was itching to get away for the weekend. Nobody foresaw the possibility that Keel and Thatcher wouldn't appear at the retrial. I travelled to Bristol because I felt a duty to attend, despite it now being Clare Edward's responsibility. The judge had no alternative but to find both defendants not guilty. I remember speaking to the press with Clare on my shoulder, hoping I wouldn't say anything controversial. I reminded the reporter that Millie's killer was still out there. You two are here again today, which means it's still the case."

"It worried you that you didn't solve Millie's murder, didn't it, Tom?" asked Grace.

"For the first year or so, Grace," said Tom. "But I've got more things to worry about now. I should go upstairs to check on Cynthia."

When he returned two minutes later, Gus and Grace were preparing to leave.

"She's awake, and once we've showered and got her dressed, I'll bring her down to the lounge. I wish you luck, Gus. Call me if you need anything else."

"We will, Tom," said Gus. "Many thanks for sparing us your time."

Gus and Grace left Primrose Cottage and were soon on the main road heading for home.

"We won't be going back, will we, Gus?" asked Grace.

"I'll remind Suzie of Cynthia's condition," said Gus. Tom Brewer may not have seen the last of officers from London Road.

MEANWHILE, Alex and Lydia were leaving Trinity Road Police Station in Old Market, Lawrence Hill, Bristol. Their meeting with DI Mick Budd and DS Lizzie Gale had passed without incident. At least, that was how Lydia felt.

"They didn't give much away, did they?" said Alex.

"Exactly what I was thinking," said Lydia. "They weren't comfortable being interviewed."

"I don't think they were hiding a badly handled investigation," said Alex. "It was more that we were from another force, and I'm only a DS. Mick Budd has been in his position for almost a decade. Did you sense a connection between those two?"

"What? You thought they were an item?" said Lydia. "Not a chance. They've worked together for ages and are a good team. Just because Lizzie finished Mick's sentences now and then didn't mean they were sleeping together."

"I suppose we did learn one thing," said Alex. "Mick Budd confirmed Justin Cannings gave him the names of the people with him on the night of the sixteenth of June."

"That would have been challenged if Millie's burglary case had ever got to court," said Lydia. "The doctors would have given him bags of pain relief for his injuries. My client didn't know what he was saying, my lord."

"We'll never know," said Alex. "Mick Budd and Lizzie Gale confirmed what Tom Brewer told Gus. They were devastated to learn Millie had been murdered. They had petitioned the court to keep Millie on remand for her safety, but the magistrate had given her bail because she had a young child. Even so, they hadn't believed the threat to kill was credible. Nathan Harvey and Craig Coombs weren't the types to resort to murder. They hadn't remained in business in Bristol South for fifteen years by making waves. Although the police made inroads into their gang when people made mistakes, the dirt never stuck to those at the top. Harvey and Coombs just filled the gaps left by the low-hanging fruit Mick and his colleagues put behind bars and carried on."

"Cameron Keel and Ivan Thatcher were different prospects, though," said Alex. "Tom Brewer reckoned Mick Budd thought they were capable of murder."

"True," said Alex, "but as Lizzie Gale said this morning, Harvey and Coombs only employed people who followed orders. Their muscle men might have taken a beating too far if left to their own devices, but the four men were in the flat together. Mick Budd said what happened in the churchyard didn't fit with how Harvey and Coombs had operated in the past."

"Maybe Keel and Thatcher did take Millie to the churchyard," said Lydia. "That's what Harvey and Coombs claimed at the first trial. No wonder they chose not to appear at the retrial."

"Could it have been that simple?" asked Alex. "They were guilty. All their Christmases came at once when their bosses were found guilty and jailed for life."

"They could have taken control of the gang in their absence," said Lydia. "The only person who could stand in their way was Micah Harvey. I've never met him, but he doesn't give me the impression he was in the same league as his brother."

"Micah still lives with his mother," said Alex. "He does feel a lightweight, doesn't he? I'm not convinced Keel and Thatcher have it in them to take control of an operation that big. They couldn't act immediately anyway because of the appeal. They must have been gutted when the Court of Appeal ordered a retrial. The obvious thing to do for them was to refuse to appear. That way, there was no risk of them getting dragged down."

"If they had thought that through," said Lydia, "they would have seen the remaining evidence was circumstantial, and the entire case would be thrown out."

"They're not the brightest bunch, are they?" said Alex. "Suddenly, Harvey and Coombs are back at the top of the tree, and Keel and Thatcher are reduced to running the skunk cannabis operation in Shortwood Road."

"Mick Budd still maintains nobody will speak out against Harvey and Coombs, even five years on," said Lydia. "The South Bristol community's collective lips were sealed, whether about the burglary, the beatings, or anything connected to the gang. They would have been in the dark if the hospitals hadn't alerted the police when victims started arriving towards the end of June."

"The last thing we learned might not be relevant. Who knows?" said Alex. "Mick Budd researched the Romany families who were regular visitors to South Bristol. One name that cropped up was Staples. Mick Budd believed Paddy was Patrick Staples. Millie's father hasn't been seen in Bristol since 1998."

"Police weren't sure whether he was abusing his daughter or not, were they?" said Lydia.

"Lizzie Gale thought they could have made a case,

based on Jeanette's evidence, but as Paddy Staples had done a runner, they moved on to other cases that offered a quick resolution."

"We'll get what Mick Budd and Lizzie Gale told us into the Freeman Files when we get back to the office," said Lydia. "Then, we'll include our suggestion that Keel and Thatcher were the killers."

"It makes more sense than some of the options we've put forward," said Alex. "Next stop, Gloucester, and our meeting with Fergus and Pippa Munro."

"ACCORDING TO MY PHONE, we leave the A303 just up here on the right, Neil," said Blessing. "Then, we follow New Road into the village and turn right by the Bell & Crown pub for Chapel Lane."

"Another New Road that's been here for a century," said Neil.

He left the main road and slowed to a standstill behind a petrol tanker turning into a garage.

"You wouldn't want to be left short of fuel in a remote village like this," he said.

As he reached the pub on his left, Blessing tapped his arm.

"That must be Jeanette on the corner. I can't see the Post Office, but the sign on the motor spares building says it's in Chapel Lane."

Neil flashed his lights and drew up in front of the pub. Jeanette Clark hurried across the road and got in the back seat.

"This is DS Davis," said Blessing, "and I'm DC Umeh. We'll drive to Stourhead and get a coffee first, and then we'll chat."

"Whatever you say," said Jeanette. "Monique was suspicious about me leaving the house early, but she didn't follow me."

"How's Shania?" asked Blessing.

"A lot better, thank you. I sent her to school today with Sammy."

Neil took the next turning left, which took them directly to Stourhead along Bell's Lane.

"My parents came here recently," said Blessing. "They enjoyed the house, but the eighteenth-century landscaped gardens with lakeside walks, caves, and classical temples were amazing at this time of year. You're so lucky to have something this beautiful on your doorstep."

"We can't afford to come here," said Jeanette. "I've read about it. The lake is artificial, anyway."

"My father wanted to climb to the top of King Alfred's Tower," said Blessing. "When my mother reminded him there were two hundred and five steps to climb, he decided to give it a miss."

"They say you can see three counties from the top," said Jeanette. "Somerset and Dorset, as well as the one we live in. It's cheaper to take the bus around the nearest small towns."

Neil hoped Blessing would give the plug for the National Trust property a rest. It wasn't encouraging Jeanette to open up about her daughter and her relationships. Melody had half a dozen photographs of the five-arched Palladian bridge over the lake at home. It did look idyllic in autumn, but for many like Jeanette, the only way they would ever appreciate the splendour would be in a magazine or one of the jigsaws Gus favoured.

They were parked outside the café restaurant in minutes. Blessing hadn't mentioned her parents for the last mile. Neil opened the rear door of his car for Jeanette, something he imagined hadn't happened too often in her life. She got out, took in her surroundings, and they walked inside.

"Coffee or tea?" asked Neil.

"Builder's tea, please," said Jeanette.

"I'll get them, Neil," said Blessing.

Neil directed Jeanette to sit at a table by the window.

"What do you think I can tell you that I didn't tell the police five years ago?" asked Jeanette.

"We try not to ask the same questions," said Neil. "That can often stir a long-forgotten memory. People change, too; their relationships at the time of the murder could have ended. So things you weren't prepared to say five years ago might not have the same importance."

Blessing returned with two coffees plus a mug of tea that looked strong enough for the spoon to stand on its own.

"Go on then," said Jeanette. "Fire away. I don't suppose I can smoke in here?"

"No smoking or vaping anywhere on these premises," said Blessing. "There was a sign on the door when we came in."

"You don't miss much," said Jeanette.

"I'm a detective," grinned Blessing. "We'll try not to keep you too long."

"Tell us about Millie's abuser," said Neil.

Jeanette stopped stirring her tea.

"How did you find out about that?" she asked.

"You were unwilling to tell DI Budd his name twenty years ago," said Neil. "As I said, it's asking the right questions of the right people."

"He was a charmer," said Jeanette. "I fell for him big-time. I left school to have Millie, and we stayed together for seven years in that house on Keble Avenue. Paddy managed to get enough work to keep the wolf from the door. There was never any talk of marriage, and he didn't want any more kids. We were happy enough, I suppose, young and foolish."

"When did you suspect he was taking an unhealthy interest in Millie?" asked Blessing.

"Millie was always a Daddy's girl," said Jeanette. "Maybe I was to blame. I wasn't backward in coming forwards with boys; look where it got me. Millie would sit on his lap and wriggle."

"She was only seven when the police had to be called," said Blessing.

"Even at that age, Millie was a little minx," said Jeanette. "Monique warned me to keep an eye on her. Monique thought Millie seemed to know what effect she was having. But, as you said, I kept telling myself she was seven, and maybe we were paranoid."

"Were you and your sister using hard drugs back then?" asked Neil.

"Never," said Jeanette. "We've never gone further than smoking the occasional joint. As I said, I thought Monique was seeing things that weren't there. But once you see something like that, you can't unsee it, can you? So the next time I caught them together, I went ballistic. You know what happened next. He disappeared, and I was left alone with Millie. After that, things were never quite the same between us again."

"When did Millie start using drugs?" asked Blessing.

"I couldn't be sure, but it wouldn't surprise me if she started smoking weed at thirteen or fourteen. Without her father's wages, I was getting behind with the rent. But then, I met Tyler."

"Tyler Rowe, Sammy and Shania's father," said Blessing.

"How did you two meet?" asked Neil.

"Monique heard his name mentioned in a pub one weekend. He was new in the area, someone to go to if you needed something to get you through the week."

"Tyler became your supplier," said Neil. "What about Millie?"

"Not before she left school," said Jeanette. "Whatever Millie needed, she could get from boys at school. It was still soft drugs at that stage, but Millie was on a slippery slope before she left school. I could go days without seeing her. She would get involved with someone older, and they would give her drugs in exchange for sex. I always took her back when she managed to get away. Jenny Dodimead was someone I knew from school. Jenny gave Millie a job in her nail bar, which kept her out of trouble for a while. The money wasn't great, but it stopped the council from evicting us."

"Wasn't Tyler living with you?" asked Neil.

"Not seven days a week," said Jeanette. "I had Sammy during Millie's last year at school. After that, Tyler was there more often over the next two years, and then Shania was born."

"That was in 2009, is that right?" asked Blessing. "What was Millie doing?"

"You might well ask," said Jeanette. "She was using cocaine by then and would do anything to keep getting her fix. Denis Long got his claws into her."

"We haven't heard of Denis Long before," said Neil.

"Denis was a pimp from Bishopsworth," said Jeanette. "The money from the nail bar wasn't enough for Millie to feed her habit. She was still giving me something towards her keep, but Denis had another way she could earn extra cash. By 2011, Millie was spending more and more time away from the house, getting deeper into trouble. She spent much of her time in a squat in Withywood, just a mile from her home. That was where she met Fergus. Millie came home to tell me she was pregnant a few months later. Fergus wasn't going to marry her; he was an addict like Millie. He'd never worked since leaving school and turned to crime to get the money for his drugs."

"How did Millie feel about her stepfather?" asked Blessing.

"She despised him," said Jeanette.

"What did you think was behind Tyler's lack of commitment?" asked Neil.

"What do you mean?" she asked.

"You had two children together, and he lived with you, on and off, for seven years."

"Tyler wasn't the type to get married and settle down," said Jeanette.

"When he was absent from Keble Avenue, Tyler was sleeping with other women, Jeanette," said Neil. "Surely you must have realised that? Did you know how many children he had fathered while you were together?"

Jeanette stared at the empty mug.

"You have no idea what it's like for someone like me," she said.

"Did you know who Tyler worked for?" asked Blessing.

"He had to get his supplies from somewhere," said Jeanette. "Tyler had customers all across Bristol, not just in Withywood. So you don't ask questions. Monique heard rumours that Tyler had other women on the go. That was why he spent less and less time with me as the years passed. She also heard Tyler was part of a major drug gang based in South Bristol. As I said, it's best not to poke your nose into who's the next link in the chain."

"You relied on him," said Blessing.

"We both did," said Jeanette.

"Millie was pretty, despite her addiction," said Blessing. "How much longer she would hold onto her looks, we'll never know. Most men would be attracted to her, especially if she continued to behave as you described. I wonder if Tyler was ever tempted. It would have saved him the trouble of looking elsewhere. Millie was fifteen, going on sixteen, when he moved in."

"I already told you," snapped Jeanette. "She despised him."

"That's fair enough," said Neil. "Millie was close to her father. Another man in her mother's life wouldn't automatically earn her affection if Millie had been eight or nine. At sixteen and already sexually active, Millie was bound to be wary. She was absent during the early years you and Tyler were together. Perhaps she was on the game. Her reliance on drugs brought on all these actions. Tyler wasn't supplying her then, was he? When did that start?"

"After she had Amy," said Jeanette. "Millie had to give up working at the nail bar for a while. Then, she could only go back part-time, and times were tough. Finally, Tyler said he'd help out."

"For a price, no doubt," said Neil.

"Millie was spending more time at the squat in Withywood with Fergus," said Jeanette. "She kept bugging him to take her on the burglaries he was doing with Justin. Anything to earn the cash for her drugs."

"Perhaps, Millie didn't want to be forced to accept drugs from Tyler unless she had the money to pay for them," said Blessing. "How could you have missed the signs, Jeanette?

What about the way Tyler looked at her? Did he try to get her alone in the house? Perhaps he waited outside the nail bar for her to finish work?"

"He wasn't living with me that often by then," wailed Jeanette.

"Maybe you saw what you wanted to see," said Neil. "Monique warned you what he was like, didn't she? She spotted Millie could wrap a guy around her little finger. Maybe, Monique was looking out for you because Millie was tempting Tyler, pretending not to be interested in him but desperate for the drugs he could provide. It's not such a stretch to imagine Millie having sex with her stepfather in return for free drugs."

"You're disgusting," shouted Jeanette. "Millie's dead. She can't defend herself. You've no right."

Blessing looked over her shoulder. They were attracting attention from the café staff and customers enjoying a quiet drink.

"Come on, Jeanette," she said. "Let's take a walk, and you can have that cigarette."

They walked outside while Neil returned the empty mugs to the counter.

He showed the manager his warrant card, apologised for the disruption, and searched for Blessing and Jeanette.

Neil caught them up by the lake.

"We're nearly done," he said. "We need to tie up a few loose ends. For example, when was the last time Millie saw Fergus Munro?"

"The night they robbed Nathan Harvey's house," said Jeanette. "The police were closing in on Fergus and Jason. They nicked Fergus the day after the robbery. So there was no chance for Millie to see Fergus or for him to visit his daughter. He was on remand, we moved to Warminster, and Millie was murdered."

"Who told you Nathan Harvey was searching for Millie?" asked Blessing.

"Monique did. She came round the day after the gang hammered on her door and told her to give me a message. Tell her we're going to kill her, they said."

"Monique insisted she didn't recognise the voice of the man who made that death threat," said Neil. "Did she know any gang members that worked for Harvey and Coombs?"

"She knew Tyler," said Jeanette. "It couldn't have been his voice. She would have known."

"As soon as she told you Millie was in danger, you made arrangements to leave," said Blessing.

"I knew I had to move fast," said Jeanette lighting her second cigarette.

"Millie was hiding out at the squat, wasn't she," said Neil.

Jeanette nodded.

"Was Tyler staying at your house?" asked Blessing

Jeanette shook her head.

"So it was just you and the three children," said Blessing.

"I found the flat in Weymouth Street through an ad on Facebook. I was surprised at how cheap the rent was until I got there and saw what a tip it was, but it didn't matter. Millie came home to Keble Avenue for a change of clothes. I told her we were moving, and the next day she was arrested for the burglary. I thought we were going to be okay. If she were on remand, it would be tougher for the gang to get at her. But Millie got bail, despite the police objecting, so we packed what little we had and went to

Warminster on the train. Only Monique knew we were leaving Keble Avenue, and we thought we had made it."

"What about Tyler Rowe?" asked Neil.

"I didn't think we'd see him again," said Jeanette. "So, Millie started putting feelers out on the streets, in pubs. She knew who to approach. Millie soon had the name of a dealer, and things were sweet again for a few weeks. Monique called me and asked if I fancied taking the kids to see her, and we made arrangements for Sunday."

"We can join the dots from there, Jeanette," said Neil. "Just one more thing. How was Millie during the time you lived in Weymouth Street?"

"Anxious at first," said Jeanette. "She was always looking over her shoulder for trouble. As the weeks passed, Millie seemed calmer, but that could have the buzz of a regular fix. Then, she seemed on edge again in the days before her death. Millie told me she wasn't feeling well, but I felt it went deeper. That was why I almost postponed the trip to see Monique. I wondered whether Millie had spotted trouble."

"How are things with you and Monique now?" asked Neil.

"Nobody bothers us out here in the sticks," said Jeanette. "Fergus must be out of prison now, but he's never attempted to trace us. The same goes for Tyler. Sammy and Shania asked after Daddy for a while when we first reached Warminster, but they were among other kids in the same boat once they started school. Kids are resilient. It's not unusual for their friends to be with a single mother, two mothers, or Mummy's boyfriend. They've all but forgotten him."

"When you've finished that cigarette, we'll take you back to the Crown & Bell," said Neil.

"Is it far to walk from there?" asked Blessing.

"Nowhere is far from the pub in the village," said Jeanette.

Neil drove back along Bell's Lane.

Jeanette got out and stood and watched as Neil drove away.

"What now, Neil?" asked Blessing.

"As soon as we're out of sight, we'll find a spot on New Road to phone Monique. We need to get her side of the story."

"Will Jeanette talk to her, do you think?" asked Blessing.

"Can't be sure," said Neil. "It was an interesting chat, though, wasn't it?"

"If there was a gold nugget in that conversation, I didn't spot it," said Blessing.

"We won't know the value of what Jeanette told us until we can compare it with Monique's contribution."

"Plus, whatever the others bring to the party," said Blessing.

"Here's a lay-by. I'll call Monique," said Neil.

Blessing listened to Neil asking when they could meet. Then, she heard Neil tell Monique to be at Warminster police station at ten. If she failed to appear, uniformed officers would collect her.

"Ooh," said Blessing. "You're so masterful at times, Neil Davis."

Chapter Ten

"I THINK THEY BOUGHT IT," said Jeanette. "There was one occasion where I might have been careless. I said kids were resilient. I was referring to Sammy and Shania's reaction after Tyler went AWOL. I was lucky those two cops didn't press me on that comment."

"Amy spent so little time with her mother; they never truly bonded," said Monique. "When was the last time you heard Amy mention Millie?"

"Not since we moved here, for sure," said Jeanette.

"Hang on," said Monique, "that's my phone. Hello?"

Jeanette took off her coat, sat beside her sister, and lit a cigarette.

"I keep telling you. I've got nothing to say," said Monique.

Monique turned to her sister and gave her the thumbs up.

"I don't like being threatened," she said. "I'll be there, but I'll bring our solicitor."

Monique ended the call.

"Was that DS Davis?" asked Jeanette.

"He reckoned he'd send someone to march me out of here and make sure the neighbours got an eyeful if I didn't agree to meet with him."

"You had better get on the phone, then," said Jeanette. "What time do they want you to meet them?"

"Ten o'clock tomorrow morning at the police station on Station Road," said Monique. "We have to hold our nerve. You should have been more careful when talking about the kids."

"What will you tell them tomorrow?" asked Jeanette.

"Something that will persuade them to leave us alone. After all, the police know we had nothing to do with Millie's murder."

GUS AND GRACE had arrived at HMP Erlestoke a mere twenty-five minutes after leaving Primrose Cottage. First, they had to endure lengthy security checks before reaching an interview room. Then, they waited forty-five minutes until Justin Cannings limped through the door with an escort.

"I've no idea who you are or why you needed to see me," he said.

Grace felt his gaze linger on her for longer than she felt comfortable.

"Take a seat, please, Mr Cannings," said Gus.

"I'm Detective Inspector Pakenham," said Grace. "My colleague, Mr Freeman, is a consultant with Wiltshire Police. We've been reviewing the Millie Clark murder from 2013. I'm sure you're familiar with the people involved and the events that led up to it."

"Hard to forget," said Justin rubbing his thighs.

"When did you first meet Millie Clark?" asked Gus.

"At a squat in Withywood. I spent time there with Fergus Munro. Millie was looking to score. Fergus got her set up, and from then on, they were inseparable. Well, for a while, at least. If we hadn't ended up in prison, they might have stuck together."

"How long had you known Fergus?" asked Grace.

"A decade or more, we mixed with the same crowd."

"Fellow drug users," said Grace.

"We can't all be born with a silver spoon in our mouths, sweetheart," said Justin.

"Everyone has choices," said Grace. "When did you turn to a life of petty crime?"

"You do what you have to," said Justin. "We couldn't afford to wait until the end of the week to collect a paycheck. We needed cash as soon as we needed it. If you get me."

"You're making excuses about why you did what you did," said Grace. "I'm waiting to hear a date."

"Monday the first of January," said Justin. "That's a date."

"Could you be a little more accurate, Mr Cannings," said Gus. "We can have a word in the Governor's ear about a problem with your release date. That's tomorrow, I believe?"

"We'd been shoplifting, grabbing granny handbags, and mugging drunken idiots late at night for a couple of years," said Justin. "Then, Fergus had the bright idea of breaking into houses where the owners looked to be minted. We did okay for a few months and then visited Hartcliffe."

"The sixteenth of June," said Grace. "Millie Clark came along with Fergus to act as lookout."

"Millie didn't join Fergus for the first couple of houses

we hit. It was my idea to have someone keeping watch in case the homeowner came home while we were inside. That night, we'd all been partying, and after we'd scored a gold watch and some bling, we decided it would be a blast to wreck the place."

"Millie was hanging around outside far longer than she expected," said Grace.

"Yeah, it was a bad move. Fergus realised that when we woke up the next day. We should have stuck to breaking and entering with a clear head. Millie told us she would hide the gear at her place. We were going to flog it once the dust settled. I left the squat to see a mate and heard Fergus had been arrested. I kept my head down at my mate's flat and tried to find out how they had worked out that it was us so quickly. A couple of days later, I realised nobody knew about the place in Hartcliffe we'd ransacked. Fergus had been lifted for the burglaries we'd done before that night. I was bricking it. There had to be a reason the guy with the flash cars didn't report the break-in. I knew then nothing good would come from it."

"So, you stayed with Viv Whitaker in his flat," said Grace.

"We never left the place. Viv ordered takeaways and called his dealer to drop by to fix us up. We had no idea what was about to happen. The next night, the door was kicked off its hinges, and six blokes stormed in. One guy shouted my name. I stood up, and I was punched and kicked by the lot. Then they strapped me to a chair with duct tape and asked where Fergus lived. I told him he had been arrested. They thought I was lying, and the guy in charge stabbed me in the thigh with a screwdriver."

Justin rubbed his left thigh.

"What happened next?" asked Gus.

"They said they wanted to find the girl we had with us," said Justin. "I told them Millie had never stepped inside the house, but they wouldn't listen. That's when I got this."

Justin touched his right thigh.

"He was even more vicious the second time. It never healed properly. I'll always carry this right leg. They kept hitting me and asking where Millie lived."

"Did they know about the squat?" asked Gus.

"They helped create it," laughed Justin. "The only people who used that place were addicts that bought their product."

"You realised who it was you'd crossed by then," said Gus.

"Nathan Harvey," said Justin. "Of all the houses in Bristol to burgle, we had to choose one owned by Mr Big."

"I don't suppose he would advertise the fact it was one of his," said Gus. "So, they kept asking for an address for Millie?"

Justin stood up and lifted his sweatshirt. Grace stopped counting marks left by cigarette burns after ten.

"I couldn't tell them what I didn't know," said Justin retaking his seat. "The only person I knew was Monique, Millie's aunt. So I told them to try her. Instead, they hit me around the head a few more times and left me in a heap on the floor."

"Your friend didn't fare too well," said Gus. "Viv Whitaker was an innocent party."

"I told them Viv never had anything to do with the burglary," said Justin. "One guy I'd seen around the city loads of times took Viv into the bedroom. The guy went mental. I could hear Viv's screams behind the closed door. When the gang had left, a girl from an upstairs flat came down to see if we were okay. I asked her not to call the police. I didn't want Harvey's thugs coming back for seconds. She called an ambulance, and when I next saw Viv in the hospital later, I learned he'd been stabbed in the face, hit with a lump hammer, and the bloke did a number on him with his boots."

"Do you know the name of his attacker?" asked Gus.

"No. He was just a face I recognised. He was one of Nathan Harvey's goons."

"Cameron Keel?" asked Grace.

"That could have been who did this," said Justin pointing to his legs.

"What about Ivan Thatcher?" asked Grace.

"We weren't on first-name terms, sweetheart," said Justin. "But someone did call the guy who stabbed me Cam."

"You were in the hospital for a while," said Gus. "Then DI Budd popped in with a bunch of grapes and read you your rights."

"I admitted it was me, Fergus, and Millie, that did the burglaries they knew about. He expected me to tell him who had put me in the hospital and why. I knew what would happen if I did. After the docs said I was fit enough to leave, the police collected me, and I was sitting next to Fergus in here before I knew it."

"Fergus didn't escape the gang's wrath, though, did he?" asked Grace.

"Who attacked him in the showers?" asked Gus.

"Inmates who used to work for Harvey but had got careless, or people who owed him a favour. He's not the Governor here, but nothing happens without his say-so. You'll find drugs in these buildings if you know where to look. Who do you think supplies them? Harvey can get them inside and send messages to his people whenever he wishes."

"Was it you that pointed the finger at Munro?" asked Gus.

"I wouldn't do that. We were friends. Anyway, I didn't need to," said Justin. "Harvey and his mate, Coombs, have someone in a suit to monitor the courts when they're in session. They report back on who has gone down for what. If they're useful to Harvey, and he wants to ensure they keep their mouth shut inside, he'll arrange to look after their wife and kids. Or he makes sure their parents don't suffer if they're single blokes."

"One big happy family," said Gus.

"Of course, the opposite applies," said Justin. "If getting caught costs the business a lot of money, then all bets are off. Those prisoners will likely receive a visit from Harvey's enforcers. Because Fergus disrespected him, as soon as Harvey heard we'd been sent down for a string of burglaries, the word went out. I couldn't warn him or do anything to help. They would have turned on me."

"We've heard Fergus is clean these days," said Grace. "He's married and has got a proper job. So what happened to you, Justin?"

"I tried to stay on the straight and narrow, believe me," said Justin. "Once employers read you've just left prison, they start looking for whose job application form is lying under yours. My gammy leg doesn't help, either. The jobs I was suited for before I was attacked are beyond me now. I can't even turn to thieving when I get out tomorrow. Even the fattest copper would catch me. But, look, is there anything else? I want to get back to my cell."

"I think that's all, Justin," said Gus. "I hope you do a better job of staying out of trouble after tomorrow."

Grace nodded to the escort. Justin Cannings got to his feet, limped to the doorway, and disappeared from view.

"I was surprised you didn't give him what for, Grace," said Gus. "He called you sweetheart twice."

"I decided he had enough troubles, Gus," she said. "Back to the office?"

"Where I hope we'll find four smiling faces," said Gus. "With luck, someone will have the key to this mystery."

Gus and Grace were soon outside the building and reunited with the Focus.

"Getting out of Erlestoke was quicker than getting in," said Grace.

"That's not a rumour you should be spreading, Grace," said Gus. "I've lost count of the number of occasions I've read in our local free paper that someone has gone AWOL. Although, as often as not, they haven't escaped. They've failed to return from a sanctioned home visit."

"Justin Cannings clarified a couple of points, though, Gus," said Grace. "Did you pick up on anything that could help?

"Justin reckoned Millie stashed the gear they stole from Nathan Harvey's house at her place," said Gus. "I don't imagine that meant the squat she shared with a dozen drug addicts. She must have popped home to Keble Avenue before going into hiding."

"Tom Brewer told us Millie sold items from the robbery to buy drugs," said Grace. "There might not have been much left when Mick Budd caught up with her. Anyone buying watches and jewellery from a desperate druggie will only pay a fraction of its worth."

"True," said Gus. "If Jeanette reckoned Millie was at the squat in the days following the burglary, then Justin has to be wrong. Millie hung onto the stuff they stole and flogged it. I don't recall anything out of the ordinary in items taken into custody when she was arrested. She had a mobile phone, house keys, a purse with cards and loose change, and a couple of bags of her drug of choice, according to Bristol police."

Gus turned into the Church Street car park and parked next to Lydia's Mini.

"All present and correct," said Grace.

They travelled to the first floor office and, not for the first time, found the others hard at work.

"Welcome back, guv," said Neil.

"Would you like a coffee, guv?" asked Blessing.

"That would be just the ticket, Blessing," said Gus.

Blessing made her way to the restroom. Soon after the door closed, Gus heard the Gaggia rattle into action.

"Who wants to go first?" asked Gus.

"I will, guv," said Neil. "We had a lively session with Jeanette at Stourhead. She was surprised we knew about her first partner. He sounded like a piece of work, but Millie wasn't little Miss Innocent."

"Tom Brewer described her as precocious," said Gus.

"Both her and Monique were smoking weed from their teens," said Neil. "Jeanette reckoned Millie followed suit around the age of thirteen. Tyler Rowe supplied the sisters, but Millie kept her contacts at school. She despised Tyler, which was why she spent more and more time away from home. As described in the murder file, Millie's teenage life slowly descended into cocaine use after leaving school. We learned that Jeanette reckoned Millie was put to work on the streets by a pimp called Denis Long. She was eighteen or nineteen at the time. Millie met Fergus Munro at the squat in Withywood and went home to Mum when she was expecting Amy. Tyler Rowe was spending less time at

Jeanette's, but he did start supplying Millie after Amy was born. I thought it sounded like Tyler might have tried it on with Millie, you know, in return for the drugs, but Jeanette was adamant nothing happened. Millie couldn't stand the bloke."

"We haven't heard much about Tyler Rowe from the people we've spoken with today," said Gus. "Anything else?"

"Jeanette said Millie had been calmer since they got to Warminster, but in the days leading up to her murder, she was getting anxious. Millie blamed it on not feeling well. That was how Micah Harvey found her outside the pharmacy. Millie was collecting a prescription. Jeanette went to Bristol to spend the night at Monique's with the kids. Millie was meant to go but cried off, saying she needed to sleep."

"That sounds like she might have seen someone, guv," said Lydia. "Perhaps she'd spotted one of Nathan Harvey's gang?"

Blessing returned with hot drinks, and everyone took a five-minute break.

Gus tried to fit Neil's pieces into his jigsaw as he nursed his mug of black coffee.

"Dazed and confused, guv?" asked Lydia.

"That sums it up succinctly, Lydia," said Gus. "Why don't you give the team our highlights, Grace?"

"One thing before Grace starts, guv," said Neil. "Monique Clark was uncooperative, so I've arranged to interview her tomorrow morning at ten. She'll have her solicitor present,"

"Will she, indeed," said Gus. "People with something to hide are prone to do that. Which doesn't fit with how things have gone so far."

"Do you want to speak to Monique, guv?" asked Blessing. "It might unnerve her if she's expecting us to turn up and you two walk in."

"That's not a bad idea, Gus," said Grace. "Did you have us down for a trip further afield?"

"Alex and Lydia could travel to HMP Winchester in our place," said Gus. "Or we could go directly there from Warminster. It's only an hour away along the A303. So we can kill two birds with one stone."

"Perhaps we should hear what Alex and Lydia learned today first, Gus," said Grace.

"Mick Budd told us Justin Cannings gave up the names of his accomplices," said Alex. "He admitted that Fergus and Millie had been involved. Everything else that followed tracked what we heard from Tom Brewer and the others we've interviewed. Lydia thought we were missing a trick. At the first trial, Harvey and Coombs reckoned Keel and Thatcher took Millie to the churchyard and killed her. Keel and Thatcher swore it was the other way round."

"Mick Budd told us Harvey and Coombs only employed people who followed orders, guv," said Lydia. "What if Keel and Thatcher disobeyed orders and went too far? They murdered Millie. The police couldn't be sure, so they charged everyone with the murder, went to trial, and somehow the jury picked the wrong names out of the hat. Harvey and Coombs got sent down for life, which left the way clear for Keel and Thatcher to assume control of the gang's lucrative business. It made perfect sense for them to decide not to appear at the retrial if that was the case. They couldn't be found guilty if they weren't there."

"I'm not sure Keel and Thatcher had the brains to pull off something that devious, Lydia," said Gus. "We'll ask Cameron Keel when we see him tomorrow. Anything else?"

"Mick Budd was able to put a name to Millie's father,

guv," said Alex. "Patrick Staples, known as Paddy, an Irish Romany who lived with Jeanette in Keble Avenue for seven years or so. Unfortunately, the alleged abuse couldn't be proven, and nobody has seen or heard of Staples since the day he walked away from Jeanette's place."

"After we left Trinity Road, we drove to Gloucester, guv," said Lydia. "Fergus and Pippa Munro were joined at the hip. No way was she going to let us speak with her husband alone."

"Their six-month-old son was asleep in the next room, guv," said Alex.

"Fergus was meant to be serving an apprenticeship," said Gus. "Where does he work?"

"He's a full-time mechanic at a garage on Stroud Road, guv," said Lydia. "Pippa is still on maternity leave but hopes to return to work in the New Year. She told us she was a data analyst before she fell pregnant. There are plenty of vacancies in that sector in Gloucester. Pippa shouldn't have too much trouble getting fixed up."

"Did she explain how they came to meet?" asked Gus. "Pippa sounds like a decent young woman. What was it about the feckless drug addict Fergus Munro that drew her to him? Fergus already had a girlfriend and a daughter when she met him in Bristol. Thirty-five miles seems a fair old distance to travel for a night out with the girls."

"Pippa was on a crusade," said Alex.

"A strong religious background, guv," said Lydia. "Her father is a Lead Pastor in a church that's all about creating hope and joy in the community."

"That goes a long way to explain things," said Gus. "You queried yesterday whether the help of a good woman did the trick for Fergus after he left Erlestoke."

"That's right, guv," said Alex. "Saint Pippa persuaded

Fergus to seek help for his addiction. Maybe he was suscep-
tible with the net closing in on him, or he fancied her. Pippa
is an attractive young woman, but people with a religious
zeal always try too hard, don't they?"

"You mean she's attractive until she starts preaching at
you," said Neil.

"Trust you to reduce things to the common denomina-
tor, Neil," said Grace.

"I find it saves time," shrugged Neil.

"I couldn't stop wondering how she managed to cuddle
her son, guv," said Lydia. "We were with them for ninety
minutes, and Pippa had her hands crossed in her lap
throughout."

"Earnest," said Gus, nodding. "I've seen TV presenters
use that approach when they want you to believe they care
about the subject they're presenting."

"Fergus described the attack in Erlestoke, guv," said
Alex. "It matched what we already knew. Nathan Harvey
ordered it from outside, and nobody saw or heard a thing.
Fergus was in the hospital for several days. Pippa said he
was fortunate not to have suffered permanent damage."

"Pippa was upset about the level of violence and
concerned the authorities didn't seem to be able to control
the inmates. So she visited him in Great Western Hospital,
and they married soon after he was released from prison."

"She repeated her complaint that Fergus hadn't received
the support he deserved after he left prison," said Lydia.

"Fergus was tougher to live with than she had thought,"
said Blessing. "Had he been treated for his addiction?"

"It started in Erlestoke, Blessing," said Alex. "It was
ongoing. Fergus was confident the worst was behind him
now. Pippa mentioned the mood swings he'd suffered after
he left Erlestoke. Fergus admitted he'd always had a short

fuse as a teenager, but things got worse while using legal highs."

"When did he start using those?" asked Gus.

"Around the time he and Justin Cannings started committing the burglaries, guv," said Alex.

"So, these legal highs were circulating while Fergus, Justin, and Millie lived at the Withywood squat."

"Yes, guv," said Lydia. "Fergus said they were evil, not just dangerous. They had been under the influence the night they broke into the house on Court Farm Road. He knew they had screwed up big time the next day when he finally awoke."

"I can't have any sympathy for him," said Gus.

"He did tell us something that might interest you," said Alex.

"Go on," said Gus.

"It was Tyler Rowe who supplied them with the legal highs."

"So, Tyler Rowe visited the squat," said Neil. "That's interesting. Jeanette told us Millie did her best to avoid buying from Tyler whenever he stayed at her home."

"Fergus didn't mention Millie at all today," said Lydia.

"With Pippa sat beside him with her hands in her lap, I'm not surprised," said Gus.

"I wonder whether Pippa knew about Millie and Amy?" asked Blessing.

"Does it matter?" asked Grace.

"How could Alex and Lydia ask questions about that part of Fergus's life with her hovering beside him all the time?" asked Blessing. "For instance, I want to know when he last saw Amy. Did he know where Millie had gone? Why didn't he attempt to see his daughter, especially after hearing Millie had been killed?"

"Fergus spent most days stealing money for drugs and then taking them," said Neil. "I don't think Millie entered his head that much, let alone Amy. While he served his sentence, the two trials took place. Fergus was in Erlestoke when Millie died. He spent time in the hospital and started concentrating on getting clean. He had something positive to aim for because Pippa was waiting for him. His old life with Millie was no more. Fergus wasn't returning to that life even if she had still been hanging out in that squat."

"That poor little girl," said Blessing. "Amy was always destined to grow up without knowing her father."

"What was it Jeanette said today, Blessing?" asked Neil. "Kids are resilient?"

"She was talking about Tyler Rowe's children," said Blessing.

"The same would apply to Amy," said Grace. "Her mother died, and her father walked away, no matter how you look at it. That has to be damaging."

"Not according to Jeanette," said Neil. "She was suggesting Sammy and Shania had their mother's love, and for over four years, they've had their aunt living under the same roof. They are well looked after and feel safe. Tyler Rowe was there one minute, gone the next, while Jeanette lived in Keble Avenue. Those two kids might remember what their father looked like, but they haven't seen him for five years, as far as we can tell. I don't reckon they ask when he's coming back or whether it was their fault he left. The questions might come when they're older, but it's not certain."

"What about Amy, though?" asked Blessing.

"I'll jump in here, Neil, if I may?" said Gus. "Amy was only eleven months old when her mother died. Jeanette told us Millie spent most of her time at the squat. When they escaped to Warminster, Millie went out during the day, seeking a supplier for Jeanette, Monique, and herself."

"Jeanette looked after Amy so much the little mite didn't notice someone was missing," said Blessing.

"That puts a different complexion on things, doesn't it, Gus?" said Grace.

"Those two women couldn't have killed Millie, Grace," said Gus. "But I believe we have another question to add to our list for Monique."

"Perhaps we should call Fergus at work, guv," said Lydia. "To pose those questions, Blessing suggested. Surely, he has a right to know where his daughter is?"

"If we're covering HMP Winchester, then you'll have time on your hands," said Gus. "Be careful. Ask specific questions requiring a single word or brief answer. Don't reveal anything about Amy at this stage. If Fergus wishes to take matters further, he can. It doesn't fall within our remit. We're searching for Millie's killer, nothing else."

Time is relentless. Gus realised another day was slipping away, and they were still some way from uncovering the truth. He felt they were closer than yesterday but had no idea how much further they had to travel.

"There might be time for Grace and me to get the details of Tom Brewer's meeting into our digital files today," he said. "We'll have to leave our thoughts on Justin Cannings until tomorrow afternoon. I don't know how much more the rest of you have to enter, but let's make good use of the last hour."

Gus didn't hear a dissenting voice, not that he expected one. They were a good bunch. Finally, at five o'clock, everyone was on their feet and ready to descend to the ground floor.

"Will we see you later, Grace?" asked Blessing.

"The Thursday Dinner Club?" asked Gus as they crowded into the lift together.

"I'd love to, Blessing," said Grace. "But I've got too much to do before Saturday."

"Has Monty Jennings offered to help you get your stuff to the farmhouse?" asked Gus.

He knew the answer before Grace replied.

"Monty hasn't spoken to me since I handed in my notice," said Grace.

"Typical," said Gus. "What have you arranged?"

"You won't fit much into your Smart car, ma'am," said Neil as they came out of the lift into the car park.

"John Ferris said he'll be at my place at nine on Saturday morning," said Grace.

"I can just see you on the trailer, bouncing behind the tractor, making sure nothing falls off," said Lydia.

"Don't be daft, Lydia. Jackie promised me John would take the best horsebox he owns," said Blessing. "She said his horses travelled in style when he was riding point-to-point. I've seen it in one of the barns; it's the size of a single-decker bus. You'll get everything to the farm in one trip."

"And you can sit in the front with the driver," said Gus. "See you in the morning, Grace."

The grin Grace gave him assured Gus that she had taken the ribbing in good part. She was slowly turning into a team player. He hadn't seen that coming.

Chapter Eleven

Friday, 2 November 2018

GUS HAD ARRIVED at the bungalow just after five-thirty last night. Suzie stepped out of her car and waited for him to join her.

"I'm surprised I didn't see you in the lane ahead of me," said Gus.

"I came from the opposite end of the village to you for a change," said Suzie. "I stopped by the allotment to collect fresh vegetables. I hope you don't mind?"

"Of course not," said Gus. "Did you see anyone?"

"Did anyone see me, d'you mean? A cabbage thief strikes a country village. Bert and Clemency wouldn't be working this late. It was almost dark, but my headlights allowed me to locate something suitable for a veggie delight for this evening."

"I should have anticipated an antidote to my meaty feast last night."

"Moderation in everything, darling," said Suzie.

They went indoors and headed straight for the kitchen.

Later, they'd curled up in front of the TV and let a forgettable drama wash over them. During the interminable advert breaks, Suzie asked how the case was going.

"Every day adds another name to the list of people who couldn't have committed the murder," said Gus.

"That's good, isn't it?" asked Suzie. "How many suspects have you got left?"

"We can't be certain we've identified everyone yet," said Gus.

"Ouch," said Suzie. "Do you want to hear what Geoff and I were reading today?"

"Let me guess," said Gus. "Kenneth handed Geoff a report he'd had on his desk for ages. Something he thought might be relevant to your investigation but which he was reluctant to open himself. He was afraid of what might crawl out."

"You're a mind reader, too," said Suzie. "Is there no end to your talents? Do you remember the Serious Organised Crime Agency?"

"The one they closed down a couple of months after Millie Clark's murder. Yes, it preceded the National Crime Agency, where my nemesis, Brendan Curran, worked. What did that report have to say?"

"They had recorded a sharp increase over the past five years in the number of police officers dealing heroin, cocaine and amphetamines," said Suzie.

"SOCA was supposed to be a national law enforcement agency tackling the trafficking of drugs and people," said Gus. "A shame that their last target was the police."

"They also recorded an equally startling rise in the

number of officers abusing their power by bullying or cajoling suspects, witnesses, and victims into having sex with them."

"I remember the Met suspending several officers and support staff on corruption charges five or six years ago," said Gus. "Some were allowed to resign or retire with full pension rights, and some were dismissed. Only a handful of those cases went to court. Is there something in the report that mentions events outside of London?"

Suzie nodded.

"I'm afraid so. Geoff would have my guts for garters for telling you this much, but our investigation has legs."

"Ouch, indeed," said Gus. He thought of Tom Brewer caring for Cynthia in Primrose Cottage. Kenneth would be gutted if his old colleague was caught up in this mess. On the other hand, it might accelerate his retirement.

Gus awoke at seven and wondered when he'd get a good night's rest again. He'd drifted in and out of sleep all night, going over the murder case. When he did drop off, he kept seeing the Chief Constable and his wife waving goodbye to Southampton as they set off on another cruise.

He joined Suzie in the kitchen after he'd showered and changed.

"Coffee and toast?" she asked.

Gus nodded. He scoured the cupboard for honey but had to settle for marmalade.

"Where are you off to today," asked Suzie.

"Warminster police station and HMP Winchester," he replied.

"Based on your comments last night, you won't arrest anyone and take them straight to jail."

"A follow-up interview with the victim's aunt, before

chatting with a violent criminal who might have got away with murder."

"Is Grace going with you again? Or have you forgiven Lydia for wearing one of her more outrageous outfits?"

"Grace is with me today," said Gus. "We're a good combination, despite everything."

"You're still expecting her to stab you in the back," said Suzie.

"If I survive another day, I'll see you at five-thirty," said Gus. "You might need your wellies if you plan to visit the allotment this evening. Heavy rain is forecast to sweep across the county before noon."

"We could always order a takeaway tonight," said Suzie.

"That would be the second night this week," said Gus. "Leave it to me. I'll cook."

They left the bungalow at eight-thirty and headed for Devizes.

Gus parked the Focus at the end of the row of Crime Review Team cars. He and Grace would be leaving again in thirty minutes. Just time to add a little more to his digital files and ensure everyone had enough to do while he was absent.

"Morning, guv," said Neil. "Friday already, and we haven't closed the case. The Chief Constable will think we've lost our mojo."

"We're doing our best, Neil," said Lydia.

Gus had a lightbulb moment.

"Change of plan," he said. "Alex, you can speak to Fergus Munro this morning as agreed. Please stick to the things I outlined yesterday afternoon. Grace, can you call ACC Clare Edwards and get the lowdown on how she handled Millie Clark's case after Tom Brewer retired? I'll take Lydia with me to Warminster and Winchester."

"Was it the dark suit that swung it for me, guv?" asked Lydia. "I don't often wear trousers."

"Oddly enough, Lydia, I thought you might enjoy crossing swords with Cameron Keel. So you can test your theory he was responsible for stabbing Millie Clark or holding her while Ivan Thatcher did."

"You don't think my idea holds water, do you?" asked Lydia.

"It has its merits, Gus," said Grace. "We can't rule it out."

"Exactly," said Gus. "I'll even let you drive, Lydia."

He hoped he didn't regret it.

"We should have finished updating our files by lunchtime, guv," said Neil. "Is there anyone we can contact for an interview?"

"Try locating Tyler Rowe," said Gus. "Where was it he was last living?"

"Above an Indian restaurant, guv," said Alex, "on Broomhill Road in Bishopsworth."

"He could be elusive, guv," said Blessing. "We don't know the names or addresses of the other women with whom he's had children. So he could be anywhere."

"Then you won't run out of things to do, will you?" said Gus.

"I'll keep an eye on them, Gus," said Grace.

Alex was searching for the phone number of the garage on Stroud Road, Gloucester, where Fergus Munro worked.

Gus and Lydia prepared to leave the office.

"Good luck, guv," said Blessing.

"Will we need it, guv?" asked Lydia as they descended to the ground floor.

"Perhaps a little to help us reach Warminster without incident," Gus replied. "While I have my eyes closed, I'll firm up the list of questions we need to ask Monique Clark."

"Alex reckons I don't have such a heavy right foot these days," said Lydia.

She reversed the Red Mini out of her bay and caused an early-morning shopper to stand on the brakes of her Toyota Yaris to avoid a collision.

"Why would Monique think she needs legal representation, guv?" asked Lydia.

"I can only assume she has something to hide, Lydia," said Gus.

"Ooh, I didn't see that coming," said Lydia.

"Rather like the Toyota Yaris," said Gus.

"Sorry? Do we need a strategy to deal with the solicitor?" asked Lydia as they left the Church Street car park and headed for Trowbridge.

"We can't go in all guns blazing because they will simply shut us down," said Gus. "You can take the lead. Ask Monique any random question you wish to get her talking."

"When she's relaxed, you hit her with a hard question. We've done that before."

"Not until we're positive we won't provoke Monique into a 'no comment' response. If we can silence her first line of defence, her brief, then maybe we'll find an opening. Then, Monique might surprise us and give us something without the preamble."

"Yeah, right," said Lydia. "As if that's going to happen."

"My gut tells me that's exactly what's going to happen," said Gus.

"Why are you always one step ahead of us, guv?" asked Lydia.

"Indigestion?" he replied.

Trowbridge was soon a grey blob in Lydia's rearview

mirror, and she drew up in the visitor's car park for Warminster police station in Station Road.

"Did you say they were closing this place, guv?" asked Lydia.

"In time, they'll move closer to the town centre," said Gus. "Something more suited to community policing. At least it's already a small set-up, so getting from here to an interview room shouldn't be as much of an obstacle as it was at Polebarn Road. Do you know what Monique Clark looks like?"

"I saw a photograph of Jeanette, taken after the retrial, guv. That lady standing by the front door could be Monique. The file says she's five years older than her sister."

"She was waiting for the lady in the Lotus who's just parked ahead of us," said Gus.

"Tall, elegant, with expensive clothes and only recently visited the hairdressers," said Lydia. "I spy a solicitor."

"I made it too easy," said Gus. "Right, let's get inside and see what they have to say."

Gus and Lydia breezed through Reception with a perfunctory sign-in. Monique Clark and her solicitor were already seated in the only interview room when they arrived.

"Good morning," said Gus as they entered the room. He noticed the recording equipment Neil had requested was set up and ready to go.

"We'll introduce ourselves for the tape," said Gus. "I'm Gus Freeman, a consultant with Wiltshire Police."

"Lydia Logan Barre, Crime Review Team."

"Maureen Sawyer, solicitor. I'm here at the request of my client."

"Monique Clark. What happened to the detectives my sister saw yesterday?"

"I don't know whether you've attended an interview like this before, Ms Clark," said Gus. "The way it works is that we ask the questions."

"Our colleagues are carrying out enquiries on other aspects of this case," said Lydia. "Don't worry, Monique. Can I call you Monique? Did you have any trouble getting here today?"

"If we had a car, I could have been here in twenty minutes," said Monique. "I had to take the bus to Salisbury, then change for one coming to Warminster. The best part of two hours wasted. I don't know what you think I can tell you that hasn't already been said."

"I fail to see how my client can help with your enquiries," said Maureen Sawyer. "This feels like a fishing expedition, and you're fishing in the wrong lake. Why aren't you interrogating the gang members responsible for Millie's death?"

"Humour us," said Gus. "I believe at least one person we've spoken to since we re-opened Millie's case has withheld a pertinent fact."

"That fact could be the key we're searching for," said Lydia. "What did you make of Paddy Styles, Monique? Was he interfering with his daughter?"

Gus swallowed hard. What part of taking it steady had Lydia not understood? This meeting could end very quickly.

"Where did you hear that name?" asked Monique.

"Bristol," said Lydia. "It's just a matter of asking the right people the right question."

"I caught Millie touching him through his trousers," said Monique. "It was unseemly. Jeanette wouldn't have believed me if I'd told her. She had her head in the sand. Always has had with men. If you asked Jeanette why Paddy disappeared for a few months, she'd say it was because he was a Romany, and a roof over his head made him feel trapped. Rubbish. He was off with another foolish young girl from the West Country. He came back when the novelty wore off."

"Jeanette eventually saw sense, though," said Lydia.

"I'm not sure she ever did," said Monique. "I think Paddy had found another girl, told Jeanette he was leaving, and she threatened to tell the police he'd been abusing their daughter. She thought it would force him to stay—a fat lot of good that did. Paddy left Bristol and never came back. Jeanette was on the breadline, and I had to keep lending her a few quid to stop her from losing her council house."

"You met Tyler Rowe first, didn't you?" asked Gus.

"Tyler was always around," said Monique. "I wasn't tied down with a kid like Jeanette. I had a social life in those days, and Tyler used the same pubs and clubs I visited."

"You told Jeanette he could supply the cannabis you both needed, is that right?" asked Gus. "Was there more to your relationship?"

"It was just sex," said Monique. "I'd tired of him before he got to know Jeanette."

"You've never married?" asked Lydia. "What about long-term relationships?"

"I was never interested," said Monique. "A casual fling, now and then, was good enough for me. But, men can't be trusted."

"Jeanette and Tyler's relationship lasted longer," said Gus.

"He proved I was right to dump him," said Monique. "It wasn't long before he started playing away. Tyler knew better than to walk along Keble Avenue and knock on my door, but he charmed his way into many a bed in Bristol.

That's not a stable relationship, no matter how long they were together."

"A good-looking guy?" asked Lydia.

"Not especially," said Monique.

"How long had Tyler worked for Nathan Harvey when you first met him?" asked Gus.

"I didn't know who he worked for," said Monique. "Tyler was someone who always had money, was always out and about on a Friday and Saturday night, but never mentioned what he did for a living when you chatted to him. I found out for myself why he was popular with the ladies, but he had plenty of men friends too. It took a while for the penny to drop. Tyler had access to a constant supply of drugs. This explained why he slipped away to a quiet corner of a club or outside a pub car park to make his deals."

"So, Jeanette and Tyler lived together," said Gus. "Sammy and Shania are born, and Tyler starts to get itchy feet. How did he get on with Millie?"

"Millie was hardly ever home," said Monique. "She started staying out overnight before her thirteenth birthday. It was only a couple of nights a week before Tyler moved in, and then it became almost full-time. She dropped by for a change of clothes or to cadge cash from her mother. I doubt Tyler set eyes on her more than a dozen times before she was nineteen. Millie didn't like Tyler. She wasn't a fan of Sammy and Shania either."

"Millie lived at home for a while after she was nineteen, is that right?" asked Lydia.

"Stupid girl had let Denis Long get his claws in her," said Monique. "Someone gave information to the police, and they arrested him. Millie took the chance to escape that life."

"Any idea who that was?" asked Gus. "Police in Bristol reckon they met a wall of silence whenever they ask questions about any criminal activity."

"I can't be sure," said Monique. "But I have my suspicions. Soon after, Tyler asked Jeanette if Millie needed anything. He was supplying us with cannabis, and we knew he handled other stuff, too, if we wanted it. Tyler was living with Jeanette on and off, and Millie bought the occasional hit from him for a while."

"Perhaps Tyler was interested in Millie for another reason," said Lydia.

"He was wasting his time if he was," said Monique. "She always disappeared to that squat in Withywood as soon as possible. That's where she met Fergus."

"Fergus got Millie pregnant, and she returned home again," said Lydia. "That's when Tyler must have started pressuring her."

"How would I know? I wasn't living there," said Monique. "Jeanette would have known if he'd tried it on with Millie."

"That's right," said Gus. "Jeanette was adamant Millie despised Tyler. She refused to accept anything was going on."

"Does that ring a bell, Monique?" asked Lydia. "Paddy Staples all over again. Jeanette with her head in the sand, refusing to accept the truth because she didn't want her man to leave her."

"Then Millie left for the squat," said Gus, "and went housebreaking with Fergus and Justin. One by one, Nathan Harvey hunted them down. Who was it outside your door that night? Who gave you the message Millie was living on borrowed time? Are you sure you didn't recognise the voice?"

"It wasn't anyone I knew," said Monique.

"I wondered whether it might have been Tyler Rowe," said Gus.

"He wasn't someone Nathan Harvey would trust to front up an operation like that. Tyler was a lowlife, pure and simple."

"What did you think when Jeanette decided to leave as soon as you passed her the message from Harvey and Coombs?" asked Gus. "Did you consider joining her?"

"Not at once. My sister didn't need to ask my permission," said Monique. "Jeanette thought she was doing the right thing to save Millie. We will always stay in touch. We're family."

"So you stayed in contact while Jeanette lived in the Weymouth Street flat?"

"Of course we did," said Monique. "We had our phones, and I travelled to Warminster on the train from Temple Meads once or twice. It was straightforward enough. That's why I suggested Jeanette take the kids back to mine that Sunday. Sammy and Shania had friends in the street that they missed. It wasn't much fun for them cooped up in that small flat."

"Wasn't there a risk they'd be seen?" asked Lydia. "Harvey and Coombs could have had someone keeping tabs on your place."

"Jeanette was still dithering over what to do at the start of the week. Then Millie spotted a face in Warminster that scared her."

"That's what Jeanette hinted at yesterday," said Gus. "The increased anxiety made Millie ill, and Jeanette was free to take the kids to stay the night at your place. Millie planned to stay in the flat, keeping low but needed to walk to the pharmacy on The Avenue. Instead, Micah Harvey grabbed her, returned her to the flat, and somebody killed Millie early the next morning."

"Did Millie tell Jeanette who it was she'd seen?" asked Lydia.

"Tyler Rowe," said Monique.

"Why was she scared of him?" asked Lydia.

"Why do you think? Tyler may have been a long way down the pecking order in the gang, but he still worked for Nathan Harvey. Millie feared he would make a phone call, and Nathan and his goons would soon catch up with her. Millie had been in town, meeting her new supplier, and when she got home, she told Jeanette she'd seen Tyler hanging around in the town centre. She was positive he hadn't seen her, but he would have a nose for where people bought their drugs. It wouldn't have taken him long to discover the whereabouts of a new face in town."

"Why didn't Jeanette suggest they run for it?" asked Lydia. "They had done it once. Warminster isn't the only small town where someone can make themselves scarce."

"Jeanette surprised me when she did a moonlight flit from Keble Avenue," said Monique. "It wasn't like her. She usually dithered, as she did about spending the night at my place. She often asked me if she was doing the right thing. But because Millie was positive Tyler hadn't seen her that first day, Jeanette decided to give herself time to mull it over. Maybe Millie had been mistaken. Where could they go, and could they afford it? She rang and asked if we could talk things through. I sensed what was coming. She would ask me for money to help them get somewhere better than that awful flat if they did move. We had that conversation on Sunday. Little did we know Millie would die that night, but we talked about moving to a village further away from Bristol, and I would quit my council house in Keble Avenue. There wasn't anything keeping me in the city. I decided to throw my lot in with my sister and help her look after the three children. It was time to make a move."

Monique allowed herself a smile.

"Wasn't Millie included in the arrangement?" asked Gus.

"Jeanette thought Millie would soon find someone," said Monique. She'd be out from under her feet, just like she had been in Withywood. She was an addict who didn't want to get help. Jeanette thought there was one sure fate ahead of her."

"What happened next?" asked Gus.

"Two days later, Millie left the flat, and Jeanette had a visit from Tyler," said Monique. "The stupid woman thought he was a knight in shining armour coming to her rescue. But instead, Tyler told her he wasn't interested in her or his kids. He just wanted to find Millie. Jeanette knew that meant he wasn't looking for another customer for his drugs. She knew Tyler was relentless when he had his mind set on something."

"We wondered from the outset whether Tyler Rowe ever visited Jeanette in Warminster," said Gus. "He would have been playing a dangerous game, knowing where Millie was and not passing the information to Nathan Harvey."

"Who says he didn't?" asked Monique. "Did you think Micah Harvey had the nous to think where to look for Millie? He hasn't got the brains for it. Tyler wouldn't have called Nathan direct. You need to be higher up the food chain for that. He called a gopher, who called Micah."

"What a rat," said Lydia.

"So it wasn't a coincidence that brought Micah to Warminster on Sunday," said Gus. "Tyler covered his backside by passing the message to his boss. How was that helping him to get Millie under his spell?"

"Tyler is temperamental," said Monique. "I can see why he lusted after Millie. She despised him, but he still thought he had a chance. Men are like that; they don't like to be denied. When they realise nothing they do will change a woman's mind, someone like Tyler is likely to lash out. He called Micah so Millie would get a beating, then he'd remind her every time he saw her that things could have been so much different if she'd seen sense."

"Will this take much longer, Mr Freeman," said Maureen Sawyer. "My client gave most of this information to Bristol Police after the murder. I think this line of questioning has gone on long enough."

"I need to get back," said Monique. "If I miss the next bus, I won't get home until it's dark."

"We've heard enough for now," said Gus. "If we have further questions, we'll arrange to visit you in Zeals, Monique. I hope that won't inconvenience you too much, Ms Sawyer?"

"I know my way around, Mr Freeman," she replied.

The two women swept from the room, leaving Gus and Lydia pondering their next move.

"Remember what we heard about the people who worked for Harvey, guv," said Lydia. "They did what they were told. Although the mystery voice Monique heard said they were going to kill Millie, maybe that was just talk. Perhaps, she *was* only going to get a beating like Fergus and Justin. Why should they have treated her differently?"

"At the first trial, Harvey and Coombs swore Keel and Thatcher took Millie to the churchyard," said Gus. "They swore they remained in the flat. Micah went with them to ensure they followed his brother's orders."

"Are you leaning towards Keel and Thatcher, guv?" asked Lydia.

"It's just my new shoes, Lydia," said Gus. "Right, we've got another piece of the jigsaw. Let's drive to Winchester for a chat with Cameron Keel."

Lydia shook her head. Another piece of the jigsaw. Tyler Rowe had visited Jeanette at the flat and had hung around the town, hoping to bump into Millie. He was nearly old enough to be Millie's father. As she unlocked her Mini, she wondered how Neil and Blessing were getting on. Had they tracked down the elusive Tyler Rowe?

Gus got into the passenger seat and fastened his seatbelt.

"Do you want to say your prayers before we leave, guv?" asked Lydia.

"Stick to the speed limit for the A303, and you'll have no complaints from me," he replied.

They arrived at HMP Winchester one hour later. Thanks to a phone call from Alex, getting in for their meeting with Cameron Keel was a breeze.

Gus and Lydia were escorted from Reception to an interview room.

"Although we've done this together a couple of times, guv, I still get the shivers when the prisoner is walked in," said Lydia.

"So you should, Lydia, " said Gus. "The others we've interviewed have been creeps, but Keel is in a different league. We can only hope he's prepared to answer a couple of questions."

Lydia heard the sound of footsteps outside the door. Cameron Keel strode into the room, flanked by two warders. The uniformed men stood head and shoulders above the hardened criminal, but the air of menace surrounding Keel seemed to negate the height difference.

His eyes were cold and fixed somewhere between her face and her midriff.

Lydia tried to recall how long he'd been in prison.

Cameron Keel took the only seat on his side of the broad table. He switched his attention to Gus when he heard him speak.

"Thank you for agreeing to see us this morning, Mr Keel. My name's Freeman. My colleague is Ms Logan Barre. We're working with Wiltshire Police on a review of the Millie Clark murder. First, let me say our interest is solely in verifying a handful of details relating to events that occurred on the afternoon and evening of Sunday the eleventh of August 2013."

"We never did it, you know," said Cameron. "We knew our place. Micah was hovering, watching every move."

"I'm sure, Mr Keel," said Gus. "Did you join Nathan and Craig and drive to Warminster together?"

"No chance. They went in a two-seater Porsche that Nathan owned and enjoyed a sunny Sunday afternoon drive in the country with the top down. I drove to Warminster with Ivan in a Lexus."

"Very nice," said Gus.

"It was leased. It won't be waiting for me when I get out."

"I'm sure Nathan and Craig have been looking after you," said Gus. "We hear the family is important. But, as far as we can tell, you've never blotted your copybook with them."

"So two cars arrived at different times in the town centre," said Lydia. "Micah was already there. Where did you park?"

"Some place on Weymouth Street, near the flat where Micah had the girl."

"The only people in the flat when you arrived were Micah, Millie, Nathan, and Craig. Is that correct?" asked Gus.

"Yes," said Cameron.

"We know Craig made three phone calls during the day. Were you present for the first of those at around four o'clock?"

"We were there," said Cameron. "He tried to get hold of the girl's mother's boyfriend."

"Craig rang Tyler Rowe?" said Gus. "Interesting. According to others we've spoken to, the gang's hierarchy would have meant Craig didn't have Tyler's number."

"Micah rang some punk, they gave a number to him, and he read it out to Craig, who entered it in his phone. Tyler wasn't picking up, anyway."

"Craig made another call three hours later," said Gus.

"About that time, yeah. Craig tried Tyler again. No reply."

"Was he any luckier at ten to eleven?" asked Gus.

"Third time lucky," said Cameron. "Craig wasn't happy being messed around. He ordered Tyler to get to the flat pronto. He reckoned Nathan didn't want Micah involved in what was planned for the churchyard. He didn't believe he had the stomach for it."

"If Tyler left Bristol straightaway, he would have been in Warminster by midnight, guv," said Lydia.

"Nice try," said Cameron. "Tyler told Craig he was in Cardiff, but the guy didn't drive anyway. His patch was in and around BS13. So Tyler could get a bus, hitch a lift, or get one of his women to drive him wherever he needed to go."

"Craig Coombs didn't know Tyler was a non-driver, I suppose?" asked Gus.

"Why would he?" shrugged Cameron. "He was a nobody to Nathan and Craig."

"How many people in the flat had a knife?" asked Gus.

"Craig held a knife to the girl's throat," said Cameron. "No idea whether Nathan was carrying. He wouldn't have trusted his brother with a blade."

"What about you and Ivan?" asked Gus.

"We were told we didn't need them for what we had to do."

"The detectives in the original investigation assumed you walked the short distance from the flat to the churchyard," said Gus. "We believe you drove there. Who was right?"

"We piled into our car," said Cameron. "Micah sat beside me, and Ivan sat in the back with the girl. Nathan and Craig stayed in the flat until we returned."

Gus nodded. That walk with Grace had been worth more than the fresh air and exercise.

"Because Tyler was otherwise engaged, Nathan had no choice but to send Micah to ensure their orders were followed."

"The girl had tried to persuade Nathan she was never inside his house," said Cameron. "She pleaded with him, but she had to be punished. So when we reached a dark corner of the churchyard, I held her while Ivan thumped her."

"When did Craig slip one of you the knife at the flat?" asked Lydia.

"You still don't get it, do you?" said Cameron. "No weapons were to be used. That was Nathan's instructions. We left the girl on the floor by a gravestone, drove to the flat, and Micah told Nathan we'd done well. The girl was unconscious but breathing. Nathan and Craig left before us to drive back to Bristol. Micah followed five minutes later, and then I drove back with Ivan. Nathan didn't want us all leaving together. I slammed the door behind me when I left."

"What did you think when you heard a body was found the next morning?" asked Gus.

"We didn't hear a thing that day. I can't remember when Ivan rang to tell me. We met in the Queen's Head in Bishopsworth and tried to work out what happened. We agreed it had to have been Craig Coombs. He and Nathan left soon after we returned to the flat. They must have driven to the churchyard, and Craig finished the girl. You don't question people like Nathan and Craig. They must have had their reasons. That's why we used the defence we did at the first trial. We weren't going to admit we'd beaten the girl. Our brief advised us to claim Nathan and Craig did everything. It worked a charm."

"You didn't suspect Micah?" asked Gus.

"Leave it out," said Cameron. "He was crying while Ivan hit the girl."

"Once again, we've heard an explanation that fits the facts, guv," said Lydia.

She turned to Cameron Keel. "Why should we believe your version?"

"I'm inclined to believe him, Lydia," said Gus. "Ask yourself this; Mr Keel has told us how the events played out in the flat and the churchyard. At the first trial, Harvey and Coombs claimed Keel and Thatcher took Millie to the churchyard and killed her. Micah Harvey was present when the beating took place and told his brother their orders had been carried out to the letter. Where was the only knife we've heard about?"

"In the flat, guv, with Craig Coombs," said Lydia. "If we can believe this man."

"No weapon was to be used," said Gus. "If Cameron or Ivan were carrying a serrated blade, Micah would have reported it to his brother."

"Well thought out, Mr Freeman," said Cameron. "Which means the girl died at the hands of the man with the only weapon. Perhaps you could persuade Craig to confess or give up his best friend if he didn't do it. Nathan could have had a knife, but I never saw one at the flat."

"Thank you, Mr Keel," said Gus. "You've answered all our questions. The escort party will return you to your cell now."

"I hope you don't drop Ivan and me in it, Mr Freeman," said Cameron. "We'll both get out one day, and it won't take long to discover where you live."

Cameron Keel stood up, took one last look at Lydia, and marched out of the room.

"You meet the nicest people in places like this, don't you, guv," said Lydia. "He gave me the creeps."

"We can call Reception now, Lydia," said Gus. "Someone will fetch us and lead us back to civilisation. We should reach the office in ninety minutes, but not sooner."

"Got it, guv," said Lydia. She made the call and collected her things. "Alex hasn't had any joy getting through to Nathan Harvey and Craig Coombs, has he?"

"They have that London chap, Stuart Coles, on speed dial, Lydia," said Gus. "I would need to run the few scraps of fresh evidence we've gathered past DS Mercer before attempting to procure a warrant to bring them to heel."

"Back to the grindstone on Monday then, guv," said Lydia.

The door opened, and their escort appeared. Gus and

Lydia followed him along the corridor. Soon they were back in the red Mini and heading for Andover.

"You've opted for Upavon and a cross-country trip to Devizes," said Gus.

"A steady speed will give you a chance to decide which version of the facts you believe is the correct one, guv," said Lydia.

Ah, the innocence of youth, thought Gus as he closed his eyes and tried to catch up on the sleep he lost last night.

Chapter Twelve

LYDIA GOT them back to the Church Street car park at half-past three. Gus opened his eyes as they slowed for Friday afternoon traffic on the outskirts of town.

"I don't know where all these cars come from," groaned Lydia. "Nose to tail every Friday afternoon."

"With supermarkets open every day except Christmas Day, you would think the days of the weekly shop were numbered," said Gus. "It's just as bad in Devizes on Saturdays if Suzie and I go shopping. So, it's not just Friday that's a nightmare."

"I wonder how the others fared today," said Lydia as she called the lift.

"We won't have long to wait," said Gus. "Everyone's upstairs."

"We were the only ones going anywhere today, guv," said Lydia.

"If that's the case, then Neil and Blessing haven't located Tyler Rowe and gone to interview him."

"He sounds like an unsavoury character," said Lydia.

"I'll ask Neil to check that alibi for Cardiff before I pass my final judgment," said Gus.

When they exited the lift, Alex and Grace were chatting.

"Where are the other two?" asked Lydia.

The unmistakable sound of the Gaggia solved that problem. Neil and Blessing were fetching refreshments.

"Shall I add ours to the list, guv?" asked Lydia.

"Yes, please," he replied. "Grace, you can go first. How was the Assistant Chief Constable?"

"Very polite, Gus," said Grace. "She explained that Geoff Mercer had already been in touch. Clare Edwards informed me that ninety percent of the information she might have given me relating to the case at the Warminster end was embargoed. Her hands were tied."

"That's a blow," said Gus. "Was there something she was prepared to share?"

"Clare's transfer from Hertfordshire was delayed," said Grace. "Her former bosses were digging in their heels. They didn't want to lose her, but Clare was ambitious. She only had seven days with Tom Brewer to get acquainted with everything he was handling before he retired, not just the Millie Clark case. Tom then disappeared on a cruise, and Clare had to rely on several visits to DI Budd in Bristol to fill in the gaps before the retrial."

"So, ACC Edwards reckoned she was under-prepared for the retrial?" asked Gus.

"Well, she wasn't impressed with DI Budd," said Grace. "She suspected something was going on between him and DS Gale. They worked together on the burglaries."

"No matter how much she'd learned about the case before they attended the Crown Court, they couldn't have foreseen what Keel and Thatcher would do," said Gus. "What was it about DI Budd's work that disappointed her?"

"She suspected there were no-go areas," said Grace. "Mick Budd made little attempt to identify the man behind the voice Monique Clark heard. Nor did he add resources to identify Viv Whitaker's attacker. Tyler Rowe confirmed he'd been in a relationship with Millie's mother, Jeanette. However, when asked about his stepdaughter, he said as he and Jeanette weren't married or in a civil partnership, he didn't accept Millie was anything to do with him. She spent so little time at Jeanette's house that Tyler thought it was a stretch to claim it as her home address. He said Millie had all but abandoned Amy, her daughter. Tyler admitted on the rare occasions their paths crossed, he and Millie didn't get on."

"Did DI Budd and DS Gale ask Tyler Rowe when he'd learned Jeanette had left Keble Avenue?" asked Gus.

"It appears not, Gus," said Grace.

"Did ACC Edwards expand on her no-go areas comment?" asked Alex.

"Not with me; she didn't," said Grace. "I imagine Geoff Mercer might have better luck, but his investigation is restricted to the borders of this county."

"Was she suggesting someone was in Nathan Harvey's pocket, guv?" asked Neil.

"Barry Knee, the Chief Constable, took early retirement just after the retrial, guv," said Blessing.

"Grace is right, Blessing. We should follow DS Mercer's example and concentrate on our patch. If ACC Edwards passes information to him which needs investigation by another area, then so be it. We concentrate on finding Millie Clark's killer."

"Understood, guv," said Blessing.

Gus could tell Grace hadn't learned anything more from her conversation with Clare Edwards. He turned to Alex.

"What did Fergus say?" he asked.

"Fergus wasn't positive Amy was his child at first, guv," said Alex. "He didn't think he and Millie were exclusive. When Fergus saw Amy with Millie a few months later, one look at her convinced him she was his child. He and Millie were doing drugs together and robbing houses, but there wasn't a single night where they slept together with Amy as a family. Millie never talked about them having that kind of relationship. She never visited him when he was first on remand. Fergus knew Justin had been arrested in hospital and heard later Millie had been arrested and given bail. While he was in Erlestoke, Fergus didn't know what was going on with Millie, and then he was attacked and spent time in the hospital. Pippa visited him at every opportunity while recovering and serving his sentence in HMP Erlestoke. Millie and Amy became a distant memory. He heard she'd been murdered, which upset him, but he had never bonded with Amy, and nobody ever mentioned Millie had moved to Warminster."

"I take it from that Fergus hasn't visited Zeals to see his daughter since he left prison," said Gus.

"No, guv," said Alex. "Fergus doesn't have any intention of doing so. He doesn't want to upset Pippa."

"That appears to be all we can do on that score," said Gus. "Let's move on to Tyler Rowe. Have you found him, Neil?"

"We seek him here, we seek him there, guv," said Neil. "We found several addresses in Bristol where he's lived over the past decade. The women he stayed with told a similar tale."

"Most used drugs to some extent, guv," said Blessing. "Tyler Rowe provided them with their drug of choice: cannabis, methamphetamine, heroin, or cocaine. He bedded them, lived with them for a couple of days a week, and eventually disappeared. His longest relationship was with Jeanette Clark, and we know he wasn't faithful to her."

"I spoke to the owner of the Indian takeaway in Broomhill Road, guv," said Neil. "He told me he remembered Tyler leaving the flat at the end of July 2013. He was in arrears for two months with the rent and left no forwarding address. Nobody we spoke to today can recall seeing Tyler in Bristol since that time."

"Perhaps he moved to Cardiff, guv," said Lydia.

"Cardiff?" asked Alex. "Why there?"

"Cameron Keel told us it was Tyler Rowe that Craig Coombs was desperate to get hold of on Sunday afternoon and evening," said Gus. "Tyler didn't pick up the first two calls, but he did reply at ten minutes to eleven, supposedly from Cardiff. Coombs wanted Tyler to accompany Keel and Thatcher to the churchyard with Millie."

"Why?" asked Alex.

"The simple answer is Nathan Harvey didn't think his brother, Micah, had the stomach for it," said Gus. "I'm still trying to fathom why they needed to dig so deep into their gang to find a thug who could stand and watch the other two punish Millie."

"Especially after what he told DI Budd and DS Gale, guv," said Lydia. "Tyler Rowe and Millie weren't close, according to him. So why was it important for him to be there? Cameron Keel didn't have an answer to that, did he?"

"Not one he was prepared to give," said Gus. "Maybe Harvey and Coombs didn't explain."

"Do we drive to Cardiff to start searching for him, guv?" asked Neil.

"I'll give it some thought over the weekend, Neil," said Gus. "There's little we can do today. I'll give you the headlines of our two meetings. Monique had a brief relationship with Tyler before he moved in with Jeanette. Millie spotted Tyler Rowe in Warminster town centre the Monday before she died. That lines up with what the Indian takeaway owner told Neil. Tyler left Bristol and moved to Warminster. However, it wasn't to get back with Jeanette. Millie didn't think Tyler saw her, but it unsettled her. She hated the bloke but was aware he fancied her. Jeanette wondered whether they should move further away from the gang's reach. This time Monique would go with them. We've asked why Tyler didn't call Harvey and Coombs if he'd known where Jeanette had gone. Well, according to Monique, it was Tyler who contacted Micah Harvey through another gang member."

"He wanted Millie to suffer because she wouldn't be another conquest," said Blessing. "What a swine. We need to start looking for him in Warminster, Neil. But hang on, has he committed a crime?"

"Not that we're aware of, Blessing," said Gus. "Lydia and I will update our digital files as much as we can by five. I suggest we spend the first hour on Monday analysing what we've gathered, and I'll welcome ideas on where we go from here."

Five o'clock duly arrived, and everyone left the office. Blessing and Grace were involved in conversation as Gus reached the car park. Tomorrow would see Grace move to a new home. Alex and Lydia had already left for Chippenham.

"Anything planned, guv," asked Neil.

"A quiet weekend, Neil and yourself?"

"Melody isn't happy, guv, but I had an invitation from

Jake and Rick for Saturday. They arranged Jake's leaving bash, and Rick's promotion drinks, on the same night."

"Tell her to look on the bright side, Neil. You'll only be drunk once."

"That's genius, guv," said Neil. "See you on Monday."

Gus arrived home before Suzie and had just stepped out of the shower when he heard her in the hallway. Five minutes later, he had dressed and wandered into the lounge. Suzie was reading something she'd brought home from work.

"Another riveting report?" he asked.

"Homework, ready for next week," Suzie replied.

"Will you be seeing ACC Edwards?" asked Gus.

"Not that I'm aware," said Suzie. "Spill the beans."

"Clare told Grace there was little she could talk about with us because Geoff had warned her off."

"He would have set the parameters of our investigation. That's standard procedure," said Suzie.

"Clare also hinted that Harvey and Coombs, our gang leaders, had someone on the inside with Bristol Police."

"We weren't aware of that, darling. I'll mention it to Geoff. He'll inform the right people."

"Right, I was thinking what I might cook for you as we drove back from HMP Winchester this afternoon."

"Let me guess," said Suzie, "a stir fry?"

Saturday, 3 November 2018

ANOTHER DAY DAWNED, and Suzie was already in the kitchen when Gus awoke. They had wandered along the lane at nine o'clock last night for a drink in the Lamb with Brett and the Reverend.

Before leaving at closing time to dodge the puddles as they made their way home, final arrangements were made for tonight. Brett would book a table at the Waggon & Horses for seven-thirty. Clemency needed an early night because she had a full day tomorrow with services at three of her parishes.

"Boiled egg and soldiers?" asked Suzie.

"Fair enough," said Gus.

"Do you think we should drive to the farm with an offer of help?"

"I'd rather you called your mother and suggested she called *us* if there was a problem," said Gus. "I heard Blessing tell Grace that Jamie would be free this morning. We'll be falling over one another."

"Okay," said Suzie. "In that case, we can do the supermarket run this morning and look for carpets and curtains this afternoon."

"I thought we'd agreed to wait until we knew what you were having before making a decision?"

"I'm talking about the lounge," said Suzie.

Gus decided to adopt Neil's approach; go with the flow. It was an argument he couldn't win. The supermarket run produced no dramas, and everything was stored away in the fridge, the freezer, or the wine rack by one o'clock. Gus knew it wouldn't be long before he could replace the non-alcoholic bottles with the Real McCoy after the baby was born.

Suzie persuaded him to grab a baguette in the supermarket to save time making lunch. She said it would increase the time they had to browse the stores she had on her list. So when Gus parked the Focus outside the bungalow at half-past five, he felt more tired than after a full day's work.

"We've got an hour to relax now," said Suzie, "to go through the brochures I picked up. I didn't see anything that grabbed me this afternoon."

Gus groaned.

The time flew by before they were showered and changed, ready for Brett to collect them

The meal at the pub was every bit as good as they'd promised their friends it would be. They walked outside through the car park to reach Brett's car. He'd parked on the grass verge in a spot Gus had used without incident in the past.

"No damage," said Brett. "That's a relief."

"If only they'd planned ahead when this pub was built in the 1850s," said Gus. "Surely, they could see the benefit of a large space to tether horses and encourage the occasional stagecoach to break its journey here. An odd choice of name if you weren't catering to the needs of waggoners."

"You're incorrigible, Gus," said Clemency.

"I've told him he doesn't listen," said Suzie.

Brett drove them back to Urchfont. He dropped the Reverend at the rectory.

"Anyone up for a nightcap?" asked Brett when he reached the bungalow.

"My bed is calling me," said Suzie. "You two can walk to the pub if you wish."

"Just the one, Brett," said Gus. "It's been a long day."

Brett drove them along the lane and parked in the Lamb car park.

"Will you be driving home, sir?" asked Gus.

"Not tonight, officer," said Brett. "I'll have a word with

the landlord. If I ask nicely, he lets me leave the car here, and I collect it in the morning."

Gus realised that Brett wasn't going home tonight.

As they walked through the beer garden to the pub's back door, a black car drove past and moved slowly along the lane.

"Strangers," said Brett. "It looked like they weren't sure where they were going."

"What can I get you?" asked Gus when they got inside the bar.

"A single malt, please," said Brett.

Gus couldn't see any reason he shouldn't join him.

The landlord called time as they savoured the last drop of their third glass.

"What a civil way to end an enjoyable evening," said Gus.

They stepped outside the pub. Another shower looked ready to spoil the mood.

"Come on," said Brett, "If we get a move on, we'll get home before it comes on too hard,"

They reached the bungalow, and Brett patted Gus on the shoulder before trotting off towards the rectory.

"Good night," he called as Gus walked through the gateway.

Two men emerged from the shadows. One grabbed Gus by the arm, and his colleague stood beside him with his hand inside his coat. Gus didn't think he was searching for a pen.

"The boss wants to see you," the man growled.

"Can't it wait until tomorrow?" asked Gus.

The black car he and Brett had seen earlier drew up by the gateway; Gus was bundled into the back and was soon sandwiched between his two minders.

"Phone," said the talkative one and clicked his fingers.

"Where are we going?" asked Gus, handing him his phone

"A quiet spot with no cameras," came the reply.

Gus didn't know where he was going, but he knew who would be there. But unfortunately, the three malt whiskies didn't help him feel less nervous.

Nathan Harvey had ignored every request from Alex for a meeting. Had they angered him? Or was he prepared to give them something useful?

Gus could tell from the clock on the dashboard they had driven for twenty minutes before turning off a minor road onto a muddy track. His sense of direction was good, especially on his doorstep. They were on the edge of Roundway Down. A quiet spot with no CCTV cameras to record their coming and going.

They stopped, and the car's headlights were switched off.

"We wait," said the guy on his right.

Within a minute, Gus saw a large dark shape appear twenty yards ahead. It stopped, and someone got out. The headlights were switched on again, and Gus saw a tall, dark-skinned man wearing a long overcoat that would have cost him a month's wages. Behind him was the large Humvee that convinced Fergus Munro and Justin Cannings that the house on Court Farm Road would bring rich rewards.

Gus was helped from the back seat. His escorts stayed by the car.

Nathan Harvey beckoned Gus forward. "We need to talk, Mr Freeman," he said.

"You could have accepted an invitation from DS Hardy," said Gus. "We would have met during normal office hours that way."

"It doesn't do for me to be seen in an interview room," said Nathan. "I have a reputation to uphold."

"I'm sure Stuart Coles would have jumped on the first train from Paddington to accompany you to Trinity Road," said Gus. "You've picked me up me for a reason. So let's hear it."

"You've been told a few stories since you started looking into the Millie Clark murder case. I want to put you right."

"Why should I believe you, Mr Harvey?" asked Gus. "You might look like a successful entrepreneur, but we both know your business. One day, the police will find the evidence to put you away for a long time."

Nathan Harvey laughed. It wasn't a pleasant sound.

"Enough of the daydreaming. I had you brought here to listen, not ask questions. We were astounded when we heard the jury think we were capable of murdering a young woman in that way. Craig and I were never anywhere near that churchyard. We stayed in that grotty flat until Cam and Ivan got back."

"We spoke to Cameron Keel today," said Gus.

"Tell me something I don't know," said Nathan. "Cam and Ivan did what they were told. They punished Millie Clark for her part in robbing me and trashing my place. My brother confirmed they left the girl lying by a gravestone. She was out like a light but still breathing. We drove back to Bristol, one at a time, and thought no more of it until the news broke on TV that a girl's body had been found propped against a tree. After she came around, someone must have attacked her and stabbed her. It wasn't Craig and me."

"Cameron claimed it wasn't him and Ivan," said Gus. "They assumed it was either you two or Micah because they waited for you to clear the flat before they made a move."

"My brother couldn't have done it anyway," said Nathan. "The pathologist swore the killer was right-handed. Nathan's a leftie and frightened of his own shadow."

"Well, somebody stabbed Millie Clark several times in the chest," said Gus.

"I don't know if I can shed light on that," said Nathan. "However, I want you to understand why people have tried to mislead you. Millie sold the jewellery for peanuts, but she held onto something sentimental to me. The gold watch I bought when I'd made my first million."

"Detectives believed Millie returned to her home in Keble Avenue after the burglary," said Gus. "Then she hid in the squat in Withywood. There was no mention of the watch when police caught up with Millie and arrested her. So what happened to it?"

"Millie's mother found my watch in the house," said Nathan. "She and her sister, Monique, kept it. I had my people put the word out that if anyone tried to sell it, I was to hear about it. So none of the fences, pawn shops, or dodgy retailers would go near it. We also kept an eye out online, and soon after they moved to Zeals, they advertised it."

"If you knew where they had moved to, how come you didn't send someone to fetch it?" asked Gus.

"We felt bad about the girl being killed," said Nathan. "That was never our intention. Craig agreed with me that we needed to do something. So, I bought the watch. Jeanette and Monique never knew it was me who paid the asking price. Have you wondered how I knew my gold watch was still unaccounted for?" asked Nathan.

"You must have had someone in your pocket," said Gus. "Whether they're still working in Bristol or not, we haven't worked out yet."

"We have enough on them to ensure you never find the answer," said Nathan.

"Might I ask how much the sisters thought the watch was worth?" asked Gus.

"Almost what I paid for it," said Nathan, "thirty grand. I doubt they told you any of that. They put Tyler Rowe in the frame, didn't they? A subtle hint here and there."

"It explains several comments they made," said Gus. "One thing puzzled us. Why did Craig call Tyler Rowe when you were in the flat? He was nothing to you. Surely, you had other people who would have gone to the church-yard to check they followed your orders?"

"I can tell you don't have a high opinion of us, Mr Free-man," said Nathan. "Yes, we punish those that step out of line, but we look after our best people if they fall foul of the law. So their families don't starve or lose their homes. We also like to put things right when one of our people goes too far. Take that lad, Whitaker, for example. He had no part in the robbery, yet one of our people did a number on him and came within an inch of killing him. Craig decided that as we were in Warminster, we could…. I almost said kill two birds with one stone, but that wouldn't be appropriate. The person who stabbed Whitaker and battered him needed to suffer."

"So Tyler Rowe was responsible for the savage attack on Viv Whitaker," said Gus.

"There's very little that escapes us, Mr Freeman. We'd finally caught up with Justin Cannings, and Cam was doing the necessary. After seeing what happened in the bedroom, one of his colleagues reported the matter to Craig. We waited for an opportunity. If two injured people staggered out of the churchyard early on Monday morning, there was little chance the local cops would solve the mystery. Tyler

Rowe and Millie Clark wouldn't have talked. They knew they had it coming. Craig couldn't get hold of Tyler, so I told Micah to go along with Cam and Ivan. There would always be another time to deal with Tyler."

"Tyler claimed to be in Cardiff," said Gus. "His landlord said he left in a hurry, and nobody had seen him in Bristol for a week to ten days before the murder. However, Monique told us that Millie had seen Tyler in the town centre on Monday morning. She said that scared Millie."

"Tut, tut, Mr Freeman," said Nathan. "You might be following another false trail, I'm afraid. Perhaps the sisters wanted you to believe Tyler was hunting for Millie. Tyler Rowe has had women chasing him for years, not the other way around."

"Did you know he was using the legal highs he sold on your behalf?" Gus asked. "Justin Cannings believed those drugs were responsible for the crazed attack he carried out on Viv Whitaker."

"Careful, Mr Freeman. There's no evidence Craig and I are connected to selling drugs of any variety. Tyler will pay for his indiscretions when my people find him."

"Who was the man who passed Monique a message on the night your people were hunting for Millie," said Gus. "She'd never met you or Craig. She swore it wasn't Tyler. So who told her to tell Jeanette you were going to kill Millie?"

"Another question? Look, Mr Freeman. Craig and I didn't go on any hunting expeditions. We were at home, watching television. Craig might recall who he called for that job. Good luck getting him to speak with you."

"I thought it could be important," said Gus. "Every time I get Millie's killer in my sights, the evidence crops up to prove they didn't do it."

"Craig didn't believe Tyler when he claimed to be in

Cardiff," said Nathan. "Micah had a phone call from someone who told him Millie was in Warminster. So he drove there, and she was exactly where this person said she would be."

"We believe it was Tyler who got a message to Micah," said Gus.

"Micah told me the person who gave him the message said it came from a woman."

Gus couldn't believe what he was hearing.

"Hang on. You felt bad about Millie's death and helped Monique and Jeanette by paying for something you could have sent someone to collect."

"We all get played by a woman in time, Mr Freeman. All you have to do now is decide which one of them did it."

Nathan Harvey turned and walked to his Humvee. Gus heard footsteps behind him.

"We'll get you home."

They made the return journey in silence. That had nothing to do with Gus's three companions but everything to do with Gus mulling over who killed Millie and why.

The car stopped one hundred yards from the gateway to the bungalow. The goon on his left got out, and Gus joined him in the lane under the branches of an oak tree.

"I hope we don't meet again," the man said. "You won't get off so lightly next time."

The man got back into the car, and the driver pulled away.

Gus cursed them. The tree branches shielded him from the rain; he would be soaked before reaching home.

He stripped off his wet clothes in the bathroom and crept into the bedroom.

"That Brett Penman is a bad influence," said Suzie.

Gus slipped into bed and hoped Suzie would soon drop off to sleep.

Sunday, 4 November 2018

GUS WAS the first to rise. He'd hardly slept. As he drank his first cup of coffee, he decided his only course of action was to tell Suzie what had happened.

He let her gently scold him for drinking too much and persuading the landlord to have a lock-in. Then, after they were showered and dressed, he sat her down in the lounge and told her everything.

"That's outrageous. What are you going to do about it?" asked Suzie.

"I'm not going to risk our lives and that of our unborn child," said Gus. "The meeting was unconventional, but we've wanted Nathan Harvey to meet with us from the outset. He's happy for us to use the information to identify Millie's killer. We've been sent on a wild goose chase more than once this week by those responsible. That ends now. I'll continue to work through the answers he gave me, and unless you can pick holes in my theory later today, I'll get my team onto action first thing in the morning. Kenneth might have to postpone our case review until Tuesday, and we'll be able to let Tom Brewer know his unsolved murder is no more."

Gus sensed Suzie was less than ecstatic about her partner meeting with a hardened criminal on Roundway Down just before midnight. Gus reminded her he was unharmed, and what Nathan Harvey told him gave the Crime Review Team more positives than negatives. After a quiet day at home, Gus finally laid out his theory on who murdered Millie Clark and how at eight in the evening.

Suzie listened in silence.

"That's incredible," she said when Gus had finished. "It's genius."

"No chinks in my reasoning?" he asked.

"They played you, didn't they?"

"Like a violin," said Gus. "All of us. Nobody studied the words they used closely."

"Time to make a move," said Suzie. "Well, now it's your turn."

Monday, 5 November 2018

GUS AND SUZIE left the bungalow at eight-thirty.

"Good luck," she said, kissing him before leaving for London Road.

Gus called the custody suite on the outskirts of town. He wanted the rest of the team to watch the interview. When arrangements had been secured for an interview room, Gus called Geoff Mercer. He caught him just as he was leaving home.

Their suspects would get a visit from uniformed officers at nine-fifteen.

As Gus pulled into the Church Street car park, he spotted Blessing getting out of Grace's Smart car. She obviously called heads instead of tails. Detailed conversations about the move would have to wait, but both women seemed happy as they waited for the lift.

He parked his Focus and joined them.

"Settling in, Grace?" he asked.

"Yes, thank you, Gus," she replied. "I hate the thought of joining a gym, but if Sunday dinner were anything to go by, I'd need to take drastic measures to keep my weight down."

"Jackie doesn't believe in portion control," said Gus.

Blessing giggled. "Tell me about it," she said.

They travelled to the first floor and joined the others.

"A change of plan," said Gus once they were all together. "I know we were going to finish updating our files before discussing our next move, but events over the weekend have moved things forward. First, I spoke with Nathan Harvey."

"Blimey, guv," said Alex. "How did you manage that?"

"I had little choice in the matter," said Gus. "His minders drove me to Roundway Down after closing time at the Lamb, and he made me realise the answer was staring us in the face all along. I've alerted the custody suite, and when Grace and I conduct the interview, I want the rest of you in the viewing room next door."

"Who will we be interviewing, Gus?" asked Grace.

"Did Nathan Harvey tell you where to find Tyler Rowe, guv?" asked Neil.

"No, Neil. Harvey and Coombs have yet to catch up with the man responsible for the savage attack on Viv Whitaker. Tyler went way beyond what his employers ordered, and attacking an innocent man meant he had to be punished."

"So that's why Craig Coombs wanted to get hold of him," said Grace. "Keel and Thatcher would have dealt with him in the churchyard. That would have confused Tom Brewer."

"It does fit with Cameron Keel's version of events, guv," said Lydia. "Both Millie and Tyler Rowe would have been beaten up. But, unfortunately, Keel and Thatcher never learned what Coombs had in mind because he couldn't get Tyler Rowe to come to Warminster."

"The police would have been non-plussed, as Millie and Tyler would have known better than to name their attackers," said Neil. "OK, that's another piece of the jigsaw slotted into place. But, who killed Millie?"

"We'll leave for the custody suite now," said Gus. "Our room is booked for a ten o'clock start. I'll take Blessing and Grace in my car. Neil, you can jump in with Alex and Lydia."

Gus could see the confused glances between the others as they headed for the lift. All would be revealed in due course unless Suzie had missed a glaring error in his deductions.

The team arrived at the modern glass and brick facility within ten minutes. They checked in at Reception, and Lydia led them along the long corridor to the two interview rooms.

"I've been here with Gus before," she told Grace. "He was awesome that day. Pulled a rabbit out of the hat."

"I didn't even know we had a hat, let alone a rabbit," said Grace. "My mind was on my move last week. I must have missed something."

"We'll just be watching, ma'am," said Lydia. "You'll be on stage with the magician."

Gus and Grace entered Interview Room One. The others found four chairs waiting for them in the viewing room. They could see and hear everything that went on behind the one-way mirror.

At one minute past ten, the door opened, and Maureen Sawyer entered, followed by Jeanette and Monique Clark.

The uniformed escort closed the door behind them as they left.

"I hope you have a good reason for this," said Maureen Sawyer.

"Please be seated," said Gus. "We need to follow procedure for the record."

Grace stated her name and rank, and Gus followed. The two women on the other side of the table gave their names, and Maureen Sawyer confirmed she was their solicitor.

"We wouldn't be here if we didn't have a good reason," said Gus. "Sammy and Shania made it to school for the day, and young Amy is at nursery this morning. Is that correct?"

"We need to collect her at lunchtime," said Jeanette.

"My superior, DS Mercer, will ensure the children are cared for," said Gus.

"I must protest, Mr Freeman," said Maureen Sawyer.

"We haven't told you what we've learned since our last meeting, Ms Sawyer," said Gus. "We made the same mistake as DI Brewer when he studied the evidence in his original investigation. The murder took place in the churchyard, and he believed the only people who could have been present were five men from a Bristol gang. Two men, Nathan Harvey and Craig Coombs, were found guilty at the first trial. They swore they were innocent and claimed they hadn't even set foot in the churchyard. Their two enforcers refused to appear at the retrial, which might have suggested they were the guilty couple. But one thing their bosses insisted on was that they followed orders. The victim was to be harmed, not killed. No weapons were to be used on Millie Clark. The fifth man, Micah Harvey, told his brother that Keel and Thatcher had done exactly as asked. So, how did Millie come to die?"

"One or all five men was lying," said Monique. "They're criminals; that's what they do."

"Perhaps," said Gus, "but DI Brewer spoke with Jeanette on Monday afternoon when she was driven back from Bristol by a detective. Someone also spoke to you in Bristol, possibly DI Budd or DS Gale. You told them Jeanette and the children stayed at your place in Keble Avenue on Sunday night."

"That's right, we did," said Jeanette. "I told that detective we went to Bristol on the train after spending the afternoon at the leisure centre."

"The perfect alibi," said Gus. "Nobody queried it five years ago, and we missed the significance of the wording in your statements."

"The sisters provided one another with an alibi," said Alex in the viewing room.

"You're talking in riddles, Mr Freeman," said Maureen Sawyer. "What wording?"

"When Jeanette spoke about the events of Sunday, she said she went to stay at her sister's," said Gus. "There was no mention of whether Monique was there. I asked Monique whether she stayed in contact with Jeanette while living in the Weymouth Street flat. Monique told me she travelled to Warminster on the train from Temple Meads once or twice. It was straightforward enough, she said. Take the kids back to mine. That's what you suggested to Jeanette, wasn't it, Monique? Because it was so simple. Your word was take, not bring, which would be normal for someone expecting to be at home to meet them."

"A slip of the tongue," said Monique.

"You said Jeanette was dithering over what to do at the start of the week," said Gus. "Then Millie spotted a face in Warminster that scared her. Millie thought she saw Tyler

Rowe. You saw your chance, and on Sunday, you contacted someone from the gang, telling them where Millie was living. Nathan Harvey confirmed a woman passed that message."

"You can't prove it was me," said Monique.

"We can get the call logs from your mobile phone supplier," said Gus. "Nathan might be prepared to offer the name and number of the person you contacted. There are other ways we can show you were responsible."

"Why would I do that?" asked Monique.

"Because Millie was a liability, She'd spent fifteen years giving Jeanette grief. There was never a moment's peace from when she caught Paddy and Millie together. In her early teens, Millie often stayed out overnight, smoking weed. Then she spent two years on the game, controlled by Denis Long. Her drug dependence was getting stronger and stronger. Millie came home for a few months, using the house on Keble Avenue as a stopping point on her descent to the gutter. Then, aged twenty, Millie runs home to tell Jeanette she's pregnant. There's no sign of the father, and who will look after Amy? Jeanette, of course. Finally, there's the burglary on the sixteenth of June. Millie comes home, knowing Fergus and Justin have done something stupid. She hides the haul and takes a few pieces to sell for cash. It didn't take long to find it, did it, Jeanette? You told Monique, and that was when you hatched the plan."

"You've got a vivid imagination," said Monique.

"Money makes a lot of things easier," said Gus. "You both needed it to escape the life you were living in Withywood. Millie provided you with the means to make that break. The police had arrested her for her part in the burglaries committed in early June with Fergus and Justin. You wanted the courts to keep her on remand, but the magistrate thought Amy should be with her mother. What a joke that was. You looked after Amy 24/7, just as you do today. Did Millie query why the watch wasn't where she'd hidden it? No doubt you said the police turned the place over after her arrest. Monique kept the watch safe."

Gus sensed the objections on the other side of the table were decreasing.

"You're a ditherer, Jeanette," he said. "That's what Monique told us. She was astonished that you moved to Warminster with such haste, but it was all part of the plan. Monique knew Tyler Rowe would search for you. He may not have been interested in you and his children, but you were loyal customers, and then there was Millie. He wanted her; I'm sure of that. You said Millie despised him; she was scared of him when she saw him in Warminster. Tyler was never there, was he? He did visit the squat in Withywood, though, and you couldn't be certain what went on there. A colleague made a relevant point earlier this week. Anxiety, depression, and angry outbursts are typical effects of long-term drug abuse. Both of you have smoked cannabis since you were teenagers. It would be just a small step from all the troubles Millie had piled on her mother to add a relationship with the charmer, Tyler Rowe."

"I never saw anything between them when they were under my roof," said Jeanette. "I always wondered, though...."

"Be quiet," snapped Monique.

"I'd better get to the final part before tempers fray," said Gus. "Harvey and Coombs knew where to find Millie, thanks to your phone call. Unfortunately, you couldn't guarantee what time they would arrive in Warminster. So, Jeanette took the kids out for the afternoon and caught the train to Temple Meads. They needed to be clear of the flat.

You travelled in the opposite direction, Monique, and kept watch. All five men were in the flat before four o'clock when Craig Coombs first called Tyler Rowe. You waited for Nathan and the others to leave, and you planned to kill Millie in the flat. That would have laid the blame on the five gang members. You hadn't expected to have to follow the car on foot, but you did, and spotted it by the churchyard and heard Millie getting punched. After the men left, you crept into the churchyard, stabbed the semi-conscious Millie, and discarded the washed knife in the bin."

"The time difference between the bruises on her upper arms and face and the knife wounds was so little the pathologist couldn't tell whether different people caused them," said Grace. "Time of death was between midnight and two. The screams were heard at a quarter to one. None of the men who went to the churchyard was near it then."

"You dumped the knife and returned to the flat," said Gus. "You and Jeanette would always have spare keys to each other's place. You're family. You caught a train to Temple Meads on Sunday morning and went to Withywood to tell Jeanette it was over."

"Then you waited for the police to call," said Grace. "You must have been quite an actress. DI Budd never suspected a thing."

"The gold watch was key to solving this case," said Gus.

Jeanette Clark's shoulders slumped.

"Monique realised the watch's value, didn't she, Jeanette? A move to a quiet country village was in your grasp. You had to be patient and keep up the pretence throughout both trials. The statements to the press were a nice touch. Monique moved to Zeals with you and the three children. When you thought the dust had settled, you put the watch up for sale on eBay. It wasn't until I spoke to someone on Saturday night that I realised you'd slipped up. You wanted to rub our noses in it. We hadn't worked out how you could be involved. You had fooled Tom Brewer five years ago and thought you'd done it again. You told me you decided to throw your lot in with your sister and help her look after the three children. It was time to make a move."

"I wondered why she smiled," said Lydia. "It was out of character. She was referring to the watch. The sale of that watch helped make it possible. That watch must have been worth a fortune. I wonder who bought it?"

Gus sat back in his chair.

"Time to make a move," he said. "It was barely a smile, more of a smirk. It registered, but I couldn't quantify its importance until Nathan Harvey told me he paid you thirty thousand pounds for his own watch. He thought he was doing the right thing. He didn't feel right having Millie's death on his hands. Nathan realises now that he was fooled."

Jeanette leapt out of her chair.

"We're finished," she screamed. "He'll never rest until we're punished."

"Hold your tongue, Jeanette," yelled Monique.

She jumped out of her chair and attacked her sister, hitting her around the head with her right hand.

Grace hit the panic strip on the wall beside her. The uniformed officers rushed in, and the situation was soon under control.

"Quite the temper," said Gus.

"I'd like a word with my clients in private, Mr Freeman," said Maureen Sawyer.

"I would expect nothing less," said Gus.

vinci-books.com/redherring

When a town's dark secrets are exposed, justice's pursuit begins.

Retired journalist Sid Selman's shocking exposé uncovers a town's overlooked web of vice and slavery. Meanwhile, the senseless bludgeoning of part-time waiter Matt Archer leaves investigators grasping for answers.

Turn the page for a free preview…

Red Herring Season: Chapter One

THE ELUSIVE SCOOP

Tuesday, 6 November 2018

There had been few days since he became Chief Constable where Kenneth Truelove had wished he could have stayed in bed. Every day brought a fresh challenge, especially when the Police and Crime Commissioner was on the warpath. The phone call he'd received from the current PCC late last night had put the proverbial cat amongst the pigeons.

As he stood by his office window, gazing across the car park, Kenneth knew his planned itinerary was disappearing over the horizon. Should he have asked Vera Butler to call Gus Freeman to tell him their morning meeting would have to be postponed? He wasn't looking forward to informing Gus that, sooner rather than later, he was losing four team members.

Kenneth prayed the enforced disruption would only be temporary.

According to the PCC, a new group of activists announced they were launching a concerted civil disobedience campaign. In addition, intelligence gathered by the Metropolitan Police suggested the minor outbreaks they'd monitored over the past two weeks would escalate from the seventeenth. As a result, they sought additional regional officers to bolster their already stretched resources.

"The Met need boots on the ground, Mercer," he'd told his right-hand-man as soon as he arrived at London Road this morning. He repeated the PCC's words.

"We don't often hear the words intelligence and the Met in the same sentence, Sir," said Geoff. "Why don't they tell the Premier League they can't have police boots around the football grounds next weekend?"

"The PCC stressed that Extinction Rebellion is calling on the government to reduce carbon emissions to zero by 2025," Kenneth had continued. "They want to establish a citizens assembly to devise an emergency plan of action similar to that seen during WWII."

"I remember reading about that crowd a couple of weeks ago," said Geoff. "One hundred academics, including a former Archbishop of Canterbury, hit the headlines by backing the cause. Given the scale of the ecological crisis, they believe it's an appropriate scale of expansion. More than sixty people have already been arrested for glueing themselves to government buildings and blocking major roads in the capital. I hope it doesn't catch on and spread to the streets of Devizes."

"Groups similar to this have come and gone," said Kenneth. "Extinction Rebellion hope their campaign of respectful disruption will change the debate around climate breakdown and signal to those in power that the present course of action will lead to disaster."

"Good luck with that, Sir," said Geoff. "We've seen what happens when large groups of people hit the streets in

London. All sorts of extremists come out of the woodwork to join in the fun. It's never a good time to be a copper in uniform, even if you've got a riot shield and bulletproof vest. Respectful disruption won't last five minutes if someone like the Anarchist Federation gets wind of what's happening."

"They emerged from the Miner's Strike in the mid-Eighties, didn't they?" asked Kenneth.

"Yes, Sir, and came to prominence during the Poll Tax riots five years later," said Geoff. "They've been under the Met's watchful eye ever since, along with several other unsavoury organisations."

"The PCC wants a list of names from me by the end of today," said Kenneth. "I know it's going to be unpopular, but to reach the numbers he quoted last night, we'll need Grace Packenham and the three serving officers working with the Crime Review Team to travel to the capital."

"What, and leave Gus and Lydia Logan Barre to soldier on alone?" said Geoff. "How long will we lose the others?"

"They'll have to leave immediately," said Kenneth. "The Met has sufficient trained personnel to cope with a moderate influx of protesters, so I don't envisage all four getting sent to the Specialist Training Centre in Gravesend. Freeman's people aren't up to speed with current crowd control techniques, so I foresee their role filling gaps in other less confrontational situations. How long for is another matter altogether. The PCC wasn't prepared to commit himself on that score."

"I wouldn't want to face DI Packenham in full riot gear, Sir," said Geoff. "However, DC Umeh would probably be best behind the counter at the police station at Paddington Green."

"Quite," said the Chief Constable. "Horses for courses.

233

Hardy and Davis might find themselves at the Emirates or Stamford Bridge watching the crowd."

"What will you do with the civilians on the Crime Review Team, Sir?" asked Geoff. "I imagine Wiltshire will be losing personnel from other sections across the county."

"I'm sure Ms Logan Barre will appreciate a change of scenery," said Kenneth. "It will be another credit on her CV when the time comes for her to move up the ladder."

"You'd like me to find Lydia a special project she can handle with minimal supervision," said Geoff.

"You read my mind, Mercer," said Kenneth. "Something to occupy her for ten days."

"Did you cross your fingers then, Sir? Does that mean you're concerned this civil disobedience business will be an ongoing thorn in the Met's side?"

"If it is, and spreads countrywide, every region providing support next weekend will need their people back. Then they'll have to start hunting for additional boots on their own patch," said Kenneth. "I don't think anyone can predict how long this will last. Ours not to reason why, Mercer, we must adapt to whatever the government and the people throw in our direction. Our opinions are irrelevant."

"Message received, Sir, though I haven't got a clue what Gus will think about it all."

"I've been wracking my brains all night trying to think of the best way to break the news to him," said Kenneth.

"Don't look at me, Sir," said Geoff.

"Typical," said Kenneth. "I suppose I'd better stick to the planned meeting over lunch and tell him he's not getting another case to review until this rebellion business quietens. I don't want you sneaking off, Mercer. Is that clear?"

"Crystal, Sir," said Geoff.

DS Mercer had left the office, and Kenneth took up his

position by the window. A light tap on the door told him Vera was outside.

"Come in," he called.

"Everything's ordered for your lunch, Sir," said Vera. "I spoke to Gus just after he arrived in the Old Police Station office. He'll be here at noon with another completed case file to present."

"He never ceases to amaze me, Vera," said Kenneth.

"Gus enjoys doing what he loves, Sir. After his superiors in Salisbury decided they could dispense with his services, he thought he'd never get another opportunity."

"I hope he can pick up where he left off," said Kenneth.

Vera looked puzzled.

"Don't worry, Vera," said Kenneth. "Events in the capital have forced me to hit the pause button on the work Gus and his team are doing so ably. Yet, somehow, I must find a way to break the news to him gently."

"Oh dear," said Vera, "rather you than me."

"Not you too, Vera," groaned Kenneth.

"You're paid to make the tough decisions, Sir," said Vera. "I've every confidence you'll make the right one on this occasion too. You haven't let us down so far."

Vera crept out of the office and closed the door. She sensed the Chief Constable would be standing by that window for a while. Time to find Kassie Trotter to tell her the news.

In the Old Police Station office, Gus and the team were working hard on the housekeeping. They were otherwise engaged at the custody suite yesterday, so there hadn't been enough time to update the Freeman files when they returned to their desks after lunch.

Almost as soon as Gus had sat at his desk at nine o'clock

this morning, Vera Butler had called from London Road. He'd gone out on a limb and promised her everything would be ready to hand the completed Millie Clark case files to her boss by noon. When the call ended, Gus looked to see whether an early frost had struck the mood in the office. He needn't have worried.

"I should be finished before ten, guv," said Lydia. "I can either do the coffee run or remove street maps and crime scene photos from the walls. Which comes first?"

"I won't be far behind Lydia, guv," said Blessing. "We'll make short work of both jobs if we work together."

"That works for me," said Gus. "Grace and I had more to update this morning due to our involvement in the interview with the Clark sisters. Does anyone think we'll struggle to make the eleven-thirty deadline I recklessly agreed to?"

"We'll be ready, guv," said Alex. Neil nodded.

Gus glanced towards Amazing Grace, but she continued typing at an impressive speed without responding. He checked his notebook and calculated how long it would take him to finish his report. It wouldn't pay to slack.

By ten o'clock, Lydia and Blessing were heading for the restroom. Neil was first to break the silence after the drinks had been delivered.

"I reckon we should keep searching for Tyler Rowe, Alex. What do you think?"

"If we can prove he was guilty of the assault on Viv Whitaker," said Alex. "When we listened to what Jeanette and Monique had to say yesterday, it was hard to distinguish fact from fiction. They misled the police on so many occasions."

"Nobody could recall seeing Tyler Rowe in Bristol after he left that flat," said Neil. "My guess is he *did* move to Westbury or Warminster. Because, although the sisters convinced the police that Tyler contacted Micah Harvey, there were good reasons for him to disappear."

"Cameron Keel recognised Tyler as a guy he'd often seen around the city," said Alex. "But Harvey and Coombs had dozens of men on their books, and Keel didn't know his name or role in the gang. Coombs just needed numbers to help search properties in Withywood. Keel made sure someone reported the Whitaker incident to cover his backside. That attack brought unwanted attention to the gang's business affairs. Thanks to Jeanette and Monique's misdirection, all five gang members ended up in court on trial for Millie's murder."

"The sisters couldn't have foreseen what would happen next," said Neil. "If everything had gone to plan at the first trial, they would have been home free. Jeanette and Monique would have pinned the blame for Millie's death on the drug gang. Nobody would have queried the result. The sisters could have waited for the dust to settle, then sold the watch. Nobody would have been any the wiser."

Lydia had been listening while she helped Blessing clear the decks ready for the next case.

"I wonder if Tyler Rowe ever did go to Warminster," she said. "Monique told Gus that Tyler went to the flat in Weymouth Street, not to get Jeanette back, but to see whether he could persuade Millie to buy her drugs from him."

"I thought Tyler told the gang where Millie was because she was one woman he couldn't get into bed," said Blessing. "I was wrong about that, but Neil's right. We should start looking for Tyler Rowe. He deserves to go to prison for what he did to that poor man."

"I agree," said Lydia. "We could start by asking any unmarried mothers with kids under five if they're chasing a boyfriend for unpaid maintenance. Tyler Rowe will be among the names we hear. I'd bet on it."

"Of course, he may have moved again," said Blessing. "Nathan Harvey told Gus he and Craig Coombs could wait. They would find Tyler Rowe in time and deal with him."

As Lydia and Blessing were busy cleaning the white-boards while they still chatted about the case, Alex collected the empty cups to return them to the restroom.

"You were quieter than usual yesterday, Neil," said Alex. "Did that have anything to do with Jake Latimer and Rick Chalmers?"

"Don't remind me," said Neil. "Melody was not a happy bunny when I arrived home on Sunday."

"What time did the taxi drop you off?" asked Alex.

"Just before lunch," said Neil. "Rick had suggested I jump into a taxi with him when he left the club in Swindon Old Town at two o'clock. I wish I'd gone with him, but Jake persuaded me to go back to his place. Janina wasn't asleep when we arrived. She realised we needed plenty of coffee, but Jake topped our mugs with rum once her back was turned. According to Jake, I fell asleep at four."

"Did Jake keep drinking?" asked Alex.

"I didn't believe it was possible to drink yourself sober," said Neil. "When I surfaced at around half-past ten, feeling like death, Jake still had a glass in his hand and was as bright as a button. He asked if I wanted a fried breakfast. That finished me. When I finally left the bathroom, I rang for a taxi and crawled through my front door at a quarter to one. Safe to say, I'm grounded until after the baby's born. Melody's mother stood beside her as I crept into the kitchen to get myself a black coffee."

"It was a good night, though, apart from that?" asked Alex.

"A cracking night," said Neil. "Young Travers was a lightweight. Two pints and he was giggling like a schoolgirl. We lost track of Travers early doors. Jake and Rick know a lot of coppers who enjoy a drink, as you can imagine. Several pubs in Swindon, and the club in Old Town, probably had their best takings of the year. Apart from Christmas Eve and New Year's Eve."

Alex disappeared to the restroom. When he returned to his desk, Lydia and Blessing had just finished getting the office ship-shape.

"Is there anything the three of us can do, guv?" he asked.

"The biggest help you can offer will be to keep the noise down while Gus and I finish our reports," said Grace.

"That's us told," said Neil as he leaned back in his chair. "My contribution is ready to go, Alex. So who's in charge of collating everything?"

"Forward your files to me, and I'll do it," said Grace.

Lydia and Blessing escaped to the restroom.

"Someone's touchy this morning," said Lydia.

"I don't think Grace has got used to sleeping at the farmhouse," said Blessing. "John and Jackie Ferris are up at the crack of dawn, and there are more bird and animal noises in the countryside than Grace is used to."

"You've never complained since you moved there," said Lydia.

"I'm a heavy sleeper," said Blessing. "My alarm went off three times before I was awake enough to silence it this morning. Grace will become acclimatised in time."

"Should we risk going back to our desks?" asked Lydia.

"If we don't, she'll only have more ammunition to throw at us after Gus drives to Devizes."

Lydia could see sense in that, so they made their way quietly back to their desks.

Gus closed his notebook and read through his final summary. It had been an odd case throughout. Perhaps there were instances where Tom Brewer could have chosen a different path to follow, and he might have uncovered the truth. But it was several days before Gus realised the main characters were being orchestrated by a hidden hand. It never ceased to amaze Gus what families could do to one another.

He forwarded his file to Amazing Grace and checked the clock on the far wall. Unless Grace was struggling, he should make his noon appointment with the Chief Constable even if there were traffic delays in Seend.

"Almost there, Gus," said Grace.

"Uncanny," said Gus. "I hadn't said a word."

Grace spent a further five minutes editing and polishing her report. Then she gathered the contributions the rest of the team had provided and sent the completed file to the printer.

"I always enjoy that sound, guv," said Blessing. "It means that later this afternoon, we'll learn where in the county we're off to next. Another week, another new destination."

At twenty past eleven, Grace handed Gus the case folder.

"We'll see you later then, Gus," she said. "Have fun."

Gus slipped on his jacket, grabbed the folder, said farewell to the team. and made for the lift.

No two trips were ever the same between the Old Police Station and London Road. Gus left Church Street and headed out of town. He negotiated the first two round-abouts without needing to stop, and then he spotted a new sign as he approached the roundabout leading to the custody suite on Crook's Way.

"That wasn't there yesterday," said Gus.

He caught the gist of the message as the line of traffic drove past at a sedate thirty. Six hundred and fifty new houses were due to be built in the field on his left. Bob, the House Builder, apologised in advance for any inconvenience this would cause over the next two years.

Gus wondered whether he'd still be making this trip when the two, three, and four-bedroomed townhouses were scarring the landscape. Yet, one of the few pleasures on this stretch of road was the rolling pastures and uninterrupted view of Bowden Hill and Caen Hill.

The journey through Seend and onwards to Devizes passed without incident, but Gus was still concerned with the poor souls who would enjoy the views he cherished while struggling to find school places for their children or get registered for a doctor or dentist. So, perhaps, Bob, the House Builder, should reserve his apologies for the town's newcomers.

Gus parked in the visitor's car park at London Road, rescued the case folder from the passenger seat, and trotted up the steps of the main building. Once inside, he gave the desk sergeant in Reception a broad smile and a wink. Gus knew that would unnerve someone who spent most of his working life facing people who sneered or snarled as soon as they set eyes on them. Gus liked to do his bit to even the score.

Vera met him at the top of the stairs.

"Geoff Mercer will join you in a minute," she said. "The boss is waiting for you. Kassie will deliver your lunch within the next five minutes. I hope you're well. How's Suzie?"

"That's more words than you've shared with me for months, Vera," said Gus. "Have I missed a balloon going up somewhere? I can only assume you've heard bad news. What is it?"

"Kenneth will explain," said Vera. "He hasn't given me the full details. Kassie has her new set of wheels today, by the way. You won't hear her trolley coming across the mezzanine."

"A rapid change of subject doesn't fool me, Vera. I smell trouble."

Vera gave Gus a sympathetic look and returned to her desk. Gus spotted Geoff Mercer emerging from his office and crossed the mezzanine to join him.

"I would have appreciated a heads-up, Geoff," he said as he fell into step beside him.

"It's only temporary, Gus," said Geoff. "As far as I can tell."

Geoff knocked on Kenneth's door. They waited for a grunt from inside and then entered. The Chief Constable had completed his car park survey and sat at his desk.

"Good morning, Freeman," he said. "I see you have brought the fruits of your labours from last week with you. Another successful cold case review. Well done. I must admit it was a surprise to learn the killer was someone nobody suspected. My money was on one of the gang members. I can't wait to read your report. Perhaps you could give me the headlines?"

"I thought I was here for some kind of announcement, " Gus said. "When Vera met me at the top of the stairs, I half expected her to say she was sorry for my loss."

"All in good time, Freeman," said Kenneth. "Did Tom

Brewer emerge unscathed from your investigations? I have fond memories of working with him many years ago."

"Several opportunities were missed by detectives in Bristol and Warminster, Sir," said Gus. "The distance between Withywood and your old stamping ground might be low in mileage terms, but they were light years apart in how they were policed. Mick Budd and his team worked under a Chief Constable with a very different approach to how things were run here by the man in your chair five years ago."

"I was that man's Assistant Chief Constable, Freeman," said Kenneth. "He had his faults, but I think DS Mercer will agree; we were singing from the same hymn sheet. Barry Knee was in charge in Bristol between 2012 and 2015. Unfortunately, he left under a cloud, and although I don't expect to see a written report on the matter, it's safe to say the IOPC has held a series of interviews with senior officers working in Bristol during that period."

"A rough translation of which is that Knee's pension's safe," said Gus. "If anyone asks an awkward question, they'll get told there's nothing to see. Move along, please."

"I couldn't possibly comment, Freeman," said Kenneth. "So, the inference from what you've uncovered is that Harvey and Coombs got an easy ride from DI Budd and his team. The gang may have had someone on the inside protecting their interests. Maybe financial inducements were offered and accepted. If the Bristol team had been more diligent, they could have provided Tom Brewer with more pertinent information."

"That's a fair analysis, Sir," said Gus. "However, Monique Clark was the person pulling the strings. Her younger sister, Jeanette, was weak and easily manipulated. I learned just how much the sisters were involved on Saturday night. That's when the pieces of the jigsaw fell into place."

"I hadn't realised you were working on the case over the weekend, Gus," said Geoff. "You didn't clear any overtime for the team with me."

"I suppose I'd better come clean," said Gus. "Nathan Harvey sent his thugs to collect me. I was enjoying a nightcap in the Lamb with a friend, Brett Penman, and after he left me in the lane outside my bungalow, I was grabbed and taken to a remote spot where Harvey told me how we'd all been duped by Monique and Jeanette Clark."

"You could have been killed, Gus," said Geoff. "Why are we hearing about this now?"

"I was perfectly safe," said Gus. "Harvey would never have accepted the offer of a friendly chat, and we needed a lot more to get him into an interview room with his solicitor. So, I decided to listen to what he had to say."

Gus thought a little white lie was permitted, just this once.

"It doesn't sound like you had much choice," said Geoff. "Were they armed?"

"Of course," said Gus. "But with three of them in the car, I would have had to go to meet Harvey whether they were carrying a gun or not. Harvey insisted he and Craig were never near the churchyard. They stayed in the flat until Keel and Thatcher returned. Micah Harvey had gone with them and confirmed Millie Clark had been punished for her part in the robbery. They left the girl alive, as instructed, lying by a gravestone. The five men then made their separate ways back to Bristol. Harvey said someone attacked and stabbed Millie after they'd left."

"Very convenient," said Kenneth. "That was their

defence at the first trial, but why should you believe a word he says?"

"I reminded him that Keel and Thatcher claimed they weren't responsible," said Gus. "Those two assumed, instead of heading straight for Bristol, that someone went to the churchyard and killed Millie. Micah had driven to Warminster alone, and Nathan and Craig travelled by car together. Keel believed one of those three could have done it. Nathan pointed out that Micah is left-handed, so, as Henry Ash swore the attacker was right-handed, that ruled him out. At that point, Nathan Harvey told me about his gold watch."

"DI Budd told Tom Brewer that Millie had sold the valuables stolen from Harvey's property to buy drugs," said Geoff Mercer. "I hadn't realised Millie Clark still had anything to sell."

"Millie hid several items at her home in Withywood," said Gus. "Jeanette found the gold watch. Monique realised it could help them escape from Withywood, and that's when they hatched the plan to move to Warminster. Millie had been a thorn in her mother's side for almost fifteen years. Monique convinced Jeanette she would always have to get her out of trouble. The best they could hope for was an overdose. That's when Monique started sowing the seeds which would confuse the investigation and offer an opportunity to murder Millie and put the blame on the drug gang members."

"A tangled web," said Kenneth. "I look forward to reading the report in full."

Grab your copy...
vinci-books.com/redherring

About the Author

Ted Tayler is the international bestselling indie author of The Freeman Files and The Phoenix series. Ted lives in the English west country, where his stories are based. He was born in 1945 and has been married to Lynne since 1971. They have three children and four grandchildren.

His thought-provoking mysteries appeal to readers of Sally Rigby, Joy Ellis, Pauline Rowson, and Faith Martin. His action-packed thrillers are a must for fans of Mark Dawson and J. C. Ryan.

Gus Freeman's cold case investigations are carried out with reasoned deduction rather than bursts of frantic action. In each of the twenty-four books, unsolved murder is accompanied by romance, humor, and country life. The core message in the twelve Phoenix novels is that criminals should pay for their crimes. Unfortunately, the current system fails to deliver the correct punishment, so Phoenix helps redress the balance.

Acknowledgments

The love and support of my family; without them, this would have been impossible.